ASHORE

Staying Afloat, Book Two

Isabelle Adler

You can only put the past away for so long.

This had never been truer for the crew of Matt's ship, the Lady Lisa. Even as their engine suffers a critical malfunction and Matt scrambles to fund the costly repairs, Val, the ship's reticent engineer, unexpectedly comes face-to-face with a deadly ghost from his past. Now it's up to Matt, Ryce, and Tony to rescue him, even if it means breaking the law and striking an uneasy bargain with a local black-market kingpin—but what if this time their best efforts simply aren't good enough?

And it might be that Val isn't the only crew member Matt risks losing when his budding relationship with Ryce unexpectedly runs aground. With their love and commitment put to the test, Matt and Ryce must rally to save their friend and to keep their ship afloat, but in a race so desperate there might not be any real winners.

To D., for his continuous support in all things

Chapter One

"THAT'S IT," MATT said. "It's over."

The three of them stood around the gutted engine of the *Lady Lisa*. Well, Matt stood, while Val and Ryce crouched beside it amid piles of discarded parts, wires, and pieces of electronics. Both of them were covered in smudges of grease and looking up at Matt with expressions bordering on horror, as if unable to accept the pronouncement of judgment. It would have been quite comical, really, except there was nothing remotely funny about the situation.

Usually, it was Matt who was unwilling to acknowledge a problem he wasn't prepared to deal with, but after watching his engineer and pilot tinker with the thing for hours with absolutely nothing to show for it, even he had to grudgingly admit it was a lost cause. If two geniuses put together couldn't fix the damn engine, then it was beyond fixing.

"We need a new power converter," Val said tiredly and wiped his face, smearing the grease even further. "There's not much we can do without it."

"We're afraid the fission chamber would explode if we try to bypass it," Ryce said apologetically, as if it was his fault the engine worked the way it did. Or didn't, as the case was.

"Yeah, don't try that," Matt said. The last thing he needed was his ship exploding, taking all the crew and half the landing dock with it.

And he definitely didn't need his ship breaking down. Luckily, the engine decided to give out while they were still safely docked at the Freeport 73 station, and not in the middle of a run. Otherwise, they'd have been stranded in space, drifting with the rest of the human-made junk that orbited Elysium until somebody deigned to answer their distress call.

"Okay," Matt said, turning his mind back to the problem at hand, searching for some sort of a quick solution. They'd have to cancel the job Matt had contracted yesterday (geological survey equipment delivery to one of the moons of Elysium-4), and every day they spent docked at the station meant more fees. They couldn't afford to tarry without any immediate sources of income.

"Can you get a new power converter?" he asked Val.

"Yes," Val said, getting up. Looming at six feet five inches and built of solid muscle, some would call Valeriy Sokolov intimidating. The buzz cut and the perpetually grim expression did nothing to soften his appearance. He was also one of the smartest people Matt had ever known, and with Ryce in the same room, that was saying a lot.

"I'm sensing a 'but' coming," Matt said.

"A brand new converter would set us back fifteen grand," Val said. "I might be able to find a used one for about five thousand creds, but there's no telling how long it'll hold. Could be just a waste of money."

Matt had had a feeling he wasn't going to like it, and his hunch proved to be correct. Unfortunately, they always did.

"Shit." He stared at the discarded parts as if they could somehow magically transform into Federal credits. He wasn't prepared for it being quite so large a sum. "Shit, shit, *shit.*"

"I'll clean up in here." Val's tone clearly suggested he wanted everybody else to leave the engine room.

"Come on." Ryce got up and took Matt by the arm, steering him toward the exit and into the narrow corridor.

Ryce's touch was comforting, and Matt instinctively leaned into it. He still couldn't quite believe they were together. As in a real relationship. Ryce was way out of Matt's league—a brilliant mind, a former Fleet combat pilot, a war hero. Not to mention hot as hell, and scrupulous to a fault—an admirable trait, but one which, at times, made their lives somewhat difficult.

As the captain of the small cargo ship *Lady Lisa*, Matt Spears was a runner, an independent contractor living off odd jobs hauling goods between the various planets and outposts in the Elysium system. While Matt was not averse to bending the rules regarding the legality of his cargo or passengers every now and then, Ryce was firmly against illicit smuggling in any shape or form. Had it been any other person, Matt would have told him to bugger off, or at least keep quiet about the nature of his contracts, but he couldn't bring himself to lie or argue with Ryce on points of honor.

Over seven months ago, Ryce had been involved in one man's covert scheme that had led to him and Matt crossing paths—but which had also cost Ryce everything. A brilliant Fleet officer with a promising career, he had been discharged under questionable circumstances and cast adrift with no remaining family to fall back on and no home to call his own.

Still, a man of Ryce's capabilities could've easily found himself a job with one of the larger transport companies in the private sector, or pursued an academic career, as his late adoptive parents had always wanted. But instead, he'd chosen to cast his lot with Matt and his crew—a position that held no prospects other than bare survival and presented no challenge for his superior skills.

And now, even this paltry job was at jeopardy. The problem was, with business having been slow lately, Matt didn't have enough money to buy a new power converter. And without a running engine, they were effectively grounded and couldn't take on jobs that would earn them the money needed for repairs. It was a vicious circle, and right now, Matt could see no way out of it.

"I don't know what to do," Matt confessed once they reached the bridge and he plopped down in the copilot seat. The huge canopy window screen was shut off, a black backdrop for the silence. Outside was the bustle of a busy dock, but here, they were shielded against the noise and nonstop activity of the station.

"We'll think of something," Ryce said. "You always find a solution, and there's still no cause for panic."

He sat beside him in the pilot's chair. When Ryce first joined the crew, after his final decommission from the military three weeks ago, they did the awkward dance around the precedence of piloting the ship, taking turns and being painstakingly polite with each other. But Matt quickly gave up on that. Ryce was an ace pilot. It was only logical to let the man do what he did best—not that piloting a small hauler around a sparsely populated solar system took much effort. This arrangement left Matt with not all that much to do around the ship, other than taking care of the business side of things and making sure everything was running smoothly. Which, at present, proved rather difficult.

Matt ran a hand through his unruly auburn hair. Ryce was right; stressing about it wasn't helpful. He'd just have to calm down and consider the situation rationally.

"I might be able to scrape up about three or four thousand," he said, crunching the numbers in his head. "There is a bit left in my account from our Ghorra job, and I could sell the new heater core Val bought last week. We could do with the old one a little while longer."

"It's not much, but it's something," Ryce said.

"Yes, but we'd still be at least ten grand short. And with the docking fees adding up..."

"Can someone loan you the money?" Ryce asked carefully.

For Matt, this had always been a touchy subject. He came from a very wealthy, very respectable family. His father was no other than the renowned Fleet Admiral Thomas Cummings, while his older sister Nora was a Major and commanded her own ship. Seven months ago, she'd been the one to pull him (indeed, all of them) out of hot water after Matt had become an unwitting accessory to high treason and multiple counts of Federal offenses. But his relationship with his family had been strained for years, their difficulties further enhanced by Matt's continued refusal to keep in touch. After the death of his mother, there was no closing that gap. Despite Nora coming to his rescue, their renewed bond was still too tenuous, and Matt didn't want to have to run to his sister every time he got into trouble. Perhaps this stance was childish, but he didn't need his family being more disappointed with him than they already were.

The only other solution was borrowing money from some of his shadier business acquaintances. No proper bank would give him a loan, but people on the gray market would happily supply him with cash—at a killer interest, of course. He just wasn't sure he wanted to get involved with a loan shark, the way his luck had been going lately.

"We'll see," he said finally. The money had to come from somewhere, that much was certain. "Let's keep this option as a last resort, for now."

"I should go help Val patch things up in there," Ryce said, getting up. He hesitated a fraction of a second before planting a kiss on Matt's forehead.

Matt grinned and reached to wipe a tiny spot of grease off Ryce's cheek.

"Sorry. I'm getting dirt all over you," Ryce said, returning his smile.

Seeing Ryce smile at him never failed to make Matt's heart beat faster. They were both still learning to navigate the sometimes-tricky path of their fledgling relationship, having spent more than six months apart with little contact during Ryce's prolonged inquiry, but these little moments of quiet affection made the long wait worth it.

"I don't mind. You can get me as dirty as you want."

Ryce snickered, a tinge of blush creeping up his cheeks, and left the bridge. When the sliding door closed behind him, Matt sighed and swiveled in his chair. His faint reflection in the darkened window turned with him.

He wished he could see the stars in live view now. Seeing them so close always made him feel as though all these new worlds were within his reach, as though anything was possible if he only tried hard enough. Sometimes it was true, sometimes it wasn't. All he knew was that if he didn't fix this problem somehow, and soon, there would be no more chasing stars for him.

For the first time in months, Matt found himself badly needing a drink.

THE LIQUOR CABINET—which Matt surreptitiously kept stocked—was located in the rec room. He poured himself a glass of whiskey and sat on the battered sofa. Now, when he was able to think things through calmly, he had to concede that while the situation was certainly difficult, they had seen worse. Being short a couple of grand was infinitely preferable to being chased by hostile aliens or threatened by pirates. If he and his crew had survived that, they could take on anything.

Having finished the drink, Matt headed to the galley in much higher spirits than an hour ago. He was greeted by the din of conversation, clinking of dishes, and the heartwarming smell of Tony's cooking.

It was easy to lose track of time on a spaceship that was by no means run with military precision, but lunch hour was studiously observed by everybody. They all took turns cooking meals and cleaning up, but out of the four of them, Tony was the only one who could whip up anything worth eating. Matt and Val's idea of fixing lunch was heating up a can of soup, and while Ryce put much more effort into diversifying the menu, his food usually ended up under- or overcooked to a degree Matt had never thought possible in a fully digitalized kitchen.

The entire crew was already gathered around the table, and they all looked up expectantly when he entered. Matt offered them as cheerful a smile as he could manage under the circumstances, and took a seat.

"So, folks. I'm sure you all already know about our predicament, and I'm not going to sugarcoat this. Until we come up with the cash to fix the engine, we're basically dead in the water. Or stuck ashore, as the case is."

Tony, his first mate and *Lady Lisa*'s makeshift medic, tugged at her braid thoughtfully. "This means we don't actually have the cash."

"Not enough to cover all the expenses." It wasn't something Matt was proud to be telling his crew, but he'd done his best to manage the finances frugally. It was just that regular maintenance was damn expensive.

"It's my responsibility, and I'll find a way to get us through it," he continued. "In the meantime, I won't hold anyone to their contract, if any of you decide to leave. I know the pay is hardly what you deserve..."

Matt trailed off as Tony made a face at him and Val shook his head. Ryce merely leaned back in his chair, his arms crossed over his chest.

"Don't be a fool." For all her petite stature, Tony could certainly sound intimidating when she wanted to. "Nobody's leaving. It's not the first time we've been in a jam together, and it sure as hell won't be the last."

"I might have to sell my body at the Freeport canteen just to pay for our meals," Matt said mournfully. It was easier to turn this into a joke than acknowledge the lump suddenly lodged at the back of his throat.

"How much do you think your body might be worth?" Ryce asked.

"With all the crap he puts in it?" Tony scooped a generous portion of the stew from the steaming pot and plopped it on her plate. "I doubt it would buy us as much as a protein bar."

"It's not crap," Matt said defensively. "It's the highest quality caffeine and alcohol the black market has to offer."

"Actually, the canteen is not a bad idea," Val said in that quietly rumbling voice of his. He shrugged when everybody looked over at him in surprise. "It's as good a place as any to scout for jobs. It's true we're not going anywhere, but if Captain can work out a down payment with a prospective client, we can buy what is needed and still make the run."

It all sounded simple enough. A sufficient advance on their fee would solve their problem without the customer even knowing there was one. The trouble was finding someone to hire them before word got out about their situation. News and gossip traveled fast on Freeports, despite the stations' impressive size. Their scoping for engine parts would definitely raise questions. Nobody wanted to entrust their cargo to a faulty ship, or risk getting scammed altogether if said ship was, in fact, out of service.

"Good idea," Matt said, getting up. "I might as well get on it."

"Great," Ryce said, though for some reason, he didn't sound too enthusiastic.

Was he afraid Matt might seek out more than clients in a crowded bar? If so, he had no reason to worry. Matt was a lot of things, but he wasn't a cheater—at least where relationships were concerned. While it was true that in the past he'd been less than discerning when it came to casual dating (if a string of random one-night stands on various stations and outposts could be called dating), he hadn't been interested in anybody else ever since he and Ryce had shared their first kiss all those months ago aboard the pirate ship. Ryce had to know that, right?

"Captain, a moment," Tony said before he could leave. She nodded to the corridor, indicating she'd like to speak with him in private.

"What is it?" he asked once they were out of earshot of the galley. Tony seemed hesitant, and he wasn't used to seeing her like this.

Tony took a deep breath, as if steeling herself for what she was about to say.

"You remember I used to work for the Interstellar Medical Aid network, right?"

"Sure," Matt said, wondering where this was going. Tony had been a clinical trial coordinator for the IMA for ten years before she was accused of embezzlement and theft of expensive experimental medication. She was convicted but lucky to be sentenced to a shortened prison term due to extenuating circumstances. The court had been lenient because Tony had risked her career and freedom to help a complete stranger get the potentially lifesaving drug he couldn't otherwise afford. But the aftermath had ruined her life just the same. The conviction gave her ex-husband the leverage he needed to get sole custody of their only child, and she was blacklisted by all Federal health-care providers and large pharmaceutical companies.

"The IMA has a branch here on Freeport 73," Tony said. "It's a decent-sized operation. They might have short-term contracts available for small-time runners—there are always emergency shipments round the system. It's rarely worth the trouble for larger delivery companies to pick those up."

"Do you think they might consider hiring us?" Matt perked up a little at the thought. A contract with the IMA, even a temporary one, would do a lot to boost their ratings with other clients.

"I don't know. I guess I can ask around. I know some people who work here, but..." she trailed off, but Matt understood her meaning. Not everybody would be willing to talk to a disgraced ex-colleague.

"If you could put some feelers out, that'd be great," he said. "But if it doesn't pan out, it's okay. No pressure. There's always something else waiting in line."

Tony nodded, but Matt could still sense her apprehension. He couldn't blame her for her reluctance to call on favors that were long past their expiration date. He couldn't bring himself to do the same, after all.

He patted her on the arm. "Thanks, Tony. I appreciate it. And if any of them are giving you trouble, I'll whip their snooty asses."

"Be careful, or you'll make Ryce jealous," she said with a wry smile. "And good luck at the bar. You might pick up on something before I do."

Matt grinned back at her and headed toward the exit but found his way blocked by Val, who was waiting for him by the main hatch.

"I'll go with you," the engineer said.

"Really?"

Val didn't usually frequent bars. His favorite pastime was reading (for the most part, 19th- and 20th-century Russian literature), and when he did go out during their many shore leaves, it was prowling junkyards for pieces of equipment.

"Yeah," Val said. "Ryce thought it'd be better if we went together. If you do find us a job, I could assess the technical side."

"Huh," was all Matt could say. Val had never once weighed in on the technical plausibility of any of their runs prior to Matt striking the bargain. Usually, he presented Val with a done deal, and any issues would be worked out between them in the process. This was something else, and it hadn't come from Val. Did Ryce really think Matt needed a chaperon? Did he not trust him enough not to let his eyes and hands wander when on his own?

Perhaps Matt couldn't boast a stellar reputation when it came to romantic involvements, but this lack of faith kind of hurt. Granted, three weeks, with most of them spent in space runs, was a short time to garner absolute trust from his new partner, but so far, Matt had given him no cause to doubt his fidelity. Hadn't he?

"Okay, fine," he said, a touch grumpily. "I guess there's a first time for everything. Let's get you to a bar."

Chapter Two

THE BROKEN STAIRWAY Canteen was located at the outer ring of the Freeport. It was one of the cheapest on the station, but it was on the larger side, and the huge panoramic windows provided a stunning view of the stars and the blue planet the station was orbiting. Elysium-5, the only terrestrial planet in the system, closely resembled the old Earth in its geological makeup and atmosphere and had at one point been considered a prime destination for colonization. But the water toxicity levels were found to be too high to sustain humans, due to some peculiar compounds secreted by the local flora, and high-water-content planets were notoriously harder to terraform. So, the poorly named Elysium system only hosted human settlers on rocky moons and space stations, until a viable solution could be found for taking over the paradise planet.

The vista was truly breathtaking, but right now, Matt was more interested in what was going on inside. The bar was open at all hours, with the flow of patrons fluctuating between working shifts and transport arrivals. It was packed, but Matt and Val were lucky enough to find two freshly vacated seats at the end of the counter. Matt swiped the digital countertop and ordered them a couple of beers to start with.

Val was not the best companion for barhopping. As much as Matt appreciated his insight and companionship, the man was neither chatty, nor a social drinker, so Matt was worried his looming presence would put a damper on other people's willingness to strike a casual conversation. Besides, it still rankled that Ryce thought he needed someone to hold him back from temptation.

"I thought we were sitting pretty now we had upgraded the cooling system." He sighed, his thoughts circling back to their current trouble.

Val shrugged. "It's an old ship. It's always going to be one thing or another."

He was right, of course. Matt wouldn't trade his precious *Lisa* for anything, but the constant upgrades were eating away at any profit they managed to turn. He prided himself on the ship being extremely fast and maneuverable for a Phaeton-type vessel (which was by and large Val's doing), but he couldn't deny the heavy cost of keeping it afloat.

Matt took a swig of the cheap artificial beer the bartender put in front of him and turned around, letting the background noise of soft music and loud voices wash over him. There was no point in sitting there feeling sorry for himself when he could be doing something useful.

As always, he picked up strands of conversations from the general din. A sergeant sitting at the nearest table was complaining to her friend about a couple of privates missing one too many tactical drills because of made-up medical emergencies. At another table, a military spacecraft maintenance tech was trying (unsuccessfully, in Matt's expert opinion) to hit on a bored-looking guy whom Matt pegged as a crew member of one of the passing freight barges. To their right, a man sitting with his back to Matt was telling someone on his comm about an Onorean spacecraft that had entered Dock L28 two hours ago.

This last tidbit made Matt perk up a bit and listen in more carefully. Ryce was half-Onorean, so any mention of them was bound to arouse his interest. Onoreans rarely ventured outside their closed community, so this was somewhat curious—especially considering how remote and unimportant the Elysium system and its Freeport were. But that particular conversation ended quickly, with the purpose of the Onoreans' visit remaining a mystery.

Nothing of what he'd overheard was of any particular use, but Matt filed away any little piece of information that helped him get a better feel of the place. Every station, from tiny maintenance outposts to the city-sized Freeports, had its own distinct vibe, its own unspoken rules, and Matt found that familiarity with the ways of the place was worth the extra effort in the long run. If you treated the right people the right way, they were more amenable to persuasion and more likely to consider him one of their own. In a business where word of mouth was everything, being in the know was of utmost importance.

"I've got to get this done quick," a low baritone said somewhere on his left, making Matt's attention snap in that direction. The speaker, a portly gentleman in a green duster coat, was talking to the bartender. There were tiny metal adapters on his temples, much like Matt's, indicating he was—or at least at some point had been—a pilot. He was holding a glass of something neon-bright and colorful.

Matt leaned in just a fraction, tuning out the other noises and Val's presence, and focusing all his attention on the man with a problem and a peculiar taste in drinks.

"I know I should've scheduled it with the station control," the man said irritably in response to the bartender's muffed question. "But things had come up unexpected, and now they're acting like real jerks about it. Say they can't accommodate a rush request because of the traffic load, or some such nonsense. Bastards."

Before the bartender could offer an answer, Matt swooped in, a solicitous smile plastered on his face.

"Those petty functionaries can be such a drag to deal with, am I right? No consideration for us folks with actual work to do." He leaned on the counter, gesturing toward the portly man with his beer bottle. "What is it you need to get done, exactly?"

The man, who'd first appeared to be slightly annoyed at the interruption, nodded, somewhat mollified by the shared sentiment.

"Our ship was redirected to another dock, but the thing is, we've already unloaded some of the cargo," he grumbled. "It needs to be stored in a different warehouse now, but the station won't assign us a loading team. And they want it moved ASAP. Where's the logic in that? Now, I don't have the manpower to haul it, and those crates are damn heavy. Another day and they'll start charging me storage fines. That's what they do to make an extra cred on our backs, I tell you."

Matt clicked his tongue and nodded sympathetically. "Those fines can be killer. But you know what? I might be able to help here. It just so happens my crew and I are between jobs at the moment. We could lend you an extra hand—for a small fee. How many crates did you say you have?"

"Twelve, about a hundred pounds each." The man still sounded dubious.

"That does sound like a lot, but seeing you're in a jam, my mate and I could be willing to help." Matt gestured to Val, who grunted by way of agreeing.

The guy in the green duster sized him up, and, apparently satisfied with Val's obvious ability to handle heavy loads, nodded.

"I can't spare more than five hundred creds on this, though," he said.

"Fair enough. So, do we have an agreement, Mr....?"

"Tanner," the man said. "Captain of the *Northcott*. Hey, if you can have all the cargo sitting in Warehouse S10 by 21:00 hours, you've got yourself a deal."

They shook hands briefly, and Matt introduced himself. After a few more minutes of meaningless chatter (with Tanner complaining about every circumstance of his business he could think of, and Matt readily agreeing on the awfulness of it all), the other captain excused himself with the promise to send Matt the access codes to the cargo.

Val waited until Tanner was well out of earshot before turning to Matt and raising his eyebrows.

"We're working as dock hands now?"

"It's something," Matt retorted. It wasn't ideal, but at least it was something they could do in the meantime instead of pointlessly moping around. "Word gets out we're willing to pick up all those loose-end jobs, and we'll get more of them. It's true they don't pay much, but it all adds up, doesn't it? And we only need enough to get us running again, anyway. Now, can you get us one of those service forklifts?"

Val got up with a sigh. "I'll make some calls, but it's too noisy in here. I'll be right back."

He made his way toward the exit as Matt swiped the countertop to pay for their drinks. This job wasn't on his top list of lucrative ventures, but as he'd said, it was something. If he had to scrape for proverbial peanuts to make sure his ship stayed afloat, so be it.

Matt was about to take out his commlink to call on Ryce and Tony's assistance, but a large hand closed on his arm above the elbow and yanked him backward, nearly toppling him off his seat.

Matt spun around, glaring at the unexpected assailant. "Hey, man! What the hell?"

The other guy let go of his arm but did not step away. He was tall and muscular, with stark white hair that radiated from his head like spikes or a hedgehog's spines. He stared, unblinking, into Matt's eyes.

Matt's hackles rose. He prided himself on having an excellent preservation instinct, and right now, it was clamoring for him to get as far away and as fast as he could from this guy, ridiculous hair notwithstanding.

"Captain Spears, is it?" the man said. There was something slightly grating about his voice, like the scrape of metal against metal. "I heard you've been doing a bit of business here at the Broken Stairway."

"Maybe. What of it?"

"You're new here, on the 73," the man said, "so I'm gonna give you a heads-up. You can haul your shit in space all you want. But you don't butt in on what goes on around the station. That's Griggs's turf."

"Oh yeah? And who's Griggs?"

"My boss. And trust me, you don't wanna mess around with him."

Unfortunately, Matt had a long and tumultuous history of messing around with people he'd been warned against. While it certainly made life less boring, he preferred avoiding unnecessary trouble when he had no possible escape routes. Five hundred creds weren't worth getting on a local black-market dealer's bad side, at least not until Matt had the opportunity to find out if this Griggs fellow was really as influential as Frosty made him sound. Looking at the henchman, though, Matt's chances didn't seem promising.

"Listen," he said, holding up his hands in a pacifying gesture. In his experience, the best tactic was to play the naïve newbie, agree to everything, and hope to be able to circumvent the imposed restriction later. "I don't want any trouble. As you said, I'm not from around here. So, how about you give me the lay of the land, and we can see how we can work things out to keep Griggs happy?"

Frosty opened his mouth to answer, but in the same moment, a hurricane-like force swept him off his feet and threw him to the ground.

"I'm gonna kill you, you scum!" Val roared, punching the man in the face with bone-shattering force.

Ignoring the gasps and shouts of the startled patrons around them, Matt jumped off his seat and grabbed Val from behind in a vain attempt to contain him. It was like trying to hold back a spaceship in the middle of an interstellar jump.

"Val, stop!" Matt yelled in the engineer's ear, trying to avoid getting elbowed in the face. While he appreciated Val coming to his aid, this went beyond overreacting.

"*Kranty tebe, tvar'! Ublyudok poganyi!*" Val responded with a string of curses in Russian questioning the circumstances of Griggs's unfortunate representative's birth and his personal hygiene while making a serious effort at beating him into a pulp. However, the other man proved that Matt's instinctive assessment of him had been correct. In a blur of motion, he twisted out of Val's vise-like grip and kicked him in the groin. Val hissed in pain and fumbled backward, sending Matt, who was still holding on to him, sprawling on the dingy floor.

The white-haired man sprang lightly to his feet. Blood was streaming from his broken nose, but it hardly gave him pause. As Val scrambled to get up—fully prepared to lunge again at the other man—an electric blade appeared in Frosty's hand, glowing blue under the dim lighting. He bared his teeth, giving his bloodied appearance an even more deranged twist.

Aside from Matt, nobody else in the bar was reckless enough to try to break up the bizarre brawl. The place had emptied at the first sign of trouble. The bartender, crouched behind the counter, was talking to someone on his commlink—most likely station security.

"You think a knife's gonna help you?" Val asked with a sudden calm that scared Matt even more than his earlier blind rage. "I'll tear your heart out with my bare hands, *podonok.*"

"Val, for fuck's sake, stop it!" Matt got back to his feet and stepped between the men, holding his arms out. The hell was going on? This behavior was so unlike Val that his mind boggled. Matt had never seen the engineer be so violent with anybody.

Val swatted his hand away, his eyes blazing with murderous fury, but he didn't have the chance to renew the attack.

"Stop where you are!"

The responding officer hurried toward them across the empty canteen floor, gun drawn. Two more security guards followed on her heels.

Frosty's blade disappeared as quickly as it had come out, and he stepped back, lifting his hands docilely. Blood spattered the front of his gray T-shirt, making it obvious who'd borne the brunt of the assault.

"Now, officer, there seems to be some sort of misunderstanding—" Matt began, but the security team wasn't listening. The two guards took hold of Val, slapping a pair of magnetic handcuffs on him. Thankfully, the engineer didn't resist, but he still didn't take his eyes off the other guy, his chest heaving with barely contained rage. If looks could kill, Frosty would have been incinerated on the spot, but now, handcuffed and held at gunpoint, all Val could do was glare at him.

"What's going on here?" the officer demanded sternly, her gun still at the ready.

"This crazy fucker attacked me out of nowhere," Frosty said. "I think he broke my nose."

"He did attack him," the bartender piped in. Matt turned to glower at him, but the guy ignored him. "These guys were talking, and then he," he gestured to Val, "just came at him for no reason. Yelled something about killing him. I was afraid he was gonna do it, too."

"This what happened?" the officer asked, turning to Matt and Frosty. The other man nodded and made a point of wiping his nose with his sleeve.

"Now, wait just a moment," Matt interjected. Everything was going terribly wrong, and it seemed like he was powerless to put a stop to the absurdity of it. "There must be some kind of mistake. I'm sure Val had no intention of hurting this gentleman, right Val?"

"The hell I didn't," Val ground through his teeth. "This bastard killed my wife."

"What?" Matt looked at him in confusion. "I thought you'd...I thought *that* guy was dead."

"There were two of them," Val said. "I never tracked down the other one. Until now."

Matt turned to Frosty, but apparently the guy had taken advantage of their momentary distraction and slipped away unnoticed. It happened so fast Matt couldn't even tell which direction he'd taken. "Damn! Where did he go?"

"Make sure to find him and take him in for questioning," the officer told the other guards before holstering her weapon and gesturing to them to lead Val to the exit. "Let's go."

"Wait, where are you taking him?"

"Protective Services Office. Let him cool off a bit and see if anybody presses charges."

Matt was left to watch helplessly as Val was hauled away, still trying to process this new information.

"Fuck my life." He wearily rubbed his forehead. The piss beer had not been enough to properly prepare him for handling this kind of fiasco. "And thanks for all *your* help," he told the bartender.

The man threw his hands up. "Hey, don't look at me. I know better than to screw with the wrong people. It's more than my life's worth if I didn't back him up."

"Who is that guy, anyway?" Matt asked.

He was ready to howl with frustration, but that wasn't going to help anybody. Having his engineer arrested for battery and disorderly conduct was yet another item on the long list of things he didn't need right now, and he had to figure out quickly how to get Val out of trouble.

"Eddie Ander, Griggs's enforcer. He's one hell of a badass. In fact, both of them are. If I were you, I'd stay well out of their way," the bartender advised.

"Gotcha," Matt said, fighting the urge to flip the guy off.

What was it with him and homicidal delinquents? Was he some kind of a magnet for attracting the attention of dangerous criminals, or was it his horrible luck at work again? Typical, that the second things were beginning to pick up, the shit had to hit the fan in the most spectacular fashion. Not that he could blame Val for his blowout, given the circumstances, but absolutely none of it was conducive to their getting off this godforsaken station as soon as possible.

Matt got out his commlink to notify Tony and Ryce of the recent developments and headed to the station's Security Center to try to get his misbehaving engineer out of jail.

Chapter Three

"HOW MUCH LONGER is this going to take?" Matt grumbled.

Ryce, who was sitting next to him, put a soothing hand on his arm.

"It's just the formalities now. They have to hold him for twelve hours for inquiry even if no charges are pressed. I suppose he's lucky the security folks didn't insist on pursuing the public disturbance angle," he added as an afterthought.

Matt huffed in annoyance. "Lucky my ass. He was only lucky in that this Ander guy wasn't armed with a blaster gun. He could've been killed, going after him bare-handed." He checked the clock on his commlink for the hundredth time. "This twelve-hour thing is taking way too long."

"I've never met anyone who was as constantly offended by the concept of linear time progression as you are," Ryce said, his lips quirking. "Anyway, he should be out any minute now."

He glanced at the door of the Protective Services Office. They were sitting in the waiting area, which consisted of several rows of metal chairs and smelled faintly of disinfectant and despair.

"Wiseass," Matt said. "By the way, I had to cancel our engagement with Captain Tanner. He wasn't best pleased, but I don't know yet who this Griggs person is, and I thought it'd be best to let sleeping dogs lie until we got this whole mess straightened out. Besides, ain't much we can do by way of hauling without Val's help."

Having to give up an easy job rankled, even if the pay wasn't so great. Canceling at the last minute wasn't going to reflect positively on their reputation, especially since their next contract would be largely dependent on favorable word of mouth. But the most important thing was getting Val back from the clutches of station security. Matt suspected the only reason Val didn't get into much worse trouble was because his victim was somewhat of a known thug. Well, that, and Matt's willingness to pay the bail money in cash. He sighed heavily, imagining all those credits leaking out of his account like water out of a cracked plastic cup.

"Is it true this Eddie Ander was complicit in the death of Val's wife?" Ryce asked in a low voice, though nobody was close enough to overhear them.

"I have no idea," Matt said tiredly. "I couldn't find out anything beyond what Val had told me, but the security folks weren't especially forthcoming, and I didn't have time to dig deeper on my own. If it's true…"

If it was true, it would present a whole new set of problems because Matt was pretty sure Val wouldn't let it go. He'd served five years in federal prison for killing one of the men who'd raped and murdered his wife, and considered it a fair exchange. If there was a second killer on the loose and within Val's reach, Matt was certain no power in the universe could stop him from hunting him down. And as much as Matt sympathized with the sentiment, he couldn't let Val pursue a path which would most likely end with him locked up for good, or worse.

He was about to say so to Ryce when the heavy armored doors finally slid open, and a harried-looking officer escorted Val out. Matt jumped to his feet and rushed to meet them, with Ryce following on his heels.

"You're Captain Spears?" the officer asked.

"Yes, that's me."

"Try to keep your crew out of bar fights," the officer said in the weary tone of someone who'd made that request too many times to believe it would be granted. "You're to remain at Freeport 73 for the next forty-eight hours. Then you're free to go if no complaint is filed against Mr. Sokolov here."

"Couldn't leave even if we wanted to," Ryce observed while Matt signed the custody release form on the officer's commlink. "Are you all right, Val?"

Val nodded curtly. Since walking out of his detention cell, he'd kept ominous silence, only curling his hands in and out of fists. His knuckles were scraped raw, but Matt remembered all too well how the other guy had looked.

"Care to explain what the hell happened in there?" Matt asked once they were out of the Security Center and safely on their way back to the docks.

"No," the engineer said curtly.

"Listen here." Matt rounded on him, taking advantage of the secluded stretch of corridor they were currently in. Ryce hung back, glancing between them with concern. "I'm on your side here, remember? But I can't do anything to help if you refuse to even talk to me."

There was a pause as Val considered his words. For a moment, it seemed like he was going to say something, but finally, he only shook his head.

"You can't help me with this. And if you try, it'll only make it worse."

"Why?" Matt faced him, hands on his hips. It wasn't the best time and place to have this confrontation, but he was too damn frustrated with worry and the long wait to postpone it until they were in the privacy of *Lady Lisa*'s galley.

Val's mouth thinned into a hard line, and he stared determinately at the wall above Matt's head.

"I'll tell you why," Matt said angrily. "You think you're going to track down that fucker and finish what you started, don't you? Well, you better think again, because I'll be damned if I'm gonna let you get yourself killed or put away for life because of some lowlife scum!"

"You don't understand," Val said harshly.

"Then explain it to me because I sure as hell don't!"

"He has a point, Val," Ryce interjected before the argument could escalate. His tone was level but firm, bringing to mind that, despite his youth, he'd had plenty of experience as a commanding officer. "You certainly don't owe us any explanations, but shutting us out isn't going to make this go away."

Val took a deep breath and glanced sideways at Ryce.

"Elena was an eco-architect. She designed environmental habitats for people living and working in small colonies—the ones it wasn't cost-effective to terraform. She'd won awards for creating affordable and ergonomic living spaces. She wanted to make people happy. We wanted to start a family."

He swallowed and briefly closed his eyes but continued. "And those two bastards took it all away from her, just because they could. They took her away from me, and I wasn't there to stop it when it happened. When they arrested that trash, Corgan, he claimed they didn't intend to kill her. They only *had a little fun* with her, and she resisted too hard."

His accent, which was usually hardly noticeable, became thicker as he struggled to keep his emotions in check. "She'd been beaten so bad I had trouble recognizing her afterward. They never caught the other one. And Corgan...I couldn't take the chance of him ever walking out of prison alive. I waited until they were transporting him for the trial, and I went over there, and I bashed his face in. And it felt damn good because at least he suffered a fraction of what Elena had suffered before he died. I did the time for that, but I didn't care. My freedom meant nothing without her." He paused again, visibly calming himself, assuming his usual taciturn demeanor.

"But I didn't forget about the second guy who had been there. Eddie Ander. I tried to find him, but that piece of shit was good at covering his tracks. After joining the *Lady Lisa* and moving to the Sonora sector, I kinda lost hope of finding him. But now... Captain, I know you want to help. I know you want to keep me safe. But you can't, not this time. Just stay out of it." He looked between Matt and Ryce. "All of you."

Val turned and strode purposefully down the corridor toward the docks without waiting for Matt and Ryce to catch up.

THE ONLY THING that made the miserable day marginally better was the prospect of a fresh brew. Matt could definitely use some coffee, along with whatever he could find in the pantry to fix himself a quick snack. He was starving.

"I think I'll go talk to him," Ryce said, pausing in the main corridor.

"Really? I'm not sure it's such a good idea right now. Val's pissed."

Matt had never seen his engineer so worked up. That angry tirade in the station hallway was more words than Val had uttered over the past year, and the first time he'd opened up about his personal tragedy to anyone but Matt. He was familiar with the gist of Val's story, of course, but not with all the gruesome details.

Ryce grimaced. "I know. But I want to be sure he doesn't run off and do something rash."

He'll probably do it anyway, Matt thought wearily, but Ryce was right. Val needed to cool off, and perhaps a sympathetic ear lent by a friend would not go amiss. Ryce was a good listener, as Matt knew from his own experience. Ryce also possessed an uncanny ability for finding the right words of solace, which had never been Matt's forte.

"Fine. Good luck." He squeezed Ryce's hand in reassurance, and, once the man turned toward the cabins, made a beeline to the galley and its promise of salvation.

Tony was there eating a sandwich. "Val just stormed past here," she said, watching Matt turn on the coffee maker and pour himself a large steaming mug. "I have it that detention didn't sit well with him."

"Not even a little bit." Matt took a can of creamed corn soup out of the pantry and sat at the kitchen table without bothering to heat it up. He badly wanted to cap the day off with a shot of something stronger, but Tony was watching him, and he decided to forgo the alcohol for the moment.

Tony made a face at him, though it was hard to tell whether it was prompted by his words or his meal choice.

"Hopefully Ryce'll do a better job of reasoning with him than I did," Matt said around a spoonful of cold soup. "Otherwise, with us stuck on this godforsaken station, it's only a matter of time until he goes all vigilante again. And by *time*, I mean however long it takes him to clean up and find a weapon."

"God, what a mess." She finished her sandwich and folded her arms on the table's shiny white surface, a look of deep concern on her face. "Val's not gonna let this go, is he? What are we going to do?"

"I don't know what we *can* do, short of locking him up in his cabin. Besides, he's a grown person. He can make his own choices, however foolhardy they are. But there are other ways to bring someone to justice, besides breaking their teeth. Maybe I'll try going to the station authorities, see what can be done."

Matt scraped out the last drops of the corn emulsion from the can and leaned back in his chair, sipping his coffee. He hated involving the Federal authorities in any of his or his crew's private affairs, and the chance of them actually being helpful was slim. But it was a better option than the alternative.

"There was something else I wanted to talk to you about," Tony said.

The hesitation in her voice caught Matt's attention.

"Go on."

"I managed to get in touch with some people from the station IMA branch."

"You did? That's great," Matt said, though Tony seemed anything but enthusiastic. "What did they say?"

"As I expected, most of them weren't thrilled to hear from me." She sighed. "But the branch head used to be a friend of mine back when we both worked at the clinical trial administration division. She said they're in the market for a contractor to take over regular and emergency medical aid shipments to the outer moons of Elysium-8. There are a few colonies there, mostly mining, and one research facility that's currently under construction. There'll be a tender, of course, but since it's a lot of hard work and the job is less than stellar, there's not a lot of interest."

"It could be a good niche for us, though." This was exactly the sort of job Matt had hoped to score—small but steady, something that could allow them to get back on their feet and gain repute, albeit slowly. There was only one problem with this otherwise promising scenario.

"Provided we win the tender based on our bid," Matt continued, "do you think the IMA would be willing to give us an advance on our contract? Otherwise, the job is no good to us if we're stuck here indefinitely."

Tony shook her head. "I don't think so." She must have had the same concerns, which would explain the lack of eagerness. "As a Federal agency, they have regulations regarding these things. But I did manage to set up a meeting for us tomorrow. Perhaps we can work something out."

"That's good," Matt said, though she didn't sound convinced. "Really, don't worry about it, Tony. Even if this doesn't pan out tomorrow, it's a good option to keep in mind if we manage to set sail again soon. Thank you. I know it couldn't have been easy for you."

Tony shrugged and pulled at her braid.

"It was nice to see some old faces. Not all, but some."

Matt patted her hand. "Whoever is wrinkling their noses at you can suck it. If they can't see what an awesome person you are, it's their loss, hot stuff."

She smiled at him, but the sadness still lingered in her eyes.

WHEN MATT WALKED out of the galley, he bumped into Ryce coming up the corridor.

"Look, Val gave me a book," Ryce said.

Matt glanced at the book. It was dog-eared, the yellow pages fragile enough to crumble at the wrong touch. The faded cover read *Slime Monsters from Outer Space!* and depicted said monsters cavorting with a scantily clad busty blonde. Ryce was holding it as if it were a precious museum piece, his face alight with childlike happiness. He was always stunningly gorgeous, but when he smiled in genuine joy, it was like watching the sun rise over the ocean on old Earth. It made Matt happy in an absurd way.

"I've never actually owned a real paper book before."

"I hope that doesn't mean Val is giving away all his earthly possessions," Matt said, tearing his gaze away from Ryce's sparkling gray eyes. "Or, well, shipbound possessions."

"Of course not." Ryce turned, and they both walked down the corridor, heading toward Ryce's cabin by some unspoken mutual agreement. The cabins were too cramped for people to share comfortably on a day-to-day basis, so they just drifted in and out of each other's living quarters as the mood took them. In any case, it was a good idea to have some breathing space once in a while, seeing as they were cooped up together for days on end.

"In fact, we had a good talk," Ryce said as the door slid open before them. "He agreed his actions had reflected poorly on the rest of the crew. We can't afford getting caught in any criminal activity while looking for work."

Matt, who was far more lenient than Ryce on the concept of "criminal activity," merely grunted noncommittally. It was surprising that this argument, over all others, could convince Val to cool his head and proceed with caution, but Matt was going to take whatever he could get. Besides, Val and Ryce seemed to have some sort of special connection, so it figured Ryce would be more likely to get through to him. Sometimes Matt envied that connection, but he couldn't fault Ryce for wanting to talk to someone who came close to being his intellectual peer. God knew Matt wasn't up to par in that regard.

He sat on the bunk bed heavily, running his fingers through his hair.

"God, I'm so ready for this day to be over. Gotta go to the Freeport admin to see what they can do about this Ander guy if Val files an official report on him. But first, Tony has set up a meeting for us tomorrow morning at the IMA branch office. If we're lucky, we might get us a hauling contract."

"Do you want me to go with you?" Ryce ran his fingers gently over Matt's temple, skimming above the pilot's neuro-implants that created the link with the ship's computer during flight. Matt hardly used his anymore except for routine checkups.

Matt took his hand and turned it to kiss his palm. They were both still a bit self-conscious about these little gestures of intimacy, neither of them the overly affectionate type. Three weeks of living together as a couple were too short to negate lifelong habits—especially considering they were stumbling through the "get to know one another" phase of their budding relationship. But Matt couldn't deny it felt good. Each touch was like a sip of cool water on a hot day, like a first taste of strong coffee in the morning—something to satisfy a craving that verged on need.

"Definitely," he said. "We can use every ounce of good impression, and you're by far the most articulate. Though, to tell you the truth, I'd prefer someone stay here and keep an eye on Val, just in case."

"Don't worry so much," Ryce said. "Val promised me he wouldn't do anything impulsive."

Matt nodded, but despite Ryce's assurances, he had a very, very bad feeling about this.

Chapter Four

THE SHADOWS ALL lay in odd angles, and the perspective shifted without him moving. He knew it was a dream, but this knowledge didn't make it any less terrifying. The memories he tried so hard to repress filtered into his subconscious anyway, feeding the nightmares.

He was half-naked, strung by his arms to the ceiling with his feet barely touching the floor. He had to stand on tiptoes to ease the pain in his shoulder blades.

He wasn't alone. Every time he jerked gracelessly in his bonds, there was laughter and jeers, though he couldn't see the faces of his tormentors clearly.

Then they began beating him—deliberate, practiced blows which were meant to cause pain rather than real damage. The entertainment had just begun, after all; there was no point in him passing out so early on.

He tasted blood as someone backhanded him across the face. He tried to kick out with his legs, but that earned him a few punches to the kidneys. Soon, all he could do was simply hang there like a piece of tenderized meat and hope for it to be over. He could take a few hits, even if they made him cough and wheeze and flail.

The crewmen wouldn't kill him anyway, not until Rodgers decided he should die. He could endure until some kind of opportunity presented itself.

Then, one of the men yanked his pants down.

MATT'S EYES FLEW open. The darkness was broken only by the faint green glow of the strip of night lighting running along the edge of the ceiling. The wisps of panic that had seized him in the dream still clung to his body, choking him, making his throat spasm.

Beside him, Ryce stirred into wakefulness. The bunk was too narrow for them to sprawl on, and every unnecessary movement was bound to disturb his partner. Matt forced his breathing to relax, but it was too late to feign sleep.

"Is everything all right?" Ryce asked, sounding groggy.

"Yeah. Sorry. Go back to sleep."

Ryce wasn't falling for it, though. He turned to face Matt, his eyes glinting eerily in the green light. Through the receding haze of vague terror, Matt wondered absently if improved night vision was one of the enhanced attributes Ryce enjoyed as an Onorean. Well, half-Onorean. There was still so much Matt didn't know about him. So much he wanted to find out.

"Another nightmare?" Ryce asked softly.

Matt nodded. It was embarrassing, really. He was a grown man, not a child to be spooked by a bad dream. Val telling him about the death of his wife had probably triggered it, though God knew, he didn't need any more fuel for his bad dreams than he already had. There were enough odd and fragmented memories of his captivity on Dylan Rodgers's *Black Baza* to last him a lifetime.

Ryce brushed his fingers against Matt's cheek tenderly, soothingly, leaving traces of warmth on Matt's skin. He leaned into it, craving that warmth as badly as he'd ever craved a drink.

"Please," he whispered. "I need to know it's you."

That must have sounded odd. Matt didn't know himself exactly what he meant, except it echoed something in his nightmare, something that slipped away as he tried to recall it. But apparently, Ryce was cannier than him, as he always was, because he closed the awning gap between them and pressed his lips to Matt's.

Matt drew him closer, pulling Ryce on top of him. The thin blanket slipped, leaving their skin exposed to the cool temperature-controlled air. The kiss deepened, both of them holding on to the minute wonder of this intimacy, its simple sweetness. The lighting remained steady, but the dimness around them seemed to change quality, embracing them in a cocoon of safety rather than pressing down on them.

It was only a trick of perception, but Matt didn't care. He finally broke the kiss, gasping for air, and ran his hands over Ryce's smooth skin, the muscles flexing under his touch.

"I want you," he whispered, surprising himself with the raw desperation that laced his voice. "I want you to—"

He couldn't say "fuck me." That would be a lie. With Ryce, it would be so much more than simple fucking, enjoyable as it could be. They hadn't taken things that far yet, choosing instead to go slow with the physical aspect of their relationship. They had all the time in the world to explore each other's wants and needs without rushing, to build on the unlikely and wondrous bond that had brought them together. But now, in the embrace of darkness, Matt needed Ryce to ground him, to keep his mind from drifting off to those forgotten and forbidden places within that terrified him.

Ryce didn't respond at first, and the silence grew heavier with every second. Finally, he drew slightly back, looking down at Matt. Their bodies were still pressed together, with only the fabric of their briefs separating them, leaving no room to doubt that physically, at least, Ryce was no less aroused by their caresses than he was. But at the same time, Matt could feel the distance between them stretching, the warmth seeping away with every quiet heartbeat.

"I'm sorry," Ryce said. "It's not that I don't want to, but I don't think I can. Not yet."

Matt knew well enough by now that, for Ryce, a strong emotional connection had to precede a sexual relationship, and if he said he needed more time, then they weren't there yet. It left Matt slightly disappointed. Not with the lack of sex, but with the realization that despite them having lived together as a couple for nearly a month, sharing every aspect of their lives, it seemed like Ryce still didn't feel as strongly about Matt as Matt did about him. About them. As if he doubted Matt's feelings, his commitment.

Granted, Matt hadn't said the words Ryce might have been waiting for. He'd never said them to anyone, not in the romantic sense. The concept of love was too big for him, too intimidating; it was something that happened to other people, not to him. And if it did, it would only be a matter of time until it was taken away from him.

"It's okay," he whispered. He still held on to Ryce, but his touch softened, losing its urgency as he squashed his arousal. "There's no pressure. You know I'll wait for you for as long as you need, right?"

Ryce settled back without answering, stroking his hair, and Matt closed his eyes again, willing himself to relax and accept the affection for what it was—a precious and fragile thing, far more important than momentary satisfaction. The gentle touch and the smell of Ryce's clean skin helped calm him. His racing heart slowed, and his thoughts cleared, leaving nothing but fatigue. The nightmares had a tendency to drain him emotionally, but it was so much easier dealing with the aftermath, lying in Ryce's arms.

Eventually, Matt reached down and pulled the blanket over their cooling bodies. He thought lazily about going back to his own cabin, to give Ryce a chance to rest after effectively ruining his sleep. But he had to admit there was no way he was getting up now. In fact, he wanted to stay there in the dark for as long as he could, listening to the sound of their hearts beating together. If only they could stay like this forever, suspended in the sweet limbo between sleep and wakefulness.

But he could feel Ryce was still wide awake, and he squeezed his hand gently.

"You okay?"

"Yes. But...there was something I wanted to talk to you about."

Uh-oh. The pleasant numbness Matt had been slipping into dissipated, leaving a faint trace of anxiety. The "we need to talk" routine was never a good thing.

"Sure," he said, stroking Ryce's palm with his thumb to hide his worry. "What did you want to talk about?"

"I realize this isn't the best time to bring this up. I've been meaning to talk to you about it for a few days now, but with everything going on—the engine breaking down and Val's arrest—there hasn't been a chance to—"

"Ryce, please, just tell me what's it about."

Ryce took a deep breath, as if before a plunge, and Matt braced himself for something deeply unpleasant.

"Nora called me about a week ago."

"What?" He must have not heard correctly. Why would his sister, a Major in the Federal Fleet, be calling his ex-military boyfriend?

"Nora called me," Ryce repeated patiently.

"Why would she call you?"

"She wanted to offer me a job."

Matt sat upright on the bed, his heart once again pounding against his ribcage like a frightened bird, but for a whole different reason. A part of him wondered if he was still caught in a nightmare, one where everything he held dear evaporated even as he tried futilely to grasp it in his hands.

"What kind of job?" His voice sounded hollow and foreign in his ears.

"She wouldn't specify." Ryce sat up as well. "Apparently, most of it is classified. All she could say was that it involved the Mnirians and that she would like to bring me on as a consultant, given my expertise on the subject."

"A consultant," Matt echoed, trying to rally his scattered thoughts. "And what do you think it would require? You won't be joining the ranks again, but anything involving Mnirian technology is confidential. There's no way they'd let you even be in contact with us, much less stay on *Lady Lisa*. You'd belong to the Fleet again, for as long as they'd want you. Are you seriously considering going back there after all the crap they've put you through?"

"I'm not considering anything yet," Ryce said, a touch defensively. "And you're being entirely too dramatic. It's a job offer, not a prison sentence. Anyway, I'm still not sure what this is all about. Major Cummings told me to call her back if I'm interested, and I believe after all she has done for us, I ought to at least hear her out. Do you think..." He trailed off in the face of Matt's moody silence.

"It's not that I'm not grateful to my sister for getting me off grand larceny and treason charges after our little kerfuffle at Colanta," Matt said finally, hoping he didn't sound as caustic as he felt. "But if she wants to steal you in favor of her war games, she at least could have had the decency to notify me first."

"Be that as it may, I *am* asking for your input," Ryce said, his tone significantly colder. "I'm not seeking approval, but I'm not going behind your back, either."

Matt took a deep breath. He didn't want to get further into a pointless argument—especially seeing as Ryce's mind was apparently already made up, and Matt's opinion on the matter was all but irrelevant. And as far as Ryce was concerned, the opportunity couldn't have come at a better time. With everything that was going on, it was unclear whether they could stay afloat much longer. A gifted pilot and scholar of Ryce's caliber would have no difficulty working his way back up the Fleet career ladder, given the option to return to its ranks in any capacity.

Ryce was going to leave, and Matt couldn't—*wouldn't*—do anything to stop him. But he owed it to Ryce to be honest.

"It's your call," he said, doing his best to sound nonchalant rather than petulant. Ryce's expression told him he wasn't doing a stellar job. "You know how I feel about having any liaisons with the Federal military, and the fact my sister is the one facilitating them doesn't make it better. You'll be working for them again, getting involved in all their dirty politics. Wasn't that the reason you joined my crew—to escape this kind of bullshit?"

"That wasn't the reason," Ryce said quietly. "You were."

Matt stared at him. The planes of Ryce's face fit together like a beautiful puzzle, half shrouded in shadow, and he swallowed hard, overwhelmed by emotion.

Of course he knew it was true. Simply being together, sharing the same bed, even if it was just for sleeping, was proof enough of that. But hearing it stated outright was almost too much to process. It robbed him of all his defenses, of all his outrage.

"I'm not jumping into anything," Ryce said. "I just want to hear what they have to say."

Matt rubbed the bridge of his nose. He was too tired to continue the conversation, and he'd already made his stance clear.

"You're right. If it's important enough that they want you back on board, it wouldn't hurt to at least hear the details. Just...keep me in the loop, okay?"

"Okay," Ryce said slowly. "I'll do that."

They settled back in bed, their hands lightly touching, but neither made a move to close the distance again.

Chapter Five

"ARE YOU NERVOUS?" Tony asked.

They were sitting in the Interstellar Medical Aid reception area. It was generic, as waiting rooms went, but still much nicer than that of Station Security. A heavily pregnant woman and her partner were sitting in the corner, both too engrossed with their commlinks to pay them much attention. Three Parveni travelers, with their long, equine faces and brightly patterned garments, occupied another corner. IMA station branches often catered to aliens, especially if they could boast xenomedicine experts or actual alien physicians working for them.

Matt kept checking his commlink—studiously avoiding making eye contact with Ryce, who was sitting next to him—though what he was expecting to find there, aside from the slowly ticking time, he couldn't say. It wasn't as though a magical solution was somehow going to fall into his incoming messages tab. If anything, it was a gateway to receiving even more bad news.

"I'm not nervous," he told Tony. "I just hate to be kept waiting. Apparently, I have an issue with linear time progression."

The truth was, he was fretting. He couldn't get the conversation he'd had with Ryce out of his head. So, instead of focusing on the upcoming meeting, he was running future scenarios in his mind, and all of them appeared exceptionally bleak. He'd barely exchanged a word with Ryce this morning, and while he supposed it was asinine of him, he simply didn't know what to say that wouldn't sound sour despite his best efforts.

He couldn't control his boyfriend's decisions. Better to concentrate on the things he had any chance of influencing, namely, charming IMA officials into handing an exclusive carrier contract to a defunct ship. Which sounded totally plausible and not hard to do at all.

"Is everything all right?" Tony asked in a low voice, looking between him and Ryce. Unfortunately, she was too sharp not to sense the tension.

"Couldn't be better," Matt muttered. Ryce moved uncomfortably in his seat and gave him a sideways look.

Tony frowned and was about to say something when a red-haired person wearing an IMA badge and holding a commlink approached them.

"Ms. Joyce? Mr. Spears? And...?" They checked the commlink before raising their eyes to Ryce expectantly.

"Mr. Easom," he supplied politely.

Hearing Ryce's real name spoken aloud still felt a bit weird to Matt. He was used to thinking of him as Ryce Faine, which was what he called himself when they first met. Old habits die hard.

"Of course. I'm Mx. Conn. Please follow me."

Despite the awkwardness between them, Matt was glad Ryce had come along. His eloquence and level of professionalism was a serious advantage when it came to conducting business negotiations in any setting more formal than the local pub.

They were led into a generic meeting room, which was decorated in a stark whiteness that reminded Matt of a hospital. Taking seats around a shiny oval table, they waited while Ryce took it upon himself to fix them all coffee from the sleek machine tucked in the corner.

The coffee was actually very good, but it did little to ease Matt's anxiety. It wasn't just this meeting he was worried about, but the entire array of problems they'd found themselves entangled in with no readily available solutions in sight. The busted engine and Val's past catching up with him were bad enough, but the possibility of Ryce leaving (and there was little doubt in Matt's mind this was eventually going to happen) was the final straw that cracked his fortitude.

After a few minutes of silence, a dark-haired, middle-aged woman wearing the white IMA uniform entered the room.

"I apologize for the delay," she said, sitting at the head of the table. "It's a busy day around here. I'm Dr. Yang. Nice to see you again, Antonia."

Tony nodded politely. Matt could tell by the set of her shoulders and the tightness around her mouth that she was tense. At least no one was giving her the side-eye, and Dr. Yang, the head of the local branch, seemed nice.

"So, I understand you're interested in submitting a bid for delivery services to the Elysium-8 moon outposts?" she asked, addressing Matt.

"That's right," he said. "We have a Phaeton hauler—not a large one, but very fast. We could cut your current delivery times in third, if not more, for those emergency shipments. Mr. Easom here has all the details."

"I took the liberty of drafting a proposal," Ryce said, readily taking over. He tapped his commlink, sending the document to Dr. Yang's address. "As Captain Spears said, we estimate our flight time from Freeport 73 to the more distant moons, like Dinona and Comera, to be around three to four days. Emergency flights can be made even faster, around two to three days—at a higher price per run than the regularly scheduled hauls, of course. Still, you'll note our rates are very competitive, compared to same-sized haulers."

Emergency flights on a busted engine, Matt thought, but, of course, said nothing out loud.

"The numbers certainly look good," Dr. Yang said, skimming the proposal. "I must say I'm pleasantly surprised. And very glad you came to me with this, Antonia. I'd say you have excellent chances of winning the bid. There aren't a lot of applicants for this particular job, I'm afraid, and your technical capabilities are very impressive, at least on paper."

Tony gave a tight smile and pulled at her braid.

"There is a slight setback," Matt said. The last thing he wanted was to commit to the job and then let Tony take the blame if it fell through because he wasn't honest from the beginning. Or at least as honest as the situation allowed without scaring off a potential client right off the bat. "We're in the middle of some, um, upgrades on the engine. So we can't start flying until everything is ready."

Dr. Yang frowned. "How much longer until you're operational? The bidding ends in about a week; we're very eager to get started with the new service as soon as possible, whoever they are. Folks working in the mines on those moons need their medical equipment, and with the new research facility on Sota close to completion, the shipping schedule is bound to become hectic."

"We should be done by then," Ryce said. He sounded convincing enough to Matt, but that wasn't saying much. "And if the terms of the contract allow for an advance, we could do an even more substantial systems overhaul, to give you an extra edge."

He paused as Dr. Yang shook her head.

"There is no advance. In fact, our payments are strictly quarterly, per standard procedure. Frankly, if your ship isn't in working order, I'm not so sure I can even let you bid. We're looking for solid proposals, and this—"

"We are very interested in this job, and I can assure you we'll be fully operational in a week's time," Matt said quickly.

He had absolutely no idea how they were going to achieve that, but this opportunity was too good to pass on, especially after such a positive response from the branch head. This contract would award them that much-needed respectability, and a solid source of income for the foreseeable future, even if it meant working harder than usual. They would just have to figure something out on the fly.

"Is this right, Antonia?" Dr. Yang asked, turning to Tony.

"Yes," Tony said without hesitation, even though she was perfectly aware of how screwed up they were. It kind of warmed Matt's heart she would back him up like that without any actual ground to stand on. "If Captain Spears says we'll be ready to fly on time, then we will be."

"All right," Dr. Yang said. Judging by her expression, their assurances weren't doing a great deal for her. But apparently, Tony still had some credibility with her former colleague, because she continued: "Why don't you go ahead and submit your bid. The board will have to review everything, of course, but in the meantime, I'd like to invite you, Antonia, and your colleagues to a reception tonight. The branch will be welcoming guests from Onor, who are collaborating with the IMA on the Sota Research Center. They'll also be presenting a short seminar on the joint diagnostic nanosensors project. I expect they will be vetting most of the logistic solutions for the center now that they're here, so it might not be a bad idea to introduce yourselves in an informal setting first."

"Thank you. We appreciate the opportunity," Tony said, glancing uneasily at Matt. "Captain?"

"We'll be there," Matt hastened to say. "Wouldn't miss it for the world."

"THAT WENT PRETTY well," Matt said brightly once they were ushered out of the offices back into the waiting area.

"Terrific," Tony muttered darkly.

"Come on, we've as good as got the job," Matt argued. "You heard what she said. We were *impressive*. You can't ask for more than that."

"Sure, it's impressive when the genius crunches the numbers," Tony said, nodding to Ryce. "But that only works in theory. How in hell are you planning on being up and running in a week? We're fucking broke!"

"Would you two keep your voices down?" Ryce said with a touch of exasperation, glancing around to make sure no one was listening in. "There's hardly any point in me doing the math if our integrity is compromised."

"I'm not saying it'll be easy," Matt said to Tony, dropping his voice to a whisper. "But I haven't given up yet. I'll do everything I can, and if nothing works out, I'm gonna withdraw the bid before they even make the decision. Are you cool with that?"

She nodded, but he could tell she was still angry with him. Which she had every right to be. But now wasn't the time to turn on each other; not when they had to scramble to save their ship.

"I'm not thrilled about going to this function tonight," Tony added as they headed toward the exit and into the station corridor. "Dr. Yang might be friendly and doing me a courtesy by inviting us, but I'm not looking forward to meeting any of the others."

"I don't think I should be going either," Ryce chimed in unexpectedly.

"Why?" Matt turned to him in surprise. He'd hated social events with a burning passion ever since he was a little kid forced into attending his grandmother's elaborate soirees, but in this case, he was willing to bite the bullet if it helped their business connections.

"You won't curry any favors with the Onoreans by bringing along a half-breed."

"Don't be absurd. And if any of them dares call you names, I'll punch them in the face."

Onoreans were notorious both for practicing preimplantation genetic modification on their progeny and for maintaining a seclusive society which the Federation only put up with because of their advanced biomedical technologies. Even putting aside the abhorrent nature of Ryce's conception that made his Onorean birth mother give him up for adoption as a baby, he would have to be seen as a sort of abomination by his people, who engineered their offspring down to the last gene. The randomness of his parentage interfering with their careful selection must have been as off-putting as any genetic mistake they could have created in a lab, but it wasn't as if that particular aspect of his biography had to be advertised upon introduction.

Ryce's smile was crooked.

"Picking a fight would rather defeat the purpose of sucking up to them, wouldn't it?"

"Still, this reception thing is a solid opportunity," Matt insisted. The prospect of wading through the formal niceties alone was less than appealing. "You never know who else might be attending. We could easily score another job by getting to know the right people, even if this one's a flop. It's all about making that good impression, remember?"

"Fine." Ryce sighed, turning off his commlink and putting it in the trouser pocket of his fatigues. "If you want me to, I'll be there."

"Thank you." Matt turned to Tony. "What do you say? Can we close ranks on this one?"

"I guess," she said grumpily. "At least there'll be free food."

"I promised Val I'd go make a sweep of the local junkyard after the meeting," Ryce said, changing the subject. "See if we can at least score a decent secondhand power converter, just for the time being. If we manage to install it in the next few days, we could conceivably last a few months until we get our first payment from the IMA, and then we can splurge on a new one."

"If the thing holds for a few months," Matt said. It was actually a good plan, one that would allow them to accept the job if they ended up winning the tender and give them some wiggle room. But used spare parts were too unreliable, in his opinion, especially when their lives depended on them. His upgrades to the ship's systems had always been top-notch, and it rankled that he'd have to settle for the unknown with such a vital piece of equipment, even temporarily.

"We can at least try." Ryce's calm voice was usually comforting, but now, Matt couldn't help but feel slightly annoyed, as if Ryce was being condescending on purpose.

He knew it had nothing to do with Ryce's tone; it was simply repressed fear. Fear that Ryce was going to just up and leave, because, realistically, Matt had nothing to offer him that would entice him to stay. Nothing but himself, but he realized perfectly well that whatever Ryce had said last night about being here because of him, he simply wasn't good enough.

When Matt failed to offer a response, Ryce nodded, as if that concluded the discussion, and strode off toward the elevators.

Chapter Six

MATT HAD TO admit that his crew cleaned up nicely. Granted, none of them possessed anything remotely close to formal attire. Even so, the three of them looked rather dashing—and, as transportation providers, it was hardly expected they be decked out in finery anyway.

Ryce, in Matt's humble opinion, looked particularly good this evening, out of his usual fatigues and wearing slim-fit black trousers and a simple crisp white shirt that showed off his lean physique. This tiny hint of sensuality gave him the appearance of being approachable, less austere, and Matt had a hard time tearing his gaze away and focusing on the rest of the room.

Val had declined Matt's offer to join them this evening—which, considering both his scruffy appearance and his bad mood, was perhaps for the best. Knowing him, Matt was sure that spending time in the engine room would work much better toward lifting his spirits than boredom at some stuffy reception.

The event, which was held at the station's conference center, was much more modest and professionally geared than Matt's grandmother's famously fancy parties, but Matt still felt out of his element. There were dozens of people there, most of them IMA employees and Freeport officials, with a few civilians thrown into the mix. As far as he could tell, they were the only independent contractors in attendance. Other than the IMA representative who greeted them upon arrival, they were effectively ignored, barring a few disapproving glances thrown Tony's way—which she stalwartly brushed off.

The Onorean delegation, on the other hand, was the center of attention. It was comprised of only five or six people, but they definitely stood out among the crowd even in the spacious room. At first, Matt couldn't quite put his finger on what was off about them, but then he saw it. They were almost identical in appearance. Oh, their skin tones were different enough, ranging from milky pale to dark brown, as were their hair colors; but they were all tall, lean, and beautiful, their features an epitome of chiseled perfection and their air of aloof superiority like an additional layer of clothing over their utilitarian garments.

Truly, their resemblance to Ryce was uncanny. Matt had never met Onoreans traveling abroad before, but of course, he'd never moved in the right circles. He was willing to bet each and every member of the little delegation was smarter than all the local branch physicians put together. Considering the depth of Ryce's intellect (and he was only half-Onorean), Matt was hard-pressed to imagine what an average Onorean IQ might be.

Tony made a beeline to the buffet and its array of fresh fruit and salads, while Ryce studied the digital project poster, which displayed alternating images of various aspects of the Sota research facility. There was also a little bar in the corner, and Matt eyed it longingly. He made up his mind to head that way as soon as the seminar started. Ryce and Tony might find the scientific talk interesting, but Matt knew he was going to be bored out of his mind without something strong to boost his patience.

"Did you find us a replacement converter at the junkyard?" Matt asked Ryce, surveying the room. He was beginning to get bored already, and if they were going to just stand there, this entire outing would be a huge waste of time.

Ryce turned away from the poster and shook his head. "Nothing that would be of any use."

"Figures." Matt sighed. "Anyway, we should ask Dr. Yang to introduce us to whoever it is we're supposed to talk to."

"That'd be expedient," Ryce agreed, though Matt could tell he wasn't thrilled about the prospect. He'd been quiet and reserved ever since they'd arrived—more so than usual.

"Are you sure you're up to it?" Matt asked. He'd have preferred Ryce do the talking since he suspected the Onoreans would find his data-supported practical approach more appealing than Matt's arguable charm, but he wasn't about to force the matter. Despite the earlier tension between them, he cared too much about Ryce to make him feel uncomfortable. "Listen, I know I've been pushy about this, but if you want to leave, you only need to say the word."

"We're already here." Ryce faced the room with a suppressed sigh. "We might as well get this over with."

"It'll be okay," Matt said, patting his shoulder in reassurance. "A bit of elbow rubbing, and we're outta here. We can hang out and watch a movie afterward if you want."

"I'd like that." Ryce offered him a quick smile in response before going to fetch Tony.

They all found Dr. Yang talking to an Onorean delegate—an older man of about fifty. (Or, who at least looked to be fifty; who the hell knew how old these people really were?) The golden specks in his blue eyes matched both the deep tawniness of his skin and his honey-colored hair, streaked with white.

"Oh good, you've made it." Dr. Yang gestured toward Matt with the champagne flute she was holding. "Professor Brinan, these are Captain Spears, Ms. Antonia Joyce, and Mr. Ryce Easom of the *Lady Lisa*. They've offered their services running shipments for the Sota facility and for the Elysium-8 outposts."

"Pleasure to meet you, Professor," Matt said. The Onorean didn't strike him as a handshaking type, so he opted for a polite smile instead.

The man nodded absently, his gaze sweeping past Matt and Tony and resting on Ryce for a moment. His expression flickered, changing from mild boredom to utter disgust as some sort of recognition dawned.

Well, shit. Apparently, Matt wasn't the only one to zero in on the similitude between Ryce and the Onoreans. He glanced sideways at Ryce, who blanched slightly and pursed his lips, but didn't otherwise show he was perturbed.

"I'd be happy to present our proposal, Professor," he said, keeping his tone professionally neutral.

"That won't be necessary," Brinan said, taking half a step back with the same grimace of repugnance, as if he could somehow be sullied by Ryce's mere proximity. "Please excuse me, I must prepare for the seminar."

He nodded stiffly to Dr. Yang, who watched him with a quizzical expression, and beat a hasty retreat.

"What was that about?" Tony asked once the Onorean was safely out of earshot. She also looked baffled, her eyes flicking from Matt to Ryce.

"Nothing," Ryce said tightly.

They excused themselves to Dr. Yang and moved away from the crowd, toward the bar. Matt touched Ryce's arm again discreetly. He hadn't counted on the ghosts of Ryce's past coming back to haunt him when he'd asked him to tag along. It seemed Matt had a knack for getting whoever was joining him for some innocent outing into trouble—first Val, and now Ryce—and God only knew what he was going to do to make it all right. At what point had their carefree smuggler's life become such a huge mess?

"Do you think he has an idea of who you are?" he asked. Brinan's reaction seemed disproportionate and much too personal to be attributed to simple distaste.

"I don't know, but I'm going to find out," Ryce said determinately.

"Really?"

Matt was aware Ryce had never met any Onoreans since his birth mother had put him up for adoption at the age of five months, so he could well understand his wish for more information about his origins, but he wasn't sure this was the right venue to go about it. Even Tony was visibly troubled.

"I don't think being thrown out for harassing a foreign dignitary would better our standing with the IMA committee," she said.

"I'm not going to *harass* him," Ryce said. He had that stubborn gleam in his eyes which told Matt he wasn't about to drop the matter. For a normally super-rational person, Ryce was like a dog with a bone once he got in his head there was something he had to do. "But if he's going to sneer at me in front of my friends and potential clients, the least he can do is tell me why."

"Good luck with that," Tony said, still sounding dubious. "He doesn't seem terribly congenial."

Even though he tended to agree with her, Matt had no choice but to trail after Ryce as he headed purposefully into the lecture hall adjacent to the reception area, where the nanosensors seminar was scheduled to begin in under half an hour.

The auditorium was dim, illuminated only by the eerie glow of the large wall screen. It was designed to accommodate about a hundred people but was now empty save for Prof. Brinan, who was standing next to the podium with his back to the entrance, checking something on his commlink.

"Would you like me to talk to him for you?" Matt asked quietly when Ryce paused at the threshold. He was perhaps overstepping some boundaries with that suggestion, but the possibility of sparing Ryce a strained conversation was worth the risk of sounding patronizing.

"No." Ryce shook his head and took a deep breath. "I got this."

He descended the shallow steps toward the podium, with Matt following silently behind.

"Professor Brinan?"

"Yes?" The Onorean turned and gave Ryce a measured look, seeming unsurprised by his showing up. His tone rivaled the temperature outside the station walls in warmth. The attitude would have been intimidating, had Ryce not possessed every ounce of that same cool arrogance, and had Matt not had plenty of practice at weathering it.

"I apologize for bothering you, but judging from your earlier response, I believe you may have some information pertaining to me," Ryce said. Despite the firmness of his voice, he sounded uncharacteristically diffident. "I'm an orphan hailing from your community, and I—"

The Onorean lifted a hand.

"Enough. Yes, I know who you are, even though we've never met. You have your mother's face and your father's eyes."

That last comment left Matt baffled. From what Ryce had told him, his father was an unknown space pirate. His adoptive parents had been miners on Shyr-5, a small off-world colony that had been razed in an Alraki raid which had also claimed their lives.

Ryce, however, focused on the former statement.

"You knew my mother?"

"Yes."

It was clear nothing else would be forthcoming. Matt shifted from one foot to the other uneasily. Tony's admonition regarding possible harassment flashed through his mind, presenting him with vivid pictures of him and Ryce being hauled to the brig by Station Security. All it would take was Brinan's word. He doubted they'd be let out on parole so easily if the Onorean decided to file an official complaint against them with the station authorities.

Ryce, however, refused to be deterred by such trivial considerations.

"If you knew her, you must also know why she gave me up. The story of her rape...is it true?"

Brinan's face twisted, the subtle age lines around his eyes and mouth becoming more pronounced.

"It's true. I was...her research supervisor on a mission to the Gemma sector." The little pause the Onorean made as he refrained from mentioning Ryce's mother's name wasn't lost on anyone. "Ours was an exploration vessel on an expedition to the ice moons of Gemma-8. We were waylaid by pirates. Never heard about those prowling that particular system before, but there they were, with their black ship. None of us were armed nor trained in combat. Half the crew was killed. I had to watch that beast get his spawn on her, but at least we were lucky to survive."

Matt's hands curled into fists. He wasn't okay with anybody calling Ryce somebody's "spawn," and now, he was fully willing to make good on his promise to punch the Onorean for putting Ryce down.

Ryce pursed his lips into a thin line at the slur, but simultaneously put a hand on Matt's elbow, holding him off.

"Does she know who adopted me?" he persisted, pointedly ignoring both the direct and the implied insult.

"She doesn't want anything to do with you," Brinan gritted out. "You should forget about her altogether. She'll never acknowledge you as her own; whatever sham you have in mind, it won't work."

"With all due respect, it's not your decision to make," Ryce said fiercely, his immaculate calm finally cracking to reveal the anger underneath. "Neither on my part nor on hers. If you truly care for her as a friend, you'll leave the choice to her—no matter how distasteful my existence is to you."

With a sharp toss of his head, Ryce turned and headed back to the exit without waiting for a response. Matt glanced after him but lingered for a moment. Something the Onorean had said nagged at him. His imagination was probably running away with him, but he couldn't help but focus on this little detail.

"The pirates' ship that'd attacked you...You said it was black?" he asked Brinan.

It was nothing, Matt told himself. There were plenty of black ships out there. All it took was a couple of canisters of metal paint. And yet, he couldn't stop his heart from hammering.

"Yes," the Onorean said in a clipped tone. He looked Matt over as if he were a peculiar but slightly disgusting creature. "The *Black Baza*, I think it was called. Now, I must ask you to leave before I call security. I've been patient enough with the two of you."

Matt gave him a curt nod and hurried out of the room. Ryce was nowhere to been seen. For a while, Matt stood there in the empty hallway, staring blankly into space, until he finally fumbled for his commlink to notify Tony that she and Ryce should head home, seeing the evening was effectively ruined—and that he would be getting in late.

Chapter Seven

MATT'S HEAD WAS spinning so hard he already knew he was going to bitterly regret going on an impromptu drinking binge. It hadn't happened in a while, and his alcohol intake wasn't what it used to be. And future hangover aside, spending money on booze at a bar was a luxury he couldn't really afford—even though he'd stuck to the shitty cheap stuff.

At least his head was spinning for a better reason than it had earlier. He kept telling himself it couldn't have been right, that the Onorean guy was mistaken or misremembering. Matt hated the word "nemesis"—it smacked of low-grade action movies and sounded too cheesy to take seriously. But if there was ever a word to describe what the notorious pirate Dylan Rodgers, captain of the *Black Baza*, was to him, "nemesis" fit the bill perfectly. To consider, even for a moment, there might be a connection between that man and Ryce, *his* Ryce, was unthinkable.

So he did his darndest to avoid thinking about it. But then all their other current problems kept popping into his mind, no matter how many whiskeys he downed to chase them away.

It was an all-around bad decision, but being drunk off one's ass also brought a certain sense of freedom and fearlessness, unencumbered by sound judgment. So, Matt did one of the things he'd been telling himself he shouldn't do—namely, head to Val's cabin and have an honest talk. At least meddling in his engineer's problems would take his mind off all the stuff he didn't want to ponder at the moment.

He took a deep breath and knocked on Val's door. It opened so quickly he lost his balance and tumbled forward, catching himself from falling on his face at the last second.

Val took a step back, letting him inside. He said nothing, but his expression clearly indicated he wasn't overly impressed with Matt's performance.

Unlike Matt's cabin, which was messy and cluttered, Val's living space was almost Spartan. Everything, from clothes to books, was neatly arranged in the cupboards, and the bunk bed was immaculately made.

The only evidence of activity was the pile of old electronic circuit boards Val had been disassembling on the little table. A blaster gun lay on the edge of the table next to the commlink.

Matt zeroed in on the gun. Much like Tony and himself, Val owned a personal weapon but rarely carried it, and when he did, it was as a precaution rather than actual need. Getting in gunfights was bad for business, and Val's looks were usually enough of a deterrent to anybody considering robbing him.

"I think we should have a chat," Matt announced, plopping down on a chair without waiting for an invitation.

Val didn't respond. He hesitated a fraction of a second before sitting on the bed. At least getting him to listen was a good sign, and Matt held on to that.

"You might fool Ryce into thinking you're being sensible, but you can't fool me," he said without preamble. "I've known you for too long. I know you're planning on going after Ander."

Not that Matt could blame him, really. He could very well understand Val's need to avenge the person he'd held most dear. If something had happened to Ryce, and Matt knew who was responsible, he would have gone after that person too, consequences be damned.

The most telling thing was Val didn't even bother denying it. He merely shrugged.

"With all due respect, Captain, you can't stop me."

"I'm not here to stop you. I realize it's useless to appeal to reason and try to talk you out of it."

Frankly, it was surprising he could talk at all in his current state of inebriation, but he'd had a lot of practice over the years. Also, he'd had a chance to think about what he was going to say to Val in advance.

Val leaned back slightly, watching him with narrowed eyes.

"Then why are you here?" he asked, in a less than polite tone.

"I'm here to ask you to put that gun aside for a moment and think. Ander is an enforcer for a black-market big shot. He's successfully evaded being captured by Federal authorities on murder charges for years. He's not somebody you can just corner in some deserted nook of the station and shoot in the back."

"It wouldn't be in the back," Val said darkly.

"Even worse. What I'm saying is you want to nail the guy—fine, I get it. But give me a chance to help you do it properly before you go dashing after him with no clear idea of what you're doing and getting yourself killed. Let me gather some info, see what I can find on him. It might be my military experience talking here, but you don't go rushing into action without some solid intel."

Val stared at him. Granted, Matt was having some difficulty judging facial expressions right now, but he hoped what he was reading was thoughtfulness, and not hostility.

"I don't want you to get involved in any of this," Val said finally.

"I'm not gonna be involved," Matt said, secretly rejoicing at the lack of outright refusal. "I'll just do some digging around, that's all. Maybe after we know more about the guy and his associates, a better plan of action would present itself. Instead of, you know, running after him around the station, guns blazing."

There was another pause.

"Okay," Val said wearily. "Let's see what you manage to dig up. But if he uses this opportunity to bolt again, Matt, I swear to God—"

"He won't," Matt said hastily. "I have a plan of getting closer to him without making him suspicious. Just...try to focus on something else in the meantime, okay? I'll let you know as soon as I find out anything."

"It's not like we have a shortage of problems to focus on," Val remarked.

Matt only wished he could disagree with that observation.

THE DISTANCE FROM Val's cabin to his own seemed longer than he remembered. When Matt finally dragged himself inside, all he wanted to do was crash on the bed and sleep for the next six to seven hours—which, considering how late it was already, probably wasn't in his future.

He hadn't counted on Ryce waiting for him there, sitting primly on the only chair, still wearing that figure-hugging white shirt, and reading the ridiculous paper book Val had given him. Ryce raised his head as Matt entered and frowned.

Usually Matt was more than happy to see Ryce hanging out in his cabin, but he was cranky, tired, and nursing the beginnings of what promised to be a magnificent headache. Besides, after what he'd heard from Prof. Brinan, he was secretly hoping to avoid Ryce for a bit longer. He was more than a little freaked out about the possible implications of the Onorean's revelation, and he still had no idea what, if anything, he should tell Ryce.

"Sorry about bailing out on the movie night, but I don't think I'm gonna be much fun," he said, lowering himself on the bed heavily and stretching out with a groan, shoes and all.

Ryce snapped the book closed and got up.

"You drink too much," he said.

Matt looked up at him. It wasn't as if he wasn't aware of this, but he *was* used to his crew carefully avoiding pointing it out, so the unexpected bluntness took him aback.

Ryce's eyes, as he stared at him, were the exact shade of gray storm clouds. Now that he thought about it, Matt *had* seen this particular rare color before on a man he really didn't want to think about at the moment. In fact, he'd spent the entire evening getting wasted so as not to think about him. "Yeah, whatever works," he muttered, turning away.

"*Works*? What's so terrible about your life that you need alcohol to *work*? Aside from our financial difficulties, which, I might remind you, are hardly the most awful ordeal you've ever faced."

"Listen, this is none of your business," Matt said, growing more and more irate.

"All things considered, I think it might be a bit of my business."

A flash of panic shot through Matt's alcohol-addled brain. Could Ryce possibly have some inkling as to Matt's suspicions? Was he waiting there in hopes of discussing them? But no. That couldn't have been what he meant. He had to have been referring to their relationship. And he was right in that Matt's vices were, in fact, his business too, if they called themselves partners. No doubt, Matt's poor decisions put a strain on him as well.

"I grant you, it hasn't happened in a while," Ryce continued with the same resolute expression, as if he'd been keeping all of this bottled inside for some time, and now finally had a reason to pour it all out. "But every time you go to a bar or a canteen, even if it's ostensibly to do business, I wonder if you're going to return wasted. Not to mention that little stash you have in the rec room which keeps winking at you every time you're feeling moody."

Matt couldn't deny there was some truth to what Ryce was saying. And he couldn't deny he felt a little bit relieved that he was wrong about the subject of Ryce's mistrust. It wasn't Matt's fidelity he doubted, but his tendency to fall into bad habits. It was just that Matt couldn't deal with any of this right now.

"Fine, whatever. You can tell me off tomorrow," he said curtly. "If it's okay with you, I could use some shut-eye."

"I merely wanted to inform you that I've set up a long-distance meeting with Nora and her commander over the interstellar communications channels tomorrow morning to discuss their proposal," Ryce said. "At oh eight hundred hours. It would be nice if you could join in, but seeing as you're—"

"I'll be there," Matt cut him off. "With bells and whistles on, all chirpy. Now, can I please get some sleep before I throw up all over myself?"

Without another word, Ryce turned and left. The cabin door slid shut behind him with a low hiss.

Matt groaned and buried his head in the pillow. It seemed his tried-and-true way of dealing with crises wasn't helping him at all this time around.

MATT'S MOOD HADN'T gotten any better by the time he sat in the copilot seat. Thankfully, his sleep had been dreamless, but it hadn't been restful, and even the strong coffee gulped down on the way didn't help. There wasn't any time for this. He had some snooping around to do regarding Eddie Ander, and he really, really had to find some other job to sustain them for a few more days of docking fees. The gray market loan idea, as dubious as it might be, was beginning to sound more and more appealing.

He also wanted his stomach to stop tying itself into a knot every time he recalled what the Onorean had said about Ryce's father, but that probably wasn't happening anytime soon.

"Thank you for coming in," Ryce said when they were both settled on the bridge. He was, once again, cool and collected, despite what had to have been an unpleasant experience yesterday. Matt could tell he'd been badly shaken by the run-in with his nominal kinsman, and he felt a pang of guilt for not doing something to comfort him, too immersed as he was in his own inner turmoil. The thought fouled his mood even further. Ryce was worthy of so much more than Matt, with his emotional immaturity, could offer him.

"Sure," he said. "Um, sorry about yesterday."

Ryce shrugged, focusing on the control panel instead of looking at him.

"No, really," Matt insisted. "I was being a jerk again, and you didn't deserve that."

"Don't mention it. We were all a little upset yesterday," Ryce said, his tone softening somewhat.

"You can say that again. I didn't know you wanted to find your birth mother." Matt fidgeted in his chair.

"I'm not sure I do." The look in Ryce's eyes became distant, almost pensive. "I've never blamed the woman, whoever she might be, for abandoning me. Intellectually, at least, I can understand why she did it, and I was lucky to have grown up in a good home, with a loving family. But now, my parents are dead. I have no family left, aside from her. I know it's not my place to actively seek her out, but if she ever wants to contact me, I won't say no to that."

Sometimes, it was easy to forget how young Ryce was. No matter how tumultuous his life had been so far, he was only twenty-two. No wonder he still yearned for a parent even if his adoptive family was gone. Matt opened his mouth to respond with words of encouragement (and perhaps another heartfelt apology for not discussing something like that sooner) but was cut short by an incoming call alert.

"Ready?" Ryce asked, sitting up straight.

When Matt nodded, Ryce opened the interstellar communications channel. The image filled the huge screen in front of them, showing two uniformed women sitting alone at a large conference desk, with a holographic star map spread out on the tabletop.

One of them was Major Nora Cummings, Matt's older and, until about seven months ago, estranged sister. Her green eyes darted in Matt's direction, but she said nothing to indicate whether she was pleased to see him. He recalled, guiltily, that they hadn't spoken in a while. Apparently, old habits die hard, and that estrangement thing had proven hard to let go of entirely.

Matt didn't know the other officer, a stern-looking older woman whose slicked gray hair appeared almost white against her deep dark skin. The insignia on the collar of her jacket marked her a Colonel, and just her air of authority made him want to sit up at attention. He slouched back into his chair pointedly to resist the urge. His military days were thankfully over and done with.

Ryce, of course, was much more diplomatic.

"Colonel," he said with a polite nod. "Major. Pleasure to see you again."

"Nice to see you again too, Mr. Easom," Nora said. "This is Colonel Mensah."

"And who is this gentleman?" the Colonel asked dryly, gesturing in Matt's direction.

"This is Captain Spears of the *Lady Lisa*." Ryce hastened to introduce him before Nora had the chance to launch into explanations. "He's my partner and employer, and whatever you say to me, you can say in his hearing."

"This is highly irregular," Colonel Mensah said, glancing at Nora. "His clearance—"

"He was as much involved in the Colanta affair as Mr. Easom," Nora said a touch wearily. It had certainly required a lot of effort on her part to get Matt out of that "affair," as she put it, without him being charged with federal treason. "Besides, Mr. Easom is a civilian now. His level of clearance is also no longer relevant."

Colonel Mensah eyed Matt critically but eventually nodded.

"Let's get started, then," she said briskly. "Mr. Easom, it may come as no surprise to you that the Research and Development Branch of the Fleet has begun extensive excavation at the Mnirian site you've discovered on the Colanta-3 moon. I am the Branch Coordinator for this project, replacing Major Cummings here." She nodded toward Nora.

"Is Commodore Archer a part of this project?" Ryce asked.

James Archer had been the one to involve both Ryce and Matt in his quest for a Mnirian superweapon. At that time, Ryce had believed in the high-mindedness of his former commander in doing so but had been left sorely disappointed when it became apparent Archer intended to use the ancient weapon to wipe out the Alraki home world. The humans had been at war with the Alraki for years, locked in a bloody standstill with nothing to change the tide. While Archer's plan would certainly win them the war, luckily, no one except him was prepared to pay the price, and only his war-hero status had saved him from a dishonorable discharge over his rogue escapade.

"No," Colonel Mensah said with a tiny frown. "Commodore Archer has been reassigned back to the Salua sector. He has no bearing on this project."

"That's good to hear," Ryce said. "Seeing as you're keen on finding someone with such specific credentials, I can assume you've uncovered something of particular interest?"

"I'm sure you understand why I cannot go into much detail regarding the progress status of the excavation," the Colonel said. "But at this juncture, we need someone with both your expertise in Mnirian linguistics and technology, as well as your experience with military operations. I cannot stress enough how delicate this matter is. We'd rather not bring a civilian scholar on board—certainly not when we have someone of your academic stature whom we can hire as a consultant."

"What would that entail, exactly?" Ryce asked. He glanced at Matt, but the look was too brief to decipher his intention.

"You would be working under my direct supervision. We have established a temporary camp on the moon, as most of the work would be conducted on-site. We're offering a six-month contract with an option for extending it. The terms are negotiable, of course, but I think you'll find them very generous as they currently stand."

Matt's heart sank a little at those words. Six months was a hell of a long time, and it could potentially be even longer. This could effectively spell a death sentence for their budding relationship. Not because he didn't trust Ryce or himself to stay faithful for so long, but because it would give Ryce yet another chance to reflect on his life choices and come to the inevitable realization that by attaching himself to Matt he'd chosen poorly.

"Our goal is to explore the site while inflicting as little damage as possible to the existing structure," Colonel Mensah continued. "Major Cummings assured me you have the expertise required to decode the various writings so we might have a better understanding of what we're dealing with. And, frankly, your Fleet record speaks for itself."

"Thank you," Ryce said. "That is certainly a very interesting proposal. But I do need some time to consider it, if I may."

"Of course. Take a few days to think about it."

Matt stared at the floor while they concluded the conversation. He couldn't wait for them to disconnect and muttered his goodbyes to Nora, even though he knew it probably made him look like a petulant child.

"What do you think?" Ryce swiveled in his chair to face him. "You barely said a word."

"You can't possibly fool yourself as to the real purpose behind the excavation," Matt said. "Research might be a big part of it, but the military isn't academia. They don't do research which isn't applicative to their needs, and at present, all their needs are focused on the war effort. They're hoping to find more than one kind of weapon in the secret Mnirian base, or perhaps new technology they can harness."

"I'm aware of the possible implications in that regard," Ryce said, pursing his lips. "Without a doubt, it's something I'd have to consider carefully before making any kind of decision. But it's not quite what I meant when I asked for your opinion."

Matt took a deep breath. Please don't go, he wanted to say. Please don't leave me again. I don't want to lose you.

But he couldn't. He had to give Ryce the space to shine like the star he was always meant to be—beautiful, distant, and bright.

"It sounds like a good opportunity," he managed to say into Ryce's expectant silence. "I think you should take it."

Something close to incredulity fleeted across Ryce's features. He stared at Matt, and his jaw worked.

"I believe her when she says it's a generous contract," he said slowly. "I mean, this could probably help our financial situation a bit."

"Sure sounds like it." Matt could hear the insincerity in his voice, which meant Ryce could probably hear it too, but really, Ryce didn't have to pretend this was for their mutual benefit.

Or that he was going to come back.

Chapter Eight

MATT LOUNGED AGAINST the bar, nursing his beer. It had been the same beer for the last half an hour, and he'd barely touched it. It wasn't like he had the money to splurge on another round.

Nobody knew what he was doing, including Tony. She would definitely chew him out for getting mixed up with a black-market dealer—especially considering what they'd gone through when Matt had tried doing business with one in the past. And she'd be right, of course. But Matt wasn't planning on taking on any questionable loans or jobs this time around. The only reason he wanted to get close to this Griggs fellow was to find out more about Ander, and that required some semblance of an excuse. Being hard up for cash was the perfect pretext for wanting to meet with a loan shark. Matt just wished it had been a little less real.

He had promised Val he'd help, and he was going to do his best to try. He had to focus on things he could do something about, as opposed to things he couldn't—most of them having to do with Ryce in some form or other.

The bartender from the Broken Stairway Canteen had proven to be a big help after all. His job entailed knowing a lot of useful people on the station, and after some prodding and bribing, the guy had agreed to spread the word of Matt's interest in the right ears. So, he was hanging around, waiting on the promised meeting.

He didn't know if making him wait was some sort of tactic, or if Griggs was really that busy. But he was definitely starting to get cranky and seriously considering up and leaving when a woman plopped on the seat beside him. She wore a black faux-leather vest and had a hardened look to her face—which was accentuated by a long scar that ran from her cheek down to her neck.

"Hi," she said in a business-like tone. "I'm Tex."

"Hi," Matt said cautiously. He was no stranger to women approaching him in bars, but even his current unwaveringly monogamous status aside, she wasn't exactly his type. He preferred his hookups, of any gender, to have less of a dangerous vibe going on.

"So, I heard you're interested in a loan," Tex said.

"I was expecting to meet Griggs." If anything, this set Matt even more on edge. He didn't have time to deal with mediators, especially the kind who looked suspiciously like enforcers.

"Griggs is otherwise occupied. It's a big station."

She was making it sound for all the world like Griggs was actually running the Freeport. And as much as Matt was familiar with the workings of various gray and black markets, this time, he was inclined to disagree. If it had taken him this long to even hear of the guy, he was hardly as all-powerful as he wished to appear.

"Whatever," Matt muttered. He briefly considered walking away, but this was his only lead to finding Ander that didn't involve tracking him down on a city-sized station. If this woman was authorized to make deals on Griggs's behalf, she had to know other people who worked for him on roughly the same level. "So, what if I *am* interested in a loan?"

Tex smiled and spread her hands. It wasn't a very comforting sort of smile.

"Whatever you need, Cap'n. Up to fifty thousand creds, for two months, at ten percent, no questions asked."

"Really?" Matt's ears perked up despite himself. These were actually good terms, as these kinds of loans went, and he didn't even need that large a sum.

"Sure. We offer very lucrative funding options," Tex said, a touch mockingly, and swiped the counter to order herself a vodka. "But, as it so happens, I might have an even better proposition for you."

"I'm listening," Matt said cautiously.

"It had come to our attention you've been having some...difficulties with your ship."

Matt leaned back in his chair. He already didn't like where this was going. "Where did you hear that?"

"It doesn't matter. Word travels fast on this station, in case you haven't already noticed."

Matt huffed noncommittally and sipped his beer. "What's the proposition?"

Tex leaned in, her dark eyes intent on his.

"Griggs is willing to cut you a deal. Give you the money you need for repairs and waive the debt altogether—in exchange for a small favor."

"What kind of favor?"

"You're about to go into business with the IMA, running their far moon shipments."

Matt nearly choked on his beer. *What the hell.* This went well beyond picking up station canteen gossip. Being privy to such information spelled out not only special interest in Matt's affairs but also a pretty impressive network of informants.

"Nothing is settled yet," he said, recovering from his initial shock. "In any case, what's it to you?"

"IMA medical supplies are registered as Federal consignments. They don't get scrutinized at customs as much as the regular stuff. So, once in a while, Griggs might ask you to add a little something to your shipment without it appearing on the declaration form."

"You want me to be his drug runner?" Matt asked, lowering his voice and glancing around.

Tex scoffed, correctly interpreting his incredulous expression. "Don't get prissy all of a sudden. You're a smuggler; don't pretend like you haven't done this before. Besides, you won't be working for free. Once you work off the loan, you'll get paid for each run. Griggs is being very generous, seeing you're in a scrape. Can hardly say no to this kind of offer."

Matt made a vague sound of assent and took a swig of his beer to stall. He didn't even have to pretend to do some hard thinking, because he was doing precisely that. Tex was right in that it was a hard offer to refuse, but not because of how lucrative it was. This kind of thorough knowledge of his affairs was more than a little disconcerting. What kind of pressure might Griggs apply if he declined?

True, he was only a smuggler, but he was doing his best to stay on the straight and narrow, to carve out a new path for himself and his crew. Being caught carrying illegal drugs inside a medical supplies shipment would be the end of all their hopes and dreams.

Besides, Ryce would never go for something so illicit; he'd be appalled at the possibility. And he'd be right, of course. Even Matt was repulsed by the idea. But Ryce was leaving to pursue better opportunities anyway, and Matt still had the livelihood and safety of his crew to think about.

And he had to tread very carefully here. Being stranded ashore meant he couldn't just raise anchor when trouble came calling. No doubt these people were counting on that exact thing. But, questionable offer aside, he had a specific purpose for being here, and he had to grab the opportunity by the horns while Tex was still regarding him as either a potential client or an accomplice.

"It's a lot to think about," he said. "But first, I must apologize for what happened with your associate the other day at the Canteen. It was all truly a misunderstanding. My crewman had a bit too much to drink, mistook him for the wrong guy. You know how it is. So I just wanted to clear the air on that one."

If she was high enough on the food chain, she must have heard all about that debacle and would know exactly whom he was talking about.

Tex's expression changed ever so slightly, and she tensed, making Matt momentarily fear he'd made a mistake. But then she relaxed just as quickly and merely shrugged without answering.

"I do feel bad about what happened to Mr....Ander, was it? I'd like to offer my apologies to him in person, if possible," Matt said, risking pressing the matter just a little bit further. "We started on the entirely wrong foot, and I'd be much more at peace knowing there's no hard feelings, especially if we're to do business together."

"Don't worry about it," Tex said. "He ain't pressing charges."

"And I'm grateful for that," Matt hastened to say. "But still, if you know where I could meet him—"

"I'm not Ander's fucking assistant," she snapped, turning to him sharply. "If you're smart, you'll stay away from him anyway. So, do you want to take the deal or not?"

Matt sat back. That was a little unexpected. Not the telling off, but the fear which clearly underlined Tex's words. She looked like someone who wasn't afraid of anything. So what was it about this Ander that caused this kind of reaction?

"Sorry," he said, trying to appear as charmingly apologetic as he possibly could. "Didn't mean to ruffle any feathers. Hmm...can I think about it some more and get back to you? I might have to consult with my crew on this one."

"Just don't go thinking too long. It's a limited time offer." Tex finished her vodka in two gulps and stood up. She took a couple more seconds to send her number to Matt's commlink, and then was off.

Matt swiped the counter hurriedly to pay for his own unfinished beer. Again, he was going to do something that probably wasn't wise, but time was of the essence, and he had to follow all the leads he'd gotten. So, he trailed after Tex as she walked out of the bar and into the communal corridor, keeping as much distance as he could between them while still able to spot her in the throng of people hurrying on their daily business. He wasn't sure exactly what he was hoping to achieve by this little bit of snooping, but at least he had something to latch on to, and so he did.

The Freeport was built of two linked concentric rings, with the outer ring housing the docks and the common areas. The inner ring had restricted access and was designated for station personnel quarters and administration offices. Even on the larger outer ring, there weren't any places that could truly be called crime hubs, since the Freeports were usually pretty tightly regulated, and the 73 was no exception. But it was a large place, populated by people of all walks of life and vocations, and, as such, it was bound to attract some shady characters and develop some shady spots. This was especially true for this particular station. The Elysium system was located on the outskirts of Federation space, enjoying neither economical nor strategic importance. As such, the 73 was somewhat understaffed compared to its more central counterparts, and military presence on the station—and indeed throughout the sector—was relatively scarce.

Tex was headed to the lower levels of the guest living quarters. These were let out to the residents and guests of the station, with rates varying wildly depending on the quality of the accommodations. Matt preferred to save by staying on his ship while they were stationside, even if it was less comfortable, but there were plenty of options available for those who chose the relative luxury of fully equipped en suite bathrooms and artificial gardens.

There weren't a lot of people in this particular area, and Matt had to slow down to avoid being seen. For all he knew, Tex was going home, but he had a hunch she had some other business here.

Eventually, she stopped at an intersection of corridors that led to the individual suits. The space was designed as a lounge of sorts, with several benches facing large screens transmitting news, advertisements, and local announcements. One wall was covered with sustainable plants in an attempt to create a green spot of sorts, but a lot of them were wilted. The benches also showed signs of wear and poor upkeep.

Tex sat on one of the benches and started typing something furiously on her commlink. Matt hung back, hiding behind the corner of the corridor. It appeared she was planning on meeting somebody, perhaps another sod unfortunate enough to have to borrow creds from her boss. There was no way he could get any closer to take a peek at the message she was writing.

His own commlink vibrated in his pocket, but he ignored it. It was probably either Ryce or Tony wondering where he was, and he'd be hard-pressed to explain his whereabouts at the moment.

Another ten or so minutes passed as Tex fiddled with her commlink. Matt was beginning to question whether it was worth his while to hang around any longer, when a man strode down the opposite corridor and sat beside Tex. Matt took an instinctive step back, retreating as much as he could into the shadows. There was no mistaking that spiky snow-white hair, and the last thing he wanted was for Frosty—Ander—to catch him eavesdropping.

Thankfully, the bench the two were sitting on faced the other way. If Matt was discreet enough, there was a good chance of him listening in on their conversation while staying safely out of sight.

"So, no go with Spears?" Ander asked. He was pretty relaxed, but next to him, Tex looked decidedly uneasy, even from the back. Matt wasn't a big expert on body language, but she was definitely on edge, and he'd venture to guess it was due to Ander's presence. Going on all the bits of information he'd gleaned from Val, he wasn't surprised. He'd be nervous around a murderous psychopath too.

"Not sure yet," Tex said.

"Well, we could always make a more convincing pitch," Ander said. The tone of his voice sent chills down Matt's back. The commlink vibrated again, and he cringed, but with the added distraction of the news feed on the large screen in front of them, neither Tex nor Ander seemed to notice.

"He did ask about you," Tex said. "Like, specifically. I think they might be after you. Spears and that big Russian dude of his. Thought you should know, just in case."

"I ain't worried about them." Ander shrugged. "Besides, we've got other problems to deal with right now."

"What kind of problems?"

Ander glanced to the side and lowered his voice. Matt had to strain to hear what he was saying. "We've lost another jet over there. Crashed and burned like a fucking firecracker."

Tex made a low whistle. "It's the second one of ours. And we're yet to see any of them win a race. That's not good."

"Griggs's pissed. It's damn messy, and someone's bound to pick up on what's going on if it happens too often. That's what you get when you hire shoddy pilots too pumped up on stims. Now we have to bust our asses to get a new jet. And a new pilot," he added as an afterthought. "And that's more money out of Griggs's pocket right there."

"No shit."

This wasn't a conversation he should have been listening to. Whatever these "races" were, Griggs probably wouldn't appreciate Matt knowing anything about them. Hell, he didn't *want* to know anything about them, but any piece of information on Griggs's illegal operations could prove useful if he ever needed leverage.

Matt even ventured taking a step forward so as not to lose the rest of their exchange, but loud voices and drunken shuffling from one of the corridors made the pair look up and fall silent. Cursing his bad luck, Matt slung back to the shadows, waiting for a bunch of wasted guys to make their way home past the intersection. When he risked peeking at the bench again, it was empty.

Chapter Nine

THE WORRIED LOOK on Tony's face as she greeted him at the main hatch of the *Lisa* told Matt everything was not going well in his little kingdom.

"What happened?" he asked, not bothering with idle chitchat. Damn it, he really should have checked the messages on his commlink, he thought as he recalled the insistent calls he'd ignored while playing the spy.

"It's Val," Tony said, confirming Matt's worst fears. "We were having late lunch in the galley, all three of us, when Val got a message on his comm. I don't know who it was, but you should've seen his face, Matt. On second thought, you shouldn't have. Anyway, that was it, he just got up and ran out. Ryce tried to stop him, but he wouldn't listen. There's no getting through to him when he's in this mood, short of coldcocking him. Maybe that's what he needed." She tugged her braid and frowned. "But we were kinda afraid to. I bet he went after that Ander guy. All he was waiting for was to catch a whiff of him, and somebody must've tipped him off."

Matt swore succinctly and then shook his head. "You did what you could. Val's a grown man, and if he chooses to go back on his word and play the fool, that's on him."

It didn't mean, of course, that Matt wouldn't have to get Val's sorry ass out of trouble, because grown man or not, he was still Matt's responsibility. Matt's own family might have turned their backs on him (or him on his family—depending on whom you asked), but he wasn't about to do the same when it came to his crew.

"He took his gun with him," Tony said quietly.

"Damn it, he promised he'd let me handle this." Matt rubbed the bridge of his nose. "We have to find him, fast. Where's Ryce?"

"In the galley."

Tony followed him to the galley, where Ryce was busy cleaning up and putting away the dishes. If he was upset about the earlier confrontation with Val and the possibility of his friend running off to get himself killed by a dangerous criminal, he wasn't showing it. Then again, Ryce was notoriously skilled at keeping his cool under pressure.

"Good, you're back," he said as Matt came in, almost succeeding in making it sound nonaccusatory. "What's the game plan?"

It seemed they were all on the same wavelength, at least. That saved time on unnecessary preliminaries.

"You and I are going after Val," Matt told Ryce. "As it happens, I chanced to see the elusive Mr. Ander in the flesh not too long ago, so I have a pretty good idea where to start looking. Tony, you contact Station Security and tell them to get to Level 4 ASAP. I'll let you know in case we end up in a different location."

"Are you sure you want to get security involved?" Tony asked, her expression troubled. "This means Val violated the terms of his release. If they catch him in the middle of a fight again, he'll be arrested for real this time."

"I'd rather he be in jail than dead," Matt said curtly.

Of course, he would have preferred not to involve the authorities, but it seemed they needed all the help they could get. Val wasn't the only one he had to think about—he was going to put Ryce and himself in danger as well, and he was going to stack the odds in their favor as much as possible, even if it meant Val would have to cool his heels in the brig for a while. Perhaps letting him simmer down in relative safety wasn't such a horrible idea.

"Fine," Tony said, although she clearly wasn't happy about it. "And meaning no disrespect, Captain, I still don't understand why I'm to stay behind while you two go off on a rescue mission."

"You know you're the first person I'd call on to back me up in a fight," Matt said. "But this time, I need you to stay with the ship. If we get into trouble, as my first mate, you're the one with the legal sway to get us out."

"Nice to know you consider me the responsible adult around here."

"One of us has to be, and it sure ain't me. So, we're okay?"

He didn't mention he also had his ship to think about. Unbeknownst to Tony, he'd made all the necessary arrangements for her to inherit *Lady Lisa* if anything happened to him. He had no doubt if that ever happened, she'd take good care of the others and his ship.

"I guess," Tony said grudgingly. "But call me if you need backup, you hear?"

"I promise." He meant it, too—by all accounts, Tony was much better than him when it came to handling a situation involving the use of firearms. He just hoped it wouldn't come to that.

"We better hurry, then," Ryce said, gently nudging Matt toward the door.

"Godspeed," Tony called after them.

"I SHOULD HAVE stopped him from going," Ryce said as they hurried along the station corridor.

"It wasn't your fault," Matt said. "You have no idea how fucking stubborn Val can be sometimes."

"I think that can be said about all of us," Ryce said quietly.

Matt shot him a look, but now wasn't the time to start questioning his partner's meaning. They had to stay focused and not get distracted by their own uncertainties, so he tried to do that by bringing Ryce up to speed on everything he'd learned by talking to Tex and listening in on her conversation with Ander.

"Not entirely sure what that exchange was about," Matt told Ryce in a low voice as they got in an elevator. "But it seems like Griggs is short a pilot for whatever illegal operation he's running. My money's on speed races. Quality entertainment for folks with an adrenaline addiction and extra cash to burn."

He had never been foolish enough to enter those types of competitions himself, even when he'd been in a tight spot before purchasing *Lady Lisa*, but it was a way for many pilots who were down on their luck to make a quick cred—or die trying.

"Griggs sure has his hand in a lot of pots," Ryce observed.

Matt grunted in agreement. He kept touching the gun in his hip holster. Matt hated having to carry, but there was no way he was going anywhere near Ander and possibly other armed criminals without a weapon. Ryce didn't own a gun now that he'd been discharged, but Matt insisted he take one anyway. He didn't have to ask Ryce whether he was a good shot—it was a given he was good at everything he did (barring cooking). It had annoyed Matt no end when he first met Ryce. Now, he realized he was going to miss being able to rely on Ryce's assured competence once he was gone.

They reached the little intersection on Level 4 where Matt had listened in on Tex and Ander's conversation. It was the middle of the afternoon shift, and the corridors were almost completely empty. Their footsteps echoed a bit too loudly in the narrow space.

Matt halted at the crossroads, trying to decide which way to go. His knowledge of the station was sufficient for his needs, but by no means extensive. While the basic layout was the same on all Freeports, the unofficial subdivision of private civilian and public areas was unique to each one.

"Let's try this way," he said finally, gesturing toward the corridor on his left. As far as he knew, this one led out of the accommodation area into this level's storage space.

Ryce nodded, and they hurried in that direction, keeping an eye out for any turns or openings that could pose a threat of an ambush. But they didn't encounter anybody, not even maintenance robots scurrying about.

The oppressing silence kept them both from speaking aloud. At length, they reached the entrance to the storage area—a small atrium leading to four corridors lined with doors marked as warehouses. These were designated for the private use of guests rather than the station's logistics. Again, the atrium was empty, with nothing that would indicate a recent struggle or disturbance.

"Now what?" Matt said, wincing at how loud his voice sounded. He glanced around nervously, but thankfully no one was around to question what they were doing there.

Ryce approached a large touch screen on one of the walls and tapped it. The screen lit up, displaying a map of the warehouses and their current status.

"If they're here somewhere, we should be looking for an occupied unit," Ryce said. "One that would have been accessed recently."

He went over the charts, noting three occupied units that had been opened in the last twelve hours.

"We can't get the ownership records without a security code," Matt said. "How do we narrow it down?"

"All three are on the larger side," Ryce said, studying the map. "But this one is located right at the end of the corridor, with an empty unit flanking it. If I had to pick, it would be this one. It offers more privacy than the rest."

"Let's test it, then," Matt said, taking his gun out of the holster and striding purposefully down the corridor.

The idea of going into a warehouse which could potentially prove to be a den of criminal activity, or worse, a makeshift prison cell, made his skin crawl. He remembered all too well waking up not once, but twice in an empty storage locker after taking a beating. The thing he remembered with a lot less detail—but nonetheless featured prominently in his nightmares—was being surrounded by jeering men in a torture chamber on a pirate ship. He dreaded walking into a similar scene, this time with Val playing the role of the helpless, bound victim.

But this was precisely why he couldn't turn back now. No one had come to his rescue when he'd needed it, but now he could be there for Val. Matt swallowed around the dryness in his throat and tightened his grip on the gun. Ryce walked right beside him, and Matt allowed himself to take momentary comfort in his quiet, strong presence. At least he wouldn't have to walk in there alone.

"I'll let Tony know where we are," he said once they were standing outside the warehouse door. A green light on the control panel indicated it was in use, but not a sound traveled through the thick door.

"We're in the Level 4 storage area," he told Tony as soon as her face appeared on his comm screen. "Tell the security folks to meet us here."

"I don't think they'll be coming," Tony said grimly. "I've called them, and they said they couldn't send in a team based on someone's hunch, without a report of an actual disturbance. You're on your own unless you want me to come give you a hand."

"Fucking assholes," Matt muttered. He didn't know what Station Security's deal was, but it seemed they really were on their own. "You stay put for now, Tony. If I don't contact you in an hour, call those asses again and report a disturbance, 'cause I can guarantee there will be one."

He disconnected and slipped the commlink back into his pocket. There was no more stalling; it was now or never.

"Open it," he told Ryce, gesturing toward the control panel with his gun.

"What makes you think I can do that?"

"Please. You've opened an alien bunker which had been sealed for thousands of years; I think you can pick a simple storage locker."

Ryce huffed with annoyance mixed with amusement, but went over to the control panel and examined it.

"Despite what you may think, breaking and entering is not one of my areas of expertise," he said. "But I can try."

He reached toward the panel, but before he could touch the tiny screen, the door slid open, seemingly of its own accord.

The first thing Matt saw were the barrels of several plasma rifles pointed their way, and he instinctively moved to shield Ryce from the line of fire. He felt the other man tense behind him, but no shots came.

"Drop your weapons and get in—now," Tex said dryly. She stood in front of them with her hands on her hips, surrounded by four armed men. The warehouse, from what Matt could see, was even larger than he originally thought, and surprisingly brightly lit. Several crates were piled in the middle of the room, creating a sort of partition between the entrance and whatever was going on behind them. Matt thought he heard sounds of a scuffle coming from beyond the crates at Tex's words, and his heart rate switched into an even higher gear, though that should not have been possible at all.

He resisted the urge to call out for Val and bent slowly to put his gun on the floor. Ryce, who stepped up next to him, followed suit.

"Get in," Tex repeated, none too patiently, and they complied. The door slid shut behind them, cutting off all outside sound. One of the men went over to pick up their discarded weapons.

"Station Security are on their way here right now," Ryce said before anyone else could utter a word. "If you assault us, you will be arrested."

"We have time," Tex said, unfazed. "I figure you two are here for this jackass?"

She nodded toward the pile of crates. Matt eyed the armed henchmen cautiously, but nobody was firing at them yet, so he risked turning his back on them and walked to the back of the storage unit.

His hunch proved correct. Val was there, strapped to a metal chair with his hands tied behind his back and a piece of tape plastered over his mouth. One of his eyes was swollen shut, and his cropped hair was matted with blood on the left side of his head, but he was definitely conscious, glaring defiantly at his captors. Seeing Matt, he jerked in his chair toward him, but that only earned him a hard slap from one of the men holding him down.

Matt gritted his teeth and held back everything he wanted to say about the situation. Tex seemed to be the one in charge, and Eddie Ander was conspicuously absent. Either way, they were all in a pickle, especially if the security folks were going to take their sweet time coming.

"You should get a tighter rein over your men, Spears," Tex said, coming up to them from behind. Ryce gave her the eye, but even he couldn't possibly argue with the sentiment. "I've warned you to leave Ander the fuck alone."

"I don't see him anywhere, so I doubt he's in any danger," Matt said, turning to face her. He had to somehow talk their (and especially Val's) way out of this. They were still alive, so that, at least, was a sign Tex could be reasoned with.

"All this"—he gestured toward Val's chair, trying to ignore his crewman's condition—"is a personal matter that can be resolved. As I recall, you'd made me a mutually beneficial proposal. Do we really want to let one unfortunate mishap affect our business? We're all adults here. I'm sure we can all agree to keep our emotions, justified as they may be, in check for our benefit. So, why don't you let us go, and I promise Mr. Sokolov here won't make any more trouble for any of you, so we can go back to discussing our deal?"

He did his best to sound as calm and nonchalant as possible. No amount of fake charm would help him here, but letting panic show would be even worse.

"Yes, business," Tex said with a little smirk as she crossed her arms over her chest. "I believe now may be a good time to negotiate slightly different terms for our deal."

"How about a trade?" Ryce said, stepping forward.

"What did you have in mind?"

"IMA shipments aside, there might be something else we could help you with. You need a pilot for your races, don't you?"

Matt bit his lip not to show his surprise. Where exactly was Ryce going with this? And where *were* those security guys?

"Good guess," Tex said, unperturbed by Ryce's knowledge. "You're making it a little difficult for me to let you walk out of here, kid, but go on."

"You're in need of a skilled pilot," Ryce continued. "Well, I'm an ex-combat pilot. A good one, too, if I do say so myself. I'll fly for you if you will release Mr. Sokolov."

Matt rounded up on him so fast he almost gave himself whiplash, but Ryce only raised his hand to silence him. He leveled his gaze at Tex, not meeting Matt's eyes.

"That's ballsy of you," Tex said finally. She gave Ryce a once-over, as if appraising his worth, her gaze lingering on his top-notch flight adapters. "You sure you're up to it? We're talking about a high-speed race over rough terrain, down planetside. Any kind of aircraft—aerojets, strike fighters, even upgraded pods. Ain't no rules, except you follow the course and come in first place. The prize is twenty thousand credits, cash. If you win, Griggs might even let you keep it."

"You want me to win a race without a trial run?" Ryce asked while Matt was still struggling to process the possibility of Ryce actually participating and the amount of money involved.

"Hell, yes," Tex said, showing signs of annoyance for the first time during the conversation. "No point in you entering otherwise, is there? Griggs's not the only one with stakes in this game. High stakes."

"It would be nearly impossible for someone to win on the first try, no matter how skilled they are," Matt argued. "You don't need a pilot, you need a miracle."

"Then you better hope your mate is a wizard," Tex retorted.

"Is Griggs the organizer, or is he only playing the ponies?" Matt asked suspiciously. Griggs sounded like the sort of fellow to be on the moneymaking side, not the side that was bound to be picked clean by the house. This was his backyard, after all; the station had virtual control of the planet, even if it was uninhabited. And if Griggs was the one running the show, there was no reason for him to have a stake of his own in it, since he'd be getting a cut from both the racers' entrance fees and the bets.

"It's none of your business," Tex said. Seeing Matt's expression, she deigned to clarify: "He's not the only organizer. A lot of powerful people are involved, and he wants to have all his bases covered."

"So he scams his partners by using a proxy to rig the odds?"

"All you need to do is win," Tex said impatiently. "What's going on behind the scenes is hardly your concern."

"I don't have a suitable aircraft available," Ryce said, cutting through their exchange. "The ship's shuttle isn't fast enough to compete with aerojets."

"We could provide you with one," Tex said. "But if you crash it, that's on Mr. Sokolov. Not that you'd care either way when you're smeared over a canyon wall, kid, but your friend might."

Matt took a deep breath before letting Tex know exactly what he thought about that, but Ryce beat him to it—just not in a way Matt would have liked.

"Fine," he said. "Do we have a deal?"

"How about this. If you're not shitting me about being a combat pilot, I'll let you fly. You win, we let this troublemaker run right back to Mommy Spears. You lose—and he might go 'missing.' Considering all the shit he pulled lately, no one will think twice about it. Same goes if you try to breathe any of this to Station Security, not that they're of much help to you anyway. Now, you go back to your ship, all nice and quiet, and we'll let you know when the next race is set up."

Tex turned to Matt. "You handle this well, and we'll go ahead on your engine fixes and the IMA shipments arrangement. Try to pull a fast one on us, and you're all dead in the water. And for some of you, it'll be quite literal. I'm handling this thing for now, but if you fail to keep your end of the bargain, I'll hand your friend over to Ander, just like he wanted in the first place."

As if to emphasize her words, one of the men kicked Val in the knee. The engineer grunted, though it sounded more like an angry growl than a moan of pain.

"Don't worry, Val," Matt said with as much conviction as he could muster, reining in his anger. "It'll be all right. We got your back."

Val made a sound of protest, his blue eyes blazing furiously, but their session was over. At a sign from Tex, the men shoved the now-discharged guns back in Matt and Ryce's hands and ushered them outside, into the empty storage corridor. The door slid shut behind them with a soft but resigned click.

Chapter Ten

"ARE YOU OUT of your goddamn mind?" Matt demanded once they were safely outside the storage area, hurrying along the long curved corridors back to the docks. "Do you have some kind of death wish? Why the hell did you offer to enter their race?"

"You know why." Ryce was walking briskly at his side, avoiding his gaze. "If I hadn't, we'd likely all have ended up dead."

"They can't just go about killing people on a Freeport," Matt said, though more from natural stubbornness than an objective assessment. "I don't know why Security didn't show up, but they would have eventually if Tony reported us missing. We're not some drifters who can disappear unnoticed; there are docking fees in my name."

"I seriously doubt that woman cares about your docking fees," Ryce said.

A tandem Station Security on-duty patrol passed them by, and Matt involuntarily scowled at them. Tex was right; they were no help at all when folks really needed them. That earned him suspicious looks, but Ryce grabbed him by the hand and led him away before Matt could air his grievances and most likely get arrested on sheer principle.

"You're not actually thinking about going through with it, are you?" Matt asked once they were out of earshot. The thought of Ryce meeting the same fate as those poor souls Ander had so casually mentioned sent his stomach roiling. How in hell had they ended up in a situation where they'd even have to consider doing something like this?

"Let's not discuss it here, please," Ryce said in a low voice. They entered the docks, which, unlike the living quarters, were milling with people. Private and commercial vessels traveled through the adjacent jumpgate round the clock, so the bays were always fully manned to monitor the departures and arrivals.

"Fine."

Matt couldn't wait to get back to the ship anyway. He was tired, angry, and utterly miserable. Not only had he failed to rescue his teammate, but he'd also gotten them all in even worse trouble, and he was in too much turmoil to deal with it adequately. He needed time to calm down and rest before he could think rationally and come up with some sort of a solution for all of this. But all that came to his mind was his trusty whiskey bottle stashed under the bed, so handy for getting himself blissfully numb. There was absolutely nothing he could do right now anyway, besides snapping at Ryce for jumping in over his head, so a break wasn't such a bad idea.

Tony was hanging around by the main hatch, waiting for them. The way her face fell when she saw it was just the two of them was like a knife plunged in his heart.

Some captain you are, he thought bitterly. You swore you'd keep your crew safe, and look where you've gotten them—stuck on a grounded ship on a backwater Freeport, held hostage by a black-market racketeer, forced to risk their lives because of your own incompetence.

"Ryce will bring you up to speed," he said without breaking stride as he headed to his cabin. "We'll have a crew meeting first thing tomorrow morning."

"Didn't you want to talk?" Ryce called after him, but Matt walked away as fast as he could, pretending not to hear him. He had a much more pressing appointment, and there was no way anybody was keeping him away from it.

THE WHISKEY TASTED bitter.

There was nothing actually wrong with it. It was perfectly fine contraband single malt, but this time, the familiar caramel-tinged smokiness didn't bring Matt the solace he craved. All he could taste was the flavor of his worry and disappointment. He finished the last drops in his tumbler anyway, and leaned back in his chair, staring at the window screen. It showed yet another newsreel, but he wasn't paying attention.

It was Ryce's fault he couldn't even enjoy a proper drink anymore. Who asked him to point out Matt's problems anyway? They were perfectly fine as they were, swept neatly under an imaginary carpet so he wouldn't have to face them.

But he wasn't mad at Ryce, not really. He had only himself to blame for everything, and he was perfectly aware drinking wasn't going to make it better. Matt had to figure something out, fast, because he damn well couldn't live with himself if he let anything happen to Val when he was supposed to be protecting him.

He even went as far as contemplating going to Nora and begging for help. He was loath to go running to his older sister to get the big bad bullies off his back, but he had to admit he and his crew were at a huge disadvantage. While his modus operandi was relying solely on himself, this time, it might not cut it. He doubted Nora would go traipsing around the station after Griggs with her gun drawn, but as a Major in the Federal Fleet, she could definitely pull some weight with the station officials, forcing them to take an interest in Val's kidnapping.

But in Val's precarious situation, going to the authorities would have to be the last resort. With folks like Eddie Ander running the show, Matt would have to tread carefully.

There was a knock on the door and Matt sighed, pushing the whiskey bottle aside on the small foldout table. It wasn't hard to deduce who was standing on the other side.

"Come in."

Ryce stepped in as the door slid shut behind him. He didn't say a word, but Matt was becoming quite familiar with the extensive array of Ryce's neutral expressions, and this one meant he was pissed off.

"I'm not drunk," Matt declared. "Yet."

"I see." Ryce sat on the edge on the bed, forcing Matt to turn to face him. "Are you going to talk to me like a fucking grown up, or are you going to mope around all night long feeling sorry for yourself?"

Matt's eyebrows shot up. Ryce was seriously angry if he was using swear words. And in that case, an offense was the best tactic.

"Yeah, let's talk." Thankfully he hadn't drunk enough for his speech to be slurred, so his voice sounded firm enough. "Starting with the obvious. No matter what kind of deal you think you've managed to score, you can't possibly be naïve enough to believe they'll actually stick to it."

"I know that," Ryce said. "I'm not placing trust in either Tex or Griggs' fairness. But it was the best I could come up with to buy Val more time and to prevent them from blackmailing us with something even worse."

"It *is* worse! Ain't no way in hell I'm letting you participate in those races. If it comes to that, I'll fly whatever piece of junk they throw at us myself."

"With all due respect to your piloting skills, I don't think that is quite up your alley," Ryce said, more gently than Matt would've expected under the circumstances. "No matter how much you want to believe it is."

"If you think I'd do it to prove I'm just as good as you are—"

"No." Ryce shook his head. "I know you, and I know you wouldn't do that out of jealousy."

"I could never be jealous of you." Perhaps it was drunken candor, but it was true nonetheless. "Not anymore. Seriously, you're, like, so far above me I might as well be jealous of a Mnirian. I haven't forgotten you're a decorated combat pilot, and all I've done in the last few years was flying the *Lisa* on autopilot. But as good as you are, it doesn't mean I'm okay with you risking your life on something so shady."

"I realize you want to protect me," Ryce said. "And not just me—all of us, because you care. But it's not something you can do all on your own. If we want to get Val back, we all have to pitch in and do our part."

Matt sighed and pinched the bridge of his nose. Ryce was right. Matt would do anything to keep him safe, but he couldn't do that if Ryce insisted on placing himself in the heart of danger.

Maybe him leaving wasn't such a bad idea, after all. If Ryce was away on a military mission, he couldn't get in trouble with local crooks.

"Even putting risk aside for a moment, you can't afford to get embroiled in this kind of shit. No matter how good an expert you are on Mnirian tech, or how much Nora wants you on her project, there's no way the Fleet would let you anywhere near a top-secret military excavation site if you're caught flying in an illegal race—on a closed-off planet, no less. You'll be ruining your potential career all over again."

But it seemed Ryce was having none of that.

"Val's my friend. Same as yours. If you're willing to risk your neck to save him, how can I do any less? You say you can't let me endanger myself; well, I can't stand aside and watch you do the same, not when there is something I can do. And besides, who said I was going to accept Nora's offer?"

"Please," Matt said wearily. "Let's keep it straight between us, at least. Of course, you're going to accept her offer. In fact, I want you to. It's a great opportunity for someone like you, and who knows? It might lead to other things. Better things than piloting a smuggler's ship, that's for sure."

Ryce was quiet for a moment. There was a different, grimmer quality to the silence.

"If that's how you feel," he said finally. "Thank you for 'keeping it straight,' as you put it. I guess you just saved me a discussion."

Matt thought he sounded doleful, even upset, but why would he? It was everything Ryce had wanted—to be back working for the Fleet, at least somewhat exonerated of the scandal that had marred his reputation thanks to his former commander's rogue exploits. Even if it meant putting everything he and Matt had shared—however briefly—behind.

The back of his throat itched dangerously, and he turned away before Ryce could notice the moisture stinging his eyes. Now was not the time to break down. He had to keep it together for both their sakes. "It's getting late. We all have to clear our heads and get some decent shut-eye while we have the chance. No more drinks, I promise."

"Okay," Ryce said slowly, uncertainly. Matt wasn't sure whether he was hesitant to leave him alone because he didn't trust him with the bottle, or for another reason. But finally, he rose and headed to the door. "See you in the morning."

Stay, Matt wanted to beg Ryce. *Don't listen to my crap. Stay with me, now, so together we can keep the despair at bay, even for a little while.*

But he didn't. Ryce had already made his decision, and it would be unfair of Matt to make it more difficult for him by being clingy and emotional.

"See you," Matt whispered, swallowing around the lump lodged in his throat as the door slid shut.

"SO, LADY AND gentleman, it seems we're up a creek without a paddle." Matt wasn't entirely sure what the phrase meant, but it sounded dire enough to describe their current situation.

They were all sitting around the galley table, bright and early. Matt and Ryce had mugs of steaming coffee in front of them, while Tony was drinking herbal tea (the smell of which Matt did his best to ignore). None of them were in the mood for a proper breakfast. Despite turning in early last night, both Ryce and Tony sported dark circles under their eyes, and Matt was pretty sure he didn't look any better. Another bout of nightmares that had haunted his sleep after he finally managed to doze off certainly didn't help his mood. Without Ryce there to hold him through it, coming to grips with reality after the panic attack had been so much harder.

"I hate to leave Val in the hands of those bastards even for another minute, but they have the upper hand now, as much as it pains me to admit it, and they call the shots. At least this woman, Tex, seems to be in charge of holding him at present, and I didn't get the impression she'd hurt him just for the hell of it."

Unlike Ander, who could apparently pull rank with Tex if he wanted to. But Matt tried not to think about that for the moment. Tony nodded agreement, her eyes brimming with concern.

"But at least it gives us time to regroup," Matt continued. The memory of Val gagged and bound, fully at the mercy of his captors, flashed through his mind, fueling both his rage and his determination. "Tex said the next race wasn't for another few days, and we can use those to come up with a game plan."

"What did you have in mind?" Ryce asked.

He seemed quiet, more subdued than usual. Some of that could be attributed to being preoccupied with Val's safety and the upcoming race, but usually, when called to action, Ryce looked anything but worried. He performed under pressure with cool, collected efficiency, even aplomb. This change in demeanor was entirely uncharacteristic of him.

"I might not be the smartest person out there, but even I know better than to trust Griggs's promises," Matt said, shifting his thoughts back to the subject. "Even if we were to do everything they ask of us, there's a good chance they won't let Val go. Having a hostage is too good a leverage; it means we'll do whatever the hell they want, for as long as they want. Like running drugs in the IMA shipments once we sign the contract."

Tony gasped. Ryce had told her about his deal regarding the races but, apparently, hadn't yet had the chance to fill her in on that particular proposal.

"We can't do that," she said. "I know we've done some shady business in the past, but there are boundaries."

"We won't," Matt assured her. The idea of smuggling drugs disguised as medicine filled him with the same loathing. "But we should give off the impression we're going along with whatever they demand. We have to figure out a way to get Val off this station before they can rope us into it."

"How?" Tony asked. "You can't go after them again the way you did. They'd have moved him already. We don't know where to start digging again, even if we weren't grossly outgunned."

"That's true. I'd risk going to the authorities for help, despite their threats, but judging from their conduct last night, Griggs might have people on pay in Station Security." Matt grimaced and ran a jerky hand through his hair. That was the downside of operating in remote systems—people tended to let a lot of things slide when they weren't under constant scrutiny of the Federal government. Usually it worked in his favor, but not when he actually needed law enforcement to do their damned job. "We're totally on our own."

"And stuck here," Tony reminded. "Even if we could extract Val somehow, we'd be sitting ducks on a grounded ship."

"All too true. That's why we have to find where their headquarters are and where they're holding Val as soon as possible. And while we're at it, figure out a way to get him out of their reach. I know other smugglers working this station. Some would be willing to pick up a stowaway on their next jump out of the system."

"That still leaves the rest of us stranded," Tony pointed out. "I'm sure Griggs would be rather angry with us."

"Val's the one in most danger and, frankly, with the shittiest judgment. I'd feel more comfortable taking on Griggs knowing Val was somewhere safe. Once we know where they're holding him, it'll be easier to plan a rescue mission. No more going in blindly, like we did yesterday. We might even have to create some sort of diversion, distract them enough so they'll lower their guard."

"If we're to get him out ourselves, we should do it during the race," Ryce chimed in. "Their attention—the big shots', anyway—will be directed planetside. They won't be watching their own backyard too closely. That's when we move in. Or, more accurately, when you two move in." He gestured between them. "Since I'll be the one racing."

Matt opened his mouth to protest, but Ryce cut him off.

"I know you're averse to the idea, and I do appreciate you trying to keep me out of harm's way. But I know I can do this, without actually risking my life in the process. And it would give you the opportunity you need to save Val. There's no other way."

Matt's emotions probably showed clearly on his face, because Ryce added softly, looking into his eyes: "You know me. You know I can."

And Matt did. He'd seen what Ryce was capable of. He'd never met a better pilot in his life. But that knowledge did nothing to quell the cold dread which settled in his stomach.

Yet, Ryce was right. They needed all the help they could get if they wanted to see Val safely back in their midst.

"Fine," he said with a heavy sigh and an even heavier heart. "You do what you have to do. In the meantime, Tony and I got ourselves a recon mission."

Chapter Eleven

"WELL, THAT'S...INTERESTING," Ryce said.

"'Interesting' my ass. It's a damn piece of junk," Matt retorted.

They walked around the jet, examining the hull. A call from Tex had come in just a short while after breakfast, informing Ryce curtly that the aircraft he was to use in the competition was waiting inside a transport vessel at Dock F57. The race itself was scheduled in three days, which didn't leave them enough time to inspect it properly, much less do any needed alterations.

Matt had no idea how Griggs had managed to score a jet on such short notice, but he could hardly argue with the proof standing right there in front of them. The old single-engine Sparrow aerojet had definitely seen better days. Military outposts and the more affluent colonies that could afford their own aerial security patrols usually used this smaller model for surveillance and strategic reconnaissance. The paint had peeled off the fuselage, which was dented in several places, and the serial numbers under the wings had been filed off. It didn't look like a plane that could race a truck, much less speed pods and other jets.

"They wouldn't have given me a defunct plane if they want me to win," Ryce reasoned. "It doesn't matter how battered it is. We just have to make sure the critical systems are in working order."

"It's one hell of a time to be missing our engineer, that's for sure," Matt grumbled. "Of course, our missing engineer is the reason we're here in the first place."

He glanced around at the other machines huddled in the belly of the spacious hauler. He guessed a lot of them were intended for the races, as they were aerial craft that would need transporting from the station to the planet and released in the atmosphere. There were about ten other planes of various makes and models, ranging from simple aerojets to strike fighters. All appeared to be in much better condition than the one they were assigned.

"Tex said they'll pay for the repairs, but we'll have to do them ourselves," Ryce said. "That leaves us no time for...other things."

By "other things," he meant, of course, their rescue operation, which, in his mind, Matt had dubbed "Crime and Punishment" in honor of Val's literary tastes. They still hadn't the vaguest idea of where to start searching or even carefully inquiring about him, and on a station this big, three days were simply not enough to set things in motion.

"We'll talk about it later," Matt said. They were currently alone inside the holding chamber, but the maintenance crew came in and out as they pleased, and discussing such sensitive issues out in the open was a bad idea anyway (even if the term "open" was being used loosely). "Let's just see what we're up against first."

He fished an electric screwdriver out of his pocket. Ryce climbed into the cockpit, and Matt paused to admire the way the coarse fabric of the fatigues tightened over his long, lightly muscled limbs. He shouldn't be ogling, but he couldn't help himself. The fact that he'd been lucky enough to actually hold this man in his arms almost every night for the past few weeks still mystified him, and sadness lanced through his chest at the thought of losing him again.

Shaking his head, he opened the lower back panel. The plane trembled slightly as Ryce activated his adapters and switched on the computer.

"The specs don't look too bad," Ryce said after a few minutes. "Nothing major needs to be replaced. Just some fine-tuning and switching out a few parts. The sensor array needs a bit of work, though."

"We'll make sure to focus on that." Matt peered inside the jet's belly. The sensors were super important in rough terrain conditions, but he was more worried about the integrity of the fuselage and the condition of the engine. With only one of those on board, there was no room for error. Whatever the plane's computer indicated, they'd have to pick the engine apart to ensure everything was working like it was supposed to. Ryce's safety was paramount.

"Nice tin can," a slightly mocking voice said from behind.

Matt pulled his head out of the jet's innards and straightened, turning around in annoyance. A tall man stood a few feet away, roughly in his fifties, wearing a bomber jacket and a crooked grin. The adapters on his temples marked him a pilot, but as far as Matt could tell, they were far from the latest model.

"You're the owner?" the guy asked, nodding at the open jet.

"I am," Ryce said, climbing down from the cockpit. He jumped nimbly onto the metal floor and dusted his hands on his fatigues. "And who are you?"

"Sandy Cobb. Seems like we be flying in the same event."

"Perhaps," Ryce said.

"My advice is, go easy at first, son. There's always some new guy thinks he's a hotshot and misses a sharp curve 'cause he ain't paying attention." Cobb shook his head ruefully.

Ryce drew himself up with that air of superior haughtiness he had mastered to perfection. But his age and striking good looks made it difficult for strangers to take him seriously. Matt had made the exact same mistake when he first met him and had been quickly set straight. So, it was understandable Cobb might think nothing of the new upstart competitor—an assumption he'd be very likely to regret once the engines started roaring.

Provided, of course, the damn engine actually worked. After *Lady Lisa*'s untimely malfunction, Matt wasn't leaving anything to chance.

"You seem like someone who's been around in this sort of thing," Matt said, reining in his annoyance at the unsolicited intrusion and making a pacifying gesture at Ryce. Cobb was the chatty type, and any tidbit of information that wasn't passed down from Tex and her buddies was welcome. "And like you said, we're new. Any more tips you could give us?"

Cobb shifted his attention to Matt. "You his navigator? Most of us fly solo."

"His mechanic," Matt said.

The man eyed his pilot adapters but just shrugged. Pilot or not, these days, with the war hitting hard on a lot of colonies, lots of people of various professions and skill levels found themselves unemployed and scraping for the odd job to make ends meet. A mechanic was as good a position as any other.

"You both seem like fine lads," Cobb decided. "If you're in to make some cash on the side, no harm in that. It's only the top three places that'll get you paid, mind you, so don't get any ideas. Slow and steady wins the race, as they say. Take your time to learn the ropes first, before you go charging ahead."

"I know how to deal with an obstacle course," Ryce said coolly, still unable to hide his affront at his experience being doubted.

"I bet you do," Cobb said in the soothing tone of somebody trying to appease a cranky toddler. "But it ain't just the obstacles. Some folks will do anything to win, and things can get pretty ugly out there. And I mean, vicious. Makes for a better show, too."

"Is there someone in particular we should be watching out for?" Matt asked.

"Pretty much everybody, if you're smart. But there's one pilot, Stahl... He's a mean son of a bitch and no mistake. Kept the lead for two races now with his Waxwing jet, so I reckon he won't give up his place too easily, if he does the next one as well."

"So he's dangerous?"

The dark brown skin around Cobb's eyes creased as he grinned at them.

"Hey, the rules are there ain't no rules. He can do whatever the hell he pleases. I'd keep my distance till I knew what's what. Maybe sit the next one out entirely if he shows. There'll still be plenty opportunities to fly."

"Thanks," Matt said. "That's mighty helpful of you."

"Just a bit of a friendly warning," Cobb shrugged. "You lads take care."

He waved goodbye and walked toward the back exit, whistling softly.

"Old busybody," Ryce said under his breath.

"He sure took pains to warn us off," Matt said. "Psychological warfare to shake the competition? But he was right in one thing—we should remember it's a dirty race. The terrain is not the only thing you'll need to be watching out for."

Ryce lifted his chin. "I've chased Alraki fighters in a Falcon under laser cannon cross fire. I think I can handle this Stahl person being belligerent."

Matt sighed. There was no getting through to Ryce when he was caught up in his cocky attitude. He'd have to have the safety talk with him later, when his feathers wouldn't be as ruffled.

"Fine, ace. Let's just forget all the well-wishers and see what we can do about those sensors."

IT WAS WELL past midnight when they finished working on the jet. In fact, they weren't as much finished as Matt simply called for a break. The engine shaped up to be in pretty good condition, but some parts of the cooling system needed to be replaced, and with Ryce still tinkering with the sensor array and Val absent entirely, it was taking Matt twice the time to get anything done.

"I'm going to take a shower," Ryce informed him once they stepped inside the *Lady Lisa*. They were both sweaty and covered in dust and grease.

"You go ahead," Matt said. "I'm gonna grab a quick bite first."

He hadn't had anything to eat since their somber breakfast that morning—which consisted of nothing but coffee. As if to emphasize his words, his stomach rumbled loudly.

A brief smile touched Ryce's lips but was gone almost as soon as it had appeared. Merely days ago, they would have laughed and joked about it, but now, even such harmless, good-natured ribbing seemed out of place. The inevitability of Ryce's departure hung over them like a heavy cloud, poisoning the brief time they had left together with a miasma of bitterness.

Matt swung by the galley for his dinner. Unfortunately, the contents of their cupboards were in a particularly sorry state. The notion of having to choose between food and other current necessities had proved only too true.

After a short search, he fished out a can of corned beef hash. The artificially flavored ration was the least popular one with the crew, and right now, he was so hungry he didn't care what it tasted like.

The light in the galley was too glaring for his tired eyes, so Matt opted to take his meager meal in the rec room. He was surprised to find Tony there, curled up on the sofa in front of the screen with a blanket thrown over her legs, watching a movie on mute.

"Couldn't sleep," she said when she spotted him in the doorway.

The room was blissfully dark, the only light coming from the flickering images on the screen. Matt sat heavily in the armchair and dug into the can with a disposable spoon, forgoing the extra effort of heating it first.

"You sure you don't want to fix yourself something nicer?" Tony asked, watching him gulp down the cold, sticky food.

"Nah. I'm good." He wiped his mouth and looked at her. "Did you hear anything from the IMA regarding the contract?"

Tony sighed. "Not yet. God, I hope they don't hear about the mess we're in."

"Yeah," Matt frowned. If either the IMA or the Onoreans caught wind of their involvement with the station's black market and illegal gambling, their only chance of getting a decent job would disappear faster than a ship falling through a jumpgate.

"I'm gonna need your help tomorrow if we want to get the repairs done on time," Matt said, changing the subject. He suspected that the less than perfect condition of the jet was at least partly intentional—to keep them busy tinkering with it instead of focusing on rescuing Val. So far, it was working. "I have a list of parts we have to procure ASAP. Don't haggle too much; Griggs will be the one footing the bill. Just stress we want them right away, if not sooner."

"Sure thing." Tony was looking at him with that expression Matt didn't like. The one which meant she was gearing up for a serious talk. Even with the heavy food currently lining his stomach, he just couldn't do any more serious talks.

"Is everything okay between you and Ryce?" Tony asked, confirming his suspicions.

He'd snap at any other person for sticking their nose where it didn't belong, but Tony was different. She was like a caring, slightly meddlesome sister. Perhaps even more than a sister, since Matt and Nora had never been close enough to be asking such personal things of each other.

"Why?" Matt edged away from a direct response. Tony knew nothing about Nora and Colonel Mensah's offer to Ryce, and he was obligated to maintain the secrecy.

"I don't know, you guys seem distant all of a sudden," Tony said carefully. "I know it's not my business or anything, just... I can feel there's something going on under the surface with you two. I thought you were doing fine."

"Me too," Matt muttered. He didn't want to talk about it, not right now. He'd need her support later, when he'd have to somehow collect the pieces and move on with his life after the inevitable breakup. "It's... complicated."

"Is it?"

No. No, it wasn't. It was all pretty simple, really. Matt cared for Ryce more than he wanted to admit, even to himself. But like most people in his life he'd cared about, Ryce wasn't going to stick around, because Matt had nothing to offer that was worth staying for.

"It's late and I'm tired," he said, getting up and picking up his trash. "I'll see you in the morning, okay?"

"Okay," Tony said slowly, but Matt was already escaping to the corridor, making for the welcome solitude of his empty cabin.

Chapter Twelve

MATT SHUT THE little panel on the jet's side with far more force than was necessary and wiped the sweat off his forehead. He was probably smearing grease on it instead, but cleanliness was a lost battle at this point. His fatigues were already stained with all the inner fluids of a half-disassembled aircraft.

"I fixed the leak," he called. "The coolant levels should hold steady now."

"Running diagnostics," Ryce answered from the cockpit, and after a few moments, "All seems to be in order."

"Finally," Matt muttered. The engine cooling unit had been giving them hell for the past few hours. Thankfully, the arrival of new carbon-steel pipe fittings helped fix the problem, but with everything still needing to be done, including sensor calibrations, they were going to pull an all-nighter.

Matt didn't mind the hard work. Hell, if it meant boosting Ryce's chances of emerging on the other side of the racecourse unscathed, he would have happily worked nonstop for a week. But every minute they spent in the giant cargo hold fixing the jet was a minute they didn't spend searching for Val. Time was slipping through their fingers, and there was nothing Matt could do to mend this particular leak. Even Tony was too busy running around the station making sure they had all they needed, and despite her promise to poke into Griggs's holdings while at it, Matt didn't count on her making much progress.

Ryce climbed down from the cockpit to stand next to him.

"You should go rest," he told Matt. "I can run the calibrations myself."

"If anybody needs his rest, it's you," Matt said, offended at the proposal. He knew Ryce was looking after him, but there was no way he was going to get his beauty sleep before they were done. "The fucking race is tomorrow. You should be on top of your game, not working till the last minute."

"There's no need to get upset," Ryce said levelly. "I'll be fine. It's only minor adjustments now. This thing is as ready to fly as it'll ever be."

"It might be ready, but we sure as hell aren't. We still don't even know where to start searching for Val, much less how to do something about it even if we did. Unless you've figured out a way for us to canvass all the private quarters of the outer ring in the next six hours."

"No." For a moment, Ryce looked as weary as Matt felt, his sharp gray eyes going dim, his mouth turning into a hard line.

Matt felt a stab of guilt. It wasn't fair of him to demand answers of Ryce. For all his intelligence, he wasn't omnipotent, and he was no less worried about Val than Matt or Tony were.

"I don't see what else we can do tonight, not with the time we have. As much as I hate to say it, we will have to gather information after I get back and wait till the next...event for the extraction," Ryce said.

For a brief second, Matt thought he'd misheard or failed to understand through the fog of his fatigue.

"You're not actually thinking about doing it twice?"

"If I have to."

"Absolutely not!" Matt sputtered. "Once is bad enough. Who knows what could happen? This is way too risky."

"We might not have a choice," Ryce said. "We're no closer to having a solid plan of action than we were two days ago. We need more time."

"Then we just tell Tex we're not ready. Tell her the damn jet is still malfunctioning. Can't race without an aircraft, can you? Then we'll have all the time we need without you endangering yourself."

"And what if she takes it for what it is—some sort of a stalling tactic? Do you really want to take that chance?"

Matt deflated. He knew he was grasping at straws. It killed him that he had to choose between Ryce and Val's safety—and ultimately, it wasn't even his choice to make. It still didn't make any of this less his responsibility. Or his fault, if anything bad happened.

The defeat must have shown on his face, because Ryce stepped up and grabbed his hand, squeezing it in reassurance. Matt squeezed back, yearning for more of this warm, anchoring touch. Their eyes locked, the irresistible and familiar connection pulling them together like a magnet as the moment stretched into infinity. Ryce's lips parted, as if he was about to say something, and Matt's heart sped up in anticipation. He made an involuntary step forward.

His comm buzzed, and the spell shattered. Ryce's expression faltered and closed off. Matt broke contact reluctantly to answer the call, clamping down on his disappointment.

"Hey, Captain," Tony said. She looked tired too, as far as Matt could make out on the little screen. The stress was certainly weighing heavily on all of them. "I think I might have found something."

The tone of her voice indicated she wasn't talking about spare parts. Matt motioned for Ryce to get closer, and they huddled over the commlink, keeping close to the side of the jet.

"What is it?"

"When I was ordering a fuel refill for you, I chatted up the supplier's technician," Tony said. "And apparently, they've been supplying fuel for a Javelin-type yacht named *Medusa* right here at Dock B11. It's been going out nearly every week, sometimes even more frequently, for the past few months, and it's always back after less than a day."

"Okay," Matt said. "I gather there's more to it than posh joyriding?"

Tony nodded. "The yacht is registered to a private company. But after some prodding, the technician implied its owner is a big shot in the station private commerce sector. And by that, he meant the underground market."

"You think it's Griggs's," Ryce said, his voice only a whisper above the steady hum of the jet's machinery.

"Yes," Tony said. "And those short off-station runs? There's nothing close enough to be reached in a 24-hour roundabout trip. I think he uses it to monitor the races in planetary orbit."

There was a short pause as they let the information sink in.

"That is plausible," Ryce said finally, but without his usual confidence. "I'm sure somebody like that would want to keep a close eye on such a sensitive operation."

"Not to mention it'd provide one hell of a view," Matt said. "The high rollers would demand live feed of the entire race, and that way he could have it all recorded from close orbit using drone cameras."

"Do you think the yacht could also function as a headquarters of sorts?" Ryce mused. "A Javelin is a large spacecraft, as far as yachts go. Having something so readily mobile would be far more convenient than occupying a permanent location under the jurisdiction of a Federal station. If one has the money to afford it, of course. Luxury yachts of that kind aren't cheap."

"It would be convenient," Matt agreed. "A privately owned spacecraft can't be boarded and searched without a warrant. With the kind of sway Griggs seems to have with the local security, he'd be long gone before that happens, even if the system's Federal authorities took an interest in his ventures."

"Do you think he could hold a prisoner aboard?" Tony asked. "It's way more private than a storage unit. And nobody would come knocking."

"That's possible too," Ryce agreed. "And deep space is a good place to dispose of any bodies."

Matt winced, wishing Ryce wasn't so blunt in his assessment. It brought out too many unwanted memories of pirates pushing their unfortunate captives out of the airlock. The thought of Val suffering the same fate was more than he could handle.

"We can't know for sure, though," he said. "We can't even be certain it's Griggs's own vessel. And there can't be any more running blind. The warehouse fiasco was more than enough."

"I'll see what else I can find out," Tony said.

"In any case, that's a great lead. Good job, Tony," Matt hurried to say, kicking himself for not praising her right away. It was the first solid clue they had, and it was a good start. "Just be careful."

"I will. See you guys later." She disconnected, and Matt shoved the comm back into his pocket.

"Do you think we should check it out ourselves, too?" Ryce asked.

Matt shook his head. Even with the new lead on the private yacht, there was simply no time to spare to do any sleuthing.

"Let's focus on getting this thing airborne," he said. "We'll go investigating later, once you're back safe and sound."

Safe and sound, he repeated to himself as Ryce went back to calibrating the sensors. There simply wasn't any other option.

IT WAS LATE by the time they returned to the ship. Matt was so exhausted he could barely walk straight with the weight of the toolbox slung on his shoulder. Ryce looked marginally better, but there were shadows under his eyes that gave away the sheer amount of stress and fatigue he was hiding underneath a composed exterior.

Tony apparently had given up on waiting for them, because both the galley and the rec room were dark and empty. Ryce halted at the entrance to the cabin corridor, making Matt stop right along with him. His expression was that of uncertainty, or at least that was what it seemed like to Matt in the gloomy lighting.

"Would you like to stay with me for the night?" he asked softly. "What's left of it, anyway?"

Matt bit his lip. He would have liked nothing better than to hold Ryce in his arms for the short hours until dawn, pretending it was going to be all right at the end.

But it wasn't going to happen. After this whole thing with the races (*please, let there be just one*) was over, Ryce was going away to restart his career. A move to regain their intimacy might appear as if Matt would try anything to keep him from leaving, and he didn't want to put that kind of pressure on Ryce. He had to keep his head—and heart—clear if he wanted a chance to restore his reputation, to rebuild his life with the Fleet, like he'd always wanted. It was Ryce's call, a logical, smart call, and Matt's confused feelings were absolutely irrelevant.

"I don't think it's a good idea. We're not gonna have any time in the morning. You have to be at the transport vessel dock bright and early, and you do need at least a few hours of uninterrupted sleep. So...I'll just wish you good luck now and let you have your rest."

This time, Matt knew it wasn't the dimness playing tricks with his perception—the hurt in Ryce's eyes was unmistakable. His guts twisted. It wasn't fair after all the times Ryce had offered the quiet support of his presence when Matt needed someone to soothe him during a particularly bad episode of nightmares. He hated doing this, being so casually cruel to the man he'd do anything to protect. But that was what he was doing, wasn't it? He was protecting him from heartbreak, making his future choice easier by distancing himself.

The rationalization sounded shaky in his mind as the heavy silence hung between them. *Who was it he was really protecting here?*

Matt was on the verge of taking his words back, but then Ryce gave him a curt nod and strode off down the corridor. The soft click of the door was louder than a gunshot, and it rang in Matt's ears as he continued to stand there, clutching the hefty toolkit and wondering what the fuck was wrong with him.

His commlink buzzed, shaking Matt out of his stupor. He took it out, fumbling a bit as his sore fingers refused to cooperate, and stared at the number for a long moment before answering the call.

His sister's face appeared on screen. Unlike Matt, she looked as fresh and crisp in her uniform as she always did.

"Nora? Do you have any idea what time it is?" he began irritably, but then uneasiness coiled in his stomach. No unexpected midnight call had ever brought good news. "Did something happen?"

"I'm aware of the time," Nora said, sounding only mildly irritated. "As for something happening, I feel I should be the one asking, seeing as your boyfriend hasn't returned my calls."

"He's been busy," Matt said curtly.

Ryce hadn't told him anything about Nora trying to contact him. Granted, they'd had more pressing things to attend to, so this little detail could have just slipped Ryce's mind.

Except, a man who could perform course trajectory calculations in his head instead of relying on the ship's computer was unlikely to forget little details, as trivial as they might seem.

"Must I remind you how sensitive this whole project is, Matthew?" Nora fell into her best lecturing tone, reminding Matt too much of their father. Fleet Admiral Cummings had the same particular manner of putting the emphasis on "Matthew" when he wanted to convey his disappointment. "I am the one who recommended Mr. Easom for the job, and my reputation is at stake here. We cannot wait on him forever. I have to know what he intends to do."

"Look, it's a tough decision," Matt said. If Ryce was stalling giving his final answer to Nora for whatever reason, the least he could do was play along. "I'm sure he'll contact you as soon as he makes up his mind. It was all...kinda sudden, and with his military service ending on such a sour note—"

"I know perfectly well how you feel about the military, Matthew. But this is not about you. For once in your life, quit being so exorbitantly self-absorbed, and stop holding the man back. Because I've seen you two together, and I'm pretty sure the only reason he's dodging me is you being so solidly against him accepting this job."

A wave of rage rose in Matt's chest. This was exactly why he'd spent years avoiding his family—their confidence in their right to tell him what to do and how to live his life; their unwavering belief they always knew better than him. He fought the urge to turn off the commlink, or worse, throw it against the wall. But he realized not all of his anger was directed at Nora. She'd touched upon a sore point, but the fact it was such a sore point was hardly her fault.

Matt swallowed his instinctive response. He'd already been on the verge of tears from his conversation with Ryce, the accumulated tiredness and frustration of these last few days only adding to the mix. Once, perhaps, he would not have hesitated to take it all out on Nora, but not anymore. He was a better man than that, or at least he was trying to be.

He tried not to think about what—or who—had caused that change, even if he already knew the answer.

"I'm not holding him back," he said after taking a deep breath to calm himself. "Our lives here may not seem as important in comparison, but we *have* been busy." He took another breath to brace himself against his own words. "I'll talk to him and make sure he calls you back with the answer you want to hear."

Nora's frown told Matt she wasn't entirely appeased by that, but right now he couldn't care less.

"Very well," she said finally. "Just make sure he does. Otherwise, I'll be forced to retract the offer. There are other experts on Mnirian technology out there who would be thrilled to pounce on such an opportunity."

"He will," Matt said dryly. "Good night."

He disconnected, feeling even more broken than before. If there was ever a time to get drunk off his ass...but not mere hours before the race. He had to stay sharp, even if he wasn't the one flying. With a sigh, he hauled the blasted toolkit the remaining few feet of hallway to his dark cabin.

Chapter Thirteen

"I'M SURE IT'LL be fine," Tony said for the tenth time.

They were sitting on the bridge of the *Lady Lisa*, with Matt occupying the pilot seat and Tony in the navigator chair next to him. The canopy screen was turned on, but so far, it had been displaying nothing but static. After Matt had put his foot down, Tex conceded to letting them watch the encrypted channel that would broadcast live footage of the races for the benefit of those who had placed bets on the competitors. She didn't specify how or from where the footage was obtained, and Matt didn't press the matter. For now, it was enough that he could keep an eye on Ryce—even if Matt would be too far away to be of any real use should anything happen to him.

He had only seen Ryce for a few brief moments in the morning, and they'd barely exchanged words before he headed out to the transport that would bring all the tiny aerojets into Elysium-5 orbit, but perhaps it was for the best. This way, it didn't feel like saying goodbye. This way, Ryce had to come back so they could have a proper talk about things—including Nora's admonition. The notion of an openhearted chat scared Matt way more than a roomful of armed thugs, but it was infinitely more preferable to the alternative of not being able to do it at all.

Tony fidgeted in her chair.

"Are you sure she gave you the right codes?"

"Yeah," Matt said, although he wasn't sure, and it wasn't like he could do anything if Tex had pulled a fast one on him. He sighed and checked the time at the bottom of the screen. "Two more minutes. Guess they're just punctual."

"Great," Tony said sarcastically. "They might yet kill us all, but at least they'll be punctual about it."

"If something happens to Ryce today, I'm the one who's going to kill them."

He didn't care how tough Tex was, or that Eddie Ander was all kinds of homicidal, or that Griggs was too elusive to reach. In this moment, he fully understood what Val must have felt when he'd thrown away his own safety to go after the people who had hurt his wife. Just thinking about the possibility of losing Ryce—not to a chance at a better life, but to death—had him ready to do the same.

Matt could feel Tony looking at him askance, probably surprised at his vehemence, but didn't turn to meet her eyes.

The screen went pitch black, and then an image of a rocky desert plain came into view. Matt sat up sharply, intent on the picture. It was clearly being shot from somewhere well above the ground, with the live high-resolution camera zooming in on the surface, like a surveillance drone. Perhaps Tony had been right about the purpose of the mysterious private ship which they were yet to investigate. Something like that would be perfect for keeping a close eye on the planetside proceedings.

The camera zoomed in even closer as eleven small ships descended from above and lined up in a neat row at some invisible point, suspended in the air by their swiveling thrusters. Matt counted two pods and nine aerojets of various models. Ryce's plane didn't stand out in any way, but Matt's gaze went straight to it, having become familiarized with its shabby exterior over the course of the last few days.

With only ten other participants, Ryce's odds were pretty good. His skills and experience as a combat pilot were hard to match among privateers. But of course, there were always contingencies even Ryce couldn't predict.

As if at a wave of an invisible hand, the jets launched into motion, with the zooming camera following them.

Tony leaned over in her chair and squeezed Matt's hand briefly. He returned a weak smile, grateful for the support. He was glad she was there with him. It made the gnawing anxiety in his chest a little more bearable when he could share it with a friend.

"Here we go," he whispered, somewhat unnecessarily.

Elysium-5 was a lush paradise planet, but its equatorial regions were dry, riddled with vast deserts and high mountain ranges. The spot for the race was picked in one such desert, with the route winding its way along a huge canyon. Dubbed by Tex "the Pit," the canyon spanned over 300 miles, its nearly perfectly vertical walls reaching a height of 10,000 feet.

The air shimmered with the heat and the engines' exhaust as the jets glided thousands of feet above the barren surface, heading for the canyon. The feed had no sound to accompany it, but Matt could well imagine the deafening roar of so many planes contending for the same space in the otherwise serene environment.

The feed switched to a different camera, and the enormous slit of the canyon came into view, a wide gash across the craggy elevated terrain. This was where the race truly began, an obstacle course that was a challenge to navigate even for experienced pilots with nerves of steel.

The jets dived into the Pit, like ancient gladiators squaring up for a fight in the arena. The drone-mounted camera followed them overhead, the picture so crisp Matt could discern the line of the now-dry riverbed at the bottom, winding its way at a dizzying depth far below. There was no additional starting shot—the planes and the pods just picked up speed, whizzing past each other at varying heights. An abrupt change of altitude mid-flight was bound to slow a jet down, make it lose those few precious seconds, allowing another flier to pass by, but sometimes there was no other way to avoid imminent collision. The Pit was wide, but not wide enough for eleven aircraft vying for dominance without bumping into each other at every turn.

And some racers apparently weren't above intentionally sending others off-kilter. No rules, Tex had said, except you stayed on course and came in first. Matt figured "staying on course" also included holding true to the confines of the canyon, because even with frequent hopping, no aircraft rose above the rim of the stone walls. Other than that... The three top places got paid, but only the winner collected the big cash prize, and only those who bet on him collected the winnings. All the rest had to cut their losses—the entrance fee along with the cost of damages sustained by their aircraft. Coupled with impunity for playing dirty and with the organizers pushing for a violent spectacle, that was one hell of an incentive to try to eliminate the competition in any way possible.

The two pods soon fell behind the speeding aerojets. Even with the best of upgrades, a pod would be hard-pressed to compete with a jet going 1,500 miles per hour. As the canyon became more serpentine, the remaining aircraft spread out, with the slower and more cautious fliers opening bigger and bigger gaps from the leaders with every protrusion or steep slope they had to skirt. Soon, the cameras focused only on those that kept to the front, switching feeds at different intervals to keep up with the jets' progress.

Matt became more agitated as time trickled by. At these velocities, the entire race would only last about twelve minutes, but those minutes were already pushing for the dubious title of being the longest in his life.

Ryce's tiny Sparrow was currently fifth, but steadily closing in on the jet ahead. Matt thought it was Cobb's plane, but he couldn't be sure. He watched in complete silence as Ryce made a wide arc around another turn, almost brushing against the opposite wall but gaining speed and overshooting the fourth pilot as he instinctively slowed down for the difficult maneuver.

"Your boyfriend has balls of steel," Tony said with something close to awe, her gaze riveted to the screen.

Matt grunted in agreement, too busy trying to keep his heart where it belonged instead of jumping to his throat. But it wasn't over yet. The canyon narrowed to a slit of only a few miles wide in what Matt presumed to be the most dangerous section of the course.

The two leaders, Finch- and Waxwing-type jets, went in ahead. The Waxwing was dogging the other plane, sitting on its tail like a persistent horn fly. The first pilot veered to the right, trying to shake it off, but then the Waxwing rolled, angling slightly, and went for the jet from behind at full speed, as if intending to ram it. The Finch broke sharply to the left to avoid collision but miscalculated the distance it had left to disengage. It tried to pull up vertically at the last second, but crashed into the right side of the canyon, exploding in a bright fireball.

"My god," Tony whispered.

Matt couldn't have said a word even if he wanted to. He recalled Cobb's warnings regarding the Waxwing's owner, Stahl, and wished he had taken the man's tips a little more seriously. He only hoped Ryce had enough sense to stay as far away from the current leader as possible.

But of course, now running third, Ryce wasn't one to be content with his placing. His goal was to win, after all; anything short of complete victory spelled defeat. Whatever happened, he'd try to push for that coveted first place.

And it was exactly what he was doing. With no hopes of bypassing the second jet in the narrow chasm, Ryce dived right below it, skimming closely to the uneven ground where the ancient river used to flow. This was putting a strain on an engine that hadn't been in top condition to begin with; these jets were not meant to go so low. Matt held his breath as the Sparrow soared again, despite his concerns, even though he could almost physically feel the forces that were threatening to tear its battered hull apart.

The maneuver put Ryce solidly in the runner-up position. The jet now in third place still hung close to his six, but Ryce was intent on closing the distance between himself and the leader. Matt could only imagine the tensions running among the gamblers at the emergence of a completely unexpected new favorite.

The Waxwing took the sharp turns with the ease of fearless familiarity. By now he probably knew some upstart was challenging his position in the race, and Matt had a feeling he was not going to take it well.

He dug his fingers into the armrests as Ryce attempted the dive yet again. The Sparrow plunged to the ground, striving to undercut the Waxwing as it had done with Cobb's jet. But this time, it seemed Ryce had met his match, at least where nerve was concerned. The Waxwing dropped down as well, right in front of the Sparrow's nose cone, flying at just about the same altitude. With the other jet so dangerously close, Ryce could neither bypass it for risk of hitting the wall, nor pull up, effectively stuck in his position at the whim of the other racer.

Matt tasted a tang of copper on his tongue and released the lip he was biting. With all of Ryce's incredible piloting skills, it was only a matter of time until the aerojet's thrusters lost the battle against the gravitational pull, or until it crashed against a rocky protrusion of the uneven ground.

But even with a better engine, the Waxwing couldn't keep it up much longer, since he ran the same risk of crashing as Ryce did.

The canyon widened abruptly, its walls opening up to more than twice the breadth they were before. The Waxwing, who by all accounts was pretty familiar with the route, took the opportunity to pull sharply up and away into the open space.

Fortunately, Ryce's instincts were quick enough to follow suit immediately. The Sparrow visibly struggled to haul itself up, losing those invaluable seconds while the Waxwing took the lead, widening the gap between them. But once Ryce was in the clear, he picked up speed, as unrelenting in this dash to the finish as he'd been fighting hostile aliens in space battles. This was the last stretch of the course, with only a few dozen miles left to go till the finish line.

Ryce's Sparrow rolled and dropped into a turn, taking advantage of the wider expanse, in what Matt recognized to be a sort of a low Yo-Yo maneuver which allowed it to cut the Waxwing's trajectory from a lower angle and overshoot it. That brought Ryce directly in front of the Waxwing's nose, which was a bad position to be in if they'd been locked in battle where laser guns were involved.

As it turned out, it wasn't a great move in the current situation either. It might have worked against a more skittish opponent, but whoever this Stahl was, he was no less determined than Ryce, and he wasn't about to go down without a fight. The Waxwing swerved in a wide arc and accelerated, doing the same kind of maneuver it had done before, in which it went on a collision course with the other jet. Matt wasn't sure if the sharp intake of breath was his or Tony's; both of them only had eyes for the drama that was unfolding on screen.

Ryce was usually not the type to fall for those kinds of tricks. In fact, he was far more likely to employ them himself. But this time, either he judged his competitor to be too obsessively tenacious to ignore, or his nerves were much more frayed than he let on, because he rolled and veered away, just as the ground began to slope upward and the walls fell back, growing gradually lower and less steep.

Without faltering, the Waxwing turned and sped upward and forward to the invisible finish line, climbing out from the canyon. Ryce's jet followed closely, but his evasion tactic had cost him the advantage and, eventually, the race, as he crossed the finish second.

The last camera lingered on the spot, waiting for the other racers to come in. Their order didn't matter at this point, after a clear winner had emerged, but the information still had to be transmitted for the sake of future bookings. When the last pod reached the sandy elevation of the desert, the feed turned off without a warning, the screen going black again.

The momentary silence was so complete Matt was sure Tony could hear the sound of his frantic heartbeat. The quiet was heavy and oppressive, even though there'd been no audio to the live feed before.

Finally, Tony stirred and turned to him, her face a mask of shock and concern, and Matt just couldn't take it anymore. He jumped from his seat and ran into the corridor, a wave of bile rising to his throat.

He stopped only in front of the hidden liquor compartment in the rec room. His hands shook as he poured himself a glass of scotch, and he couldn't tell if it was with relief or panic. Either way, he needed to calm the fuck down.

Matt swallowed the scotch, wincing at the taste, like acid scorching his throat, despite it being the last of his top-quality stock. He poured himself another shot but lingered, staring at the paneled wall with unseeing eyes.

It's okay. Ryce is alive; he's coming back. Get a grip on yourself.

But will Ryce be as lucky next time? There was that treacherous little voice whispering in his head. Because there would be a next time. Matt had been too slow and too incompetent to get shit done on the first try, despite all the help he'd had from Ryce and Tony. Val was still being held hostage somewhere, and Ryce was forced to risk his life again and again, and they were nowhere near a solution— It was all his fault.

Matt's fingers tightened on the glass, and for a second, he wasn't sure if he wanted to drink it or smash it against the wall. Finally, after what seemed like an eternity, he made himself push it away. Now was not a good time to wallow in self-pity. There were people who depended on him—*his* people—and he had to do whatever it took to make things right for them.

First things first. Ryce had come out of the race alive and whole, even managing not to mangle the jet too badly, but he did only come in second. Griggs and his lot were bound to be displeased by that. Even if Ryce competed again and won the next race, the stakes he'd command after today's performance would be much lower, since more people would bet on him winning. It meant that even if he succeeded, Griggs's winnings would be substantially less than they could have been had Ryce won as a "dark horse" on the first try.

The thought nearly caused another bout of panic, but this time, Matt managed to stomp it down. Griggs still needed Ryce, even after today's faux pas, so it was unlikely he'd do anything to actually harm him.

In any case, there was nothing Matt could do but wait for Ryce's return. He left the glass on the table, untouched, and headed back to his own cabin.

Chapter Fourteen

MATT LOITERED IN the corridor leading up to the main hatch, like a dog waiting for his master to come home. At least, that was what he thought dogs did, because he'd never actually owned one, either real or biomechanical. He was pretty sure even a loyal pet would at some point become sorely disappointed with his caring skills.

He was debating whether calling Ryce was a good idea when the entrance panel finally lit up and the hatch slid open, admitting a very tired and—Matt could see it clearly from the tightness around his eyes and mouth—very irate Ryce.

"You're back," he blurted, leaning his hand against the wall, his knees weak with giddy relief.

Ryce cocked his head to the side, as if judging his response. His flight suit was rumpled and smelled faintly of sweat and jet fuel.

"Of course I'm back," he said with just a hint of annoyance.

Matt peeled himself off the wall and crossed his arms on his chest, trying to appear more nonchalant. He wanted to pounce on Ryce, hold him close, whisper even sillier things in his ear, but it seemed none of it would be welcome right now.

"Did they give you a hard time?"

"No," Ryce said. "No one approached me at the station docks, and I stayed as far away as I could from anyone else on the transport on the way back. Seemed like a wise thing to do."

"I guess that means they'll contact us with further instructions, then," Matt said. A part of him was glad Griggs's people had left Ryce alone instead of harping on his failure, or worse, retaliating, but another part wondered at this unexpected benevolence; it was nothing if not suspicious.

Ryce just nodded. He looked weary—not even tired, really, but sort of jaded. Coming down from an intense adrenaline rush must have been rough, but Matt knew it was more than that. Ryce was used to being the best at everything, both when it came easy and when it required hard work. Suffering defeat at something he considered his forte, his calling even, was not something he was used to dealing with, especially when there had been so much riding on his potential win.

Matt let his hands fall to his sides and took a step forward. They were now standing only a few inches apart, but the invisible wall he'd gone out of his way to erect between them was still there, a barrier not to be crossed.

He hated seeing Ryce so despondent. Maybe he couldn't touch him, but he could at least talk.

"Hey. Don't let it get to you, all right? It was the first time you've flown the route. That other guy in the Waxwing knew what he was doing. You'll get the hang of it next time. You know you're better than all those pilots; it's just a matter of getting your toes wet."

Ryce gazed at him, his expression intense and unreadable. For a moment, Matt was afraid Ryce was going to snap at him—not that he didn't have a right to. But he just sighed and ran his hand over his hair, which had grown out of its previous severe buzz cut into soft blond waves.

"I should have done better. The oldest trick in the book, and I fell for it. Lost my nerve at the last moment. It's never happened to me before. Not like this."

"You didn't know what that rabid bastard would do," Matt said, trying to think of a cogent argument which would convince Ryce to go easy on himself and not take the loss to heart. "I saw the whole thing, and I was sure he was gonna slam right into you if you didn't move out of his way."

Matt's heart sped up again at the memory, for a brief second reliving the terror at watching that unlucky Finch jet explode, and he swallowed hard to make it stop.

"You're damn lucky to have come out of it alive," he said, his voice a bit hoarser than he intended.

Ryce didn't answer. If anything, he looked even more miserable.

Fuck it, Matt thought with sudden clarity. *Even if it's all to be over between us, he's still my friend, first and foremost, and he needs me.*

Matt closed the distance between them and hugged Ryce, as tightly as he could. He was ready to let go if Ryce pulled away, but he didn't. Ryce's heartbeats mixed with his own, and he was overcome by an incredible sense of belonging. Ryce was now a part of his soul—as trite as it sounded—and even having to give him up couldn't change that.

Matt loved him.

A small amount of tension left Ryce's body as they stood there in the middle of the corridor, locked in the impromptu embrace. He sighed again and leaned into Matt infinitesimally.

The entrance alert buzzed, and Matt bit down a curse. Why couldn't they have even a brief moment to themselves? He seriously considered letting whoever it was at the door cool their heels a bit, but Ryce already stepped back, breaking the contact and leaving Matt feeling strangely bereft. His gray eyes were dark with emotion, but a second later, he schooled his features into his usual mask of cool indifference.

Matt punched the entrance panel to see who was interrupting them so rudely, itching to give them a piece of his mind, but the external camera feed showed no one outside the main hatch. Instead, there was a small cooler crate, about fifteen by ten inches, sitting at the top of the ramp.

"What the hell," Matt muttered.

He opened the hatch and peered cautiously to the sides before stepping outside. As far as he could see, nobody was lurking in the shadows, waiting to jump him. He bent down and picked the cooler. It was heavy for its size, but that was probably the added weight of the temperature-controlling electronics rather than actual contents. The crate's screen was devoid of any information—nothing to either indicate the sender or give any clue as to what might be inside.

Matt was sorely tempted to leave the thing outside unclaimed or call Station Security to investigate it, which would be the sensible thing to do. But in his position, he couldn't afford to be sensible. He either played the game or forfeited, and that was not an option he was prepared to consider—since he wouldn't be the one paying the steep price of losing.

Ryce closed the hatch as soon as Matt stepped back inside.

"What is it?"

"I have no idea. Let's check it out in the galley."

They met Tony coming their way as they hurried up the corridor.

"Oh, you're finally back!" She began with a smile as she spotted Ryce, but then her eyes fell on the cooler in Matt's hands. She frowned. "Where did that thing come from?"

"Someone left it on the doorstep," Matt said and hauled the crate onto the kitchen table. They all huddled around it.

"Are you sure you want to open it?" Tony asked. Ryce didn't say anything but looked at Matt questioningly. In the end, Matt was the captain, and the final decision fell on him.

No, he wanted to say. He had a very, very bad feeling about whatever was inside, but it was too late to back down now. Instead, he swiped the touch pad on the crate. The lid popped open with a soft hiss, and the galley filled with the coolant vapors.

"Holy fuck," Tony said into the ensuing silence.

Lying on a bedding of artificial ice packs was a finger. It was a human index finger, cleanly cut at the base with presumably a laser knife, the wound partially cauterized. The old faded burn marks at the tip made it only too easy to guess whom it belonged to. Tony had spent way too much time fixing the results of Val's tampering with faulty wiring.

Matt recoiled and fought hard not to gag at the sight. He'd seen the mangled bodies of soldiers and civilians left after Alraki attacks, so he was hardly a stranger to gore and violence. Yet somehow, this single thing, so incongruous in an otherwise perfectly normal setting, had so much more impact.

He glanced around at his companions. Tony stared at the detached body part, her hand hovering over her mouth in horror. Ryce was white as a sheet.

"Excuse me," he said in a hollow voice and ran out of the galley without waiting for their response.

"I might be sick too," Tony said faintly.

"I don't think he's sick," Matt said. He suspected that unlike him, Ryce didn't get queasy at the sight of blood. "He believes he's responsible."

He pushed the lid shut again, unable to stand looking at Val's finger any longer. Now, as the initial shock subsided, anger bubbled to the surface. This had to be Ander's doing. Oh, Griggs might have ordered it, and Tex might have thought it necessary, but Matt didn't have a doubt in his mind Ander had been the one carrying out the directive, and enjoying every last bit of it.

I hope you die, motherfucker. Next time somebody tries to beat you into a bloody pulp, I'm gonna help them.

"Can we find out who delivered it?" Tony asked, her voice still a bit shaky. "Maybe request pulling recordings from the dock surveillance cameras? Station Security would have to investigate something like that."

Matt shook his head. "What's the point? We know damn well who delivered it, and why."

Silence hung heavily around the table as they stared at the crate, its control panel lights glowing serenely.

"I'll hold on to it," Tony said finally, grabbing the cooler. "Keep it in the infirmary till Val gets back."

"You do that," Matt said. He didn't know whether it'd do any good, but it was the best they could do for the time being. "I'm gonna have a quick chat with Ryce."

"You do that," Tony echoed as he headed toward the cabins.

MATT HALTED IN front of Ryce's closed door and took a deep breath. It wasn't that he was afraid to talk to him, precisely, but he was worried about making things worse. He had never been that compassionate person to offer sage advice; if anything, he was the one who was notoriously bad at keeping his shit together during emotionally rough patches. But he couldn't leave Ryce alone right now, either. He knew what it was like to blame himself for the harm that befell his crewmates, whether the culpability was real or not.

He knocked on the door. A full minute passed before it opened.

"Are you okay?" Matt asked, stepping inside.

Ryce nodded, but the truth was he looked anything but okay. He was still wearing the smelly flight suit, and the bed he'd apparently been sitting on was rumpled. For Ryce, who was usually neatness personified, it was a sure sign of distress.

"This is not your fault," Matt said fiercely. "You know that, don't you?"

"Yes, it is," Ryce said in a lackluster voice. "I faltered, and now Val is the one paying for it."

"Like hell. You didn't do this to Val. *They* are the ones responsible."

"You know that's not how it works."

Matt bit back his response. He knew too well words only went so far in mitigating that awful feeling which came with carrying someone else's suffering as your burden. Ryce had said almost the same to him when he'd confided in him about abandoning his former crew-fellows when pirates captured the ship he'd been navigating. While he'd appreciated the sentiment, he could never bring himself to agree he wasn't to blame for their deaths.

He took Ryce by the hand. It felt cold and clammy. He sat on the bed and drew Ryce close until he had no choice but to sit next to him. Very slowly, very tentatively, Matt reached out and brushed Ryce's cheek with his fingertips. Ryce's face had always been beautifully sculpted, with high cheekbones and fine features, but now it looked and felt too thin, even gaunt. They were all exhausted, going full throttle without much food or sleep, and this recent reminder, courtesy of Griggs and his cohorts, meant they'd only be forced to work even harder.

"What happened out there?" he asked quietly. Ryce was right in one thing—the hesitation that had cost him the race was as uncharacteristic of him as the loss itself.

There was a long, tense moment.

"I guess...I wasn't focused enough," Ryce said reluctantly. "I'm ashamed to say that I was too preoccupied."

"With what?" Matt lowered his hand but let it rest in the small space between them, like a tiny bridge of warm flesh to span the gap.

"A mistake of mine," Ryce said.

"You never make mistakes."

"You were a mistake."

Matt went very still.

"By all accounts, this—us being together, living together, flying together—shouldn't have worked," Ryce continued, finally raising his eyes, so Matt could see his own reflection in their stormy depths. "But somehow, it did. Maybe falling in love with you was a mistake, but it was the happiest one I've made in my life."

"'Was'?" Matt barely recognized the sound of his own voice.

Ryce shook his head, struggling with words, his usual eloquence failing him against raw emotion. "I know this can't be enough for you. Not emotionally, not physically. I'm used to being alone. It's always been...safer that way. I'm not an easy person to get attached to, certainly not to love. Not in the sense you must be used to. Don't try to deny it," he added as Matt opened his mouth to protest. "You've been all too clear about wanting to end things with me, encouraging me to leave. And that is your right; I understand that. You don't have to sugarcoat it for my sake. I want you to be happy, Matt. And if you can't find happiness with me, then it is pointless for me to linger. Once this whole ordeal is over, I'll be out of your way."

For once in his life, speech utterly failed Matt. He couldn't even find his voice, let alone the right words, as he let Ryce's confession sink in.

Ryce thought he wasn't good enough for *Matt*? Ryce *loved* him?

Suddenly, he was truly, deeply angry at himself. Ryce had been feeling this all this time, while Matt clung to his insecurities, too afraid to say the word that would change everything? And would it change anything, really? This was how he felt. He knew that, had known that from the moment he'd seen Ryce walk into a canteen on the Messa-1 station and into his new life on *Lady Lisa*. Saying it aloud would only be admitting it to himself, and he'd been too much of a damn coward to do that.

Until now.

"Baby, I love you more than anything in this entire fucking galaxy," he said. Ryce's gray eyes widened, but Matt went on. The words finally poured freely, and he let them flow. "I'd trade anything I have—my ship, my life—for your happiness. That's why I said all that nonsense. The invitation to work for the Fleet again... It's what you wanted. God knows you deserve it far more than anything I could ever give you. And if you think it's all about being physical for me, you're wrong. Well, you'd probably be right if you were any other person, but it's *you*. I'd wait for you for as long as it would take. I'd wait for you forever."

"You've never said that before," Ryce said into the resonating silence which followed. "Not...the love part."

Matt barked a laugh that bordered on hysterical. "It's because you fell in love with a craven asshole."

"I didn't."

Ryce leaned in, and the touch of his lips on Matt's was like a bolt of electricity, the sensation coursing through his veins like a live current through exposed wires. A pitiful, humiliating sob tore out of him, but he didn't care. All he wanted was the taste of those perfectly curved lips.

The kiss was everything he wanted, yet almost more than his heart could safely handle. As their mouths locked in this intimate embrace, Matt felt it shatter and the pieces fall back in their rightful places again, making it whole and stronger for being once broken and healed.

"Stay with me tonight," Ryce whispered as they finally parted. His breath ghosted over Matt's skin, making him shiver.

Matt found Ryce's hand and brought it to his lips, kissing the tips of his fingers.

"I will, baby. Go wash up, and we'll get some sleep."

They both needed rest, desperately. But even as they lay later in the narrow bunk, having discovered anew the comfort of simple closeness, sleep didn't come easily. Matt was wrung out, his emotions having run the gamut from horror to despair to unexpected hope, but his mind was still struggling with doubt.

Ryce might love him, but he didn't say he wasn't going to take Nora's job.

Chapter Fifteen

"SO," MATT SAID the next morning, when they were all assembled in the rec room with their coffees and breakfast sandwiches. Somehow, the idea of eating at the galley dinner table with the memory of unpacking yesterday's delivery hovering over them wasn't very appealing. "We need to step up our game. Because if we don't, they surely will."

"They already have," Tony pointed out from where she was sitting in the oversized old armchair—Val's favorite reading spot—with her cup of herbal tea. "If we stick to our previous plan of making our move during the race, how much time do you think we have until the next one?"

"We don't know exactly." Ryce was sitting on the sofa next to Matt, sipping his scalding-hot coffee. A good night's rest had done wonders to erase the signs of fatigue from his face and posture. At the very least he appeared more relaxed. Matt secretly hoped that perhaps their mutual confessions had something to do with it too.

"Tex hasn't sent us the details yet," Matt said. Perhaps Griggs was so disappointed with Ryce's performance he'd abandoned the idea of using him for racing again. He wouldn't say as much aloud, though.

"It can't be too soon," Ryce said. "It's risky to arrange something so big only days apart; the scope of logistics would draw too much attention. Even if they have people on the pay among the station personnel, it would be difficult to keep under wraps. I'd say the races would have to be about a week apart, at least." He set his half-empty cup on the side table. "But it can't be much more than that, either. The organizers would want to maintain the right level of interest brewing. Not to mention the entire affair is probably seasonal."

"What do you mean?" Tony asked.

"I've assembled all the information I could find on the geography of this particular region of Elysium-5, and it seems the large canyon is flooded at winter time. Not completely, of course, but enough that it would interfere with the racing."

"So, there are only so many events they can do," Matt said. "And every one counts."

"We have to hustle, then," Tony remarked. "I'm guessing Tex won't give us a lot of head notice, either."

"Exactly," Matt said, taking a big swig off his coffee. Now that they had this short grace period, he needed to stow all his other worries and misgivings away in order to focus on not dropping the ball on "Crime and Punishment" this time around. And that meant letting go of his preoccupation with Ryce's plans for the future and whatever sinister secrets surrounded the particularities of his birth. For now, he had to draw strength from his love for Ryce, and from the fact that, as incredible and improbable as it was, his love was returned.

"The one lead we have to go on is that private yacht. Is there anything we can glean about the owner?"

"A private holding company," Tony said. "There wasn't much time to delve into it. I couldn't even get the name from the fuel supplier tech. Either he didn't know, or he didn't want to give up too much information other than throwing some vague hints around to impress me. If Griggs is involved with it somehow, I doubt we can catch on, seeing as nobody here knows who Griggs actually is."

"Can we at least establish some connection to people in his close circle?" Ryce asked. "Or at least to any of the activities Griggs is involved in on the station? I'd hate to break into somebody else's ship without being sure such an action was warranted."

"You won't be doing any break-ins," Matt said firmly. "You'll be too busy preparing for the race, remember?"

He didn't know which option was worse, but it wasn't like Ryce had much choice in the matter. His part, aside from appeasing Griggs, was providing the distraction they needed for whatever extraction scenario they came up with. That meant all the grossly illegal moves (well, slightly more grossly illegal than drag racing on a virgin planet) would fall on Matt and Tony.

Ryce inclined his head. He clearly wasn't thrilled with this idea either.

"I'm on it," Tony said, setting her empty cup aside and taking out her commlink to type in some notes. "Don't get your hopes up, though."

"We don't need an airtight proof for a court case," Matt reminded. "Just something we could go on before moving forward. Any clue, as small as it might be."

Tony nodded absently, already scrolling through some data on her comm. Matt turned to Ryce.

"Assuming this is Griggs's ship, how do we get on it? If Tony's research pans out, there would be no avoiding that. And if any of us are caught sneaking about Griggs's posh yacht, we aren't going to get as easy a pass as we did when we crashed Tex's little party at the warehouse."

Ryce crossed his long legs and leaned back on the sofa, deep in thought. Matt couldn't help but admire the languid, effortless elegance of his limbs, perfectly arranged in requiescence. Heat flushed Matt's cheeks as he remembered last night when they'd lain together, their bodies entwined. Nothing had happened between them—if one could call exposing your soul to another human being through a simple embrace nothing—but the mere thought filled his chest with warmth.

He felt Tony's gaze on the back of his head and turned. She made a lovesick face and fluttered her lashes. He stuck out his tongue at her, but she only gave him a thumbs-up and went back to whatever she was browsing on her comm.

"If you want to sneak aboard his ship without being detected, the first thing you need is the access key code," Ryce said, startling Matt a little. Thankfully, it seemed like he hadn't noticed the juvenile exchange. "I doubt the ship is guarded, but you'd want to avoid any security personnel and cameras at the dock. In fact, it would be best to disable the cameras altogether for the few minutes it'd take you to get on board."

"I'm sure there won't be any security folks checking that particular dock," Matt said. "Griggs wouldn't want any prying eyes looking too closely, especially if he keeps hostages on board. Can we really disable the cameras, though?"

"Sure, if we hack into the station's infrastructure network."

The fact that Ryce, of all people, was considering hacking into a Federation-owned computer system without batting an eye was a testimony to just how desperate they'd all become. Matt hated placing him in this position, but at this point, it was too late to balk at the possibility of committing a federal offense.

"Can you do it?"

"Yes," Ryce said without hesitation. "I just need access to one of the maintenance terminals and ten minutes undisturbed."

Matt sighed and rubbed the bridge of his nose. "What else?"

"The ship is spacious, but not huge. I'll pull the specs on Javelin yachts to see what areas would offer the best hiding places. Then all you'll have to worry about is neutralizing the guards and getting away safely before anyone pokes in to check on the prisoner and finds him gone."

"Oh, is that all?" Tony chimed in sarcastically, still intent on her comm.

"I know we talked about using the race as a distraction tactic, but once we get confirmation of Griggs's ownership of this yacht, I don't think we should wait for another one," Matt said. He was still loath to let go of the notion that Ryce participating in another event could be avoided somehow. "Whisking somebody out of a ship is much easier when it's docked. Doing that while it's hovering in orbit filming the surface is a hell of a lot trickier, not to mention we'd have to hide inside and hope we're not discovered prematurely. If we can get in and find Val, we can get out while it's still stationside."

"I know it sounds counterintuitive to wait until the ship is running," Ryce said. "And it is far riskier. However, I still believe this scenario offers the best chance of making a clean escape. The station is Griggs's playground; he can easily hunt you down minutes after you leave the ship. We'd be sitting ducks here, while in space he won't be expecting an attack. We'd have the element of surprise on our side. If we're lucky enough, he won't know anything happened until it's too late."

"But if we're unlucky, it'd be the end," Matt said quietly.

He wasn't trying to intimidate anybody, but it needed to be said to make things perfectly clear for everybody involved. "If we're caught on that yacht, me and Tony and Val would simply vanish, and you'd be dead the moment you step out of your aerojet. Nobody would even know we're missing until the station peeps come to check why the docking fees for *Lisa* haven't been paid. Are you willing to take that chance?"

"I am," Ryce said.

"Me too," Tony said firmly. "Stop beating a dead horse, Captain."

"Okay then," Matt sighed. They were all in, and there was no turning back.

"You'll have to rely on one of their own lifeboats," Ryce said. "With them having to maintain orbit to record the race, they won't be able to give chase. And even a black-market kingpin can't install long-range weapons on a cruise yacht without getting in trouble with the authorities, so you should be in the clear once you break away."

"True. I'll make arrangements for getting Val the hell out of this sector. So really, our main concern here is taking on the guards."

"Don't worry. These fuckers won't even know what hit them," Tony said acidly.

Matt and Ryce exchanged a look.

"Anyway, I think I've found something," she said before either of them could comment. "I've accessed the private vessel registry database and dug up information on the pilot."

"How did you access the registry?" Matt asked suspiciously. "It's restricted."

"I used your pilot license credentials."

"Why in the world would you have my—oh, never mind," Matt muttered. "Just tell us what you found."

"The *Medusa* yacht is registered to a company named Paragon Inc. It appears to be some sort of a holding company that encompasses local transport and technical maintenance vendors. Nothing strikes me as particularly shady about it, but the owner isn't listed anywhere on here."

"See if you can find anything about this company on the web." Matt perked up a little. A name was a name, even if it didn't belong to the actual person they'd been trying to find, and it was a good place to start digging. "I'll ask around, check if any of my contacts has heard about it. Discreetly," he added pointedly when Ryce frowned.

"We should obtain the access code in the meanwhile," Ryce said, acceding with a nod. "That way we'll be ready to move in as soon as the intel pans out—assuming it does."

"Can we get the code while we're hacking into the mainframe?"

Ryce thought about it for a moment.

"Theoretically, yes," he said, somewhat reluctantly. "But it's much riskier than simply tapping into the dock cameras' feed. Information pertaining to private spacecraft being serviced by the Freeport would be in an encrypted database. It would take longer to get into, now that I don't have the necessary security clearance, and if the unauthorized access is detected..." He trailed off into a meaningful silence.

"There must be another way," Tony said.

"Actually, there might be." Matt turned to her. "What did you say the name of that fuel supplier technician guy was?"

IN SMUGGLING, THE line between potential ally and competition was a thin one. Matt didn't exactly have friends in the business, but he knew some people who'd been willing to work with him over the years—if it benefited their interests.

Once such associate was Randy Reid. Matt liked him, because Randy was if not honest, at least more upfront than the other smugglers, and more discerning in his dealings. In fact, he was the one who recommended the Elysium system to Matt when he was looking for an alternative to Sonora as his base of operations.

Matt settled in the pilot seat and activated the link between the adapters on his temples and the ship's computer. Sitting there felt weird. This was Ryce's place now, one that Matt had ceded willingly. But he had to get used to occupying it again, didn't he? Once they had Val safely back (and Matt refused to consider any other outcome), Ryce would be gone, and it would be back to the good old days of piloting the *Lady Lisa* himself.

If only he could fool himself into thinking that would fill the aching void which had irrevocably settled deep beneath his breastbone.

Matt shook his head and focused on opening the local communications channel. After a few calls, Randy's jovial, slightly pudgy face appeared on screen. Matt couldn't make out the background very clearly because of the poor illumination, but it appeared Randy was currently on his ship, the *Siren*. Once a sleek luxury yacht, it had been converted to a hauler but had still retained its elegant appearance and superior specs.

"Spears," Randy said in a low rumble. "Long time no see."

"How's it going, Randy?" Matt leaned back in his chair and donned a casual smile. It probably clashed horribly with the rest of his haggard, worry-lined face, but there was only so much he could do about that. "Still working the 73?"

"I rarely get to Freeport 73 nowadays. Been running around the outer planets. What's up?"

"Been stuck at the station for a while. As a matter of fact, I've run into some trouble here recently."

"Oh," Randy said guardedly.

"Do you know this guy named Griggs?"

There was a short pause.

"I've heard of Griggs," Randy said finally. He didn't look scared or upset, but it took some serious shit to make Randy Reid lose his cool. "You get on this motherfucker's bad side or what?"

"Something like that." Matt wasn't about to let Randy in on all the details of his situation. Friend or no friend, smugglers dealt with prized commodities, and information was a commodity like any other.

"We stay out of each other's way," Randy said. "But he's territorial as fuck, and I've heard he can be nasty. If you're planning on staying on the 73, you better not mess around with him. I've known people who've disappeared there, just like that, and the authorities turned the other way. Nobody cares unless there's Feds or rich folks involved."

"Do you know of any legit businesses he owns on the station? Like, if I wanted to stay the hell out of his way, which ones I'd steer clear of?"

Randy gave him a look which said he wasn't fooled by Matt's attempts at subterfuge.

"I dunno, man. He has a lot of stuff going on. From what I've heard, he has joint ownership in a lot of ventures, mostly in the entertainment sector. Bars, rec rooms, lounges, those kinds of things. Not to mention underground entertainment, of course—brothels and casinos."

"What about holding companies? Like Paragon Inc.?"

"Yep, that's his," Randy said, casually confirming Matt's suspicions. "Why, you got work for them?"

"No, no. You know, just heard some rumors circulating and trying to stay out of trouble here." Matt was ready to bounce with excitement at this first major break, but for now, he had to keep his expression neutral, since his negotiations with Randy weren't over yet.

"Good. If I were you, I'd stay the fuck away from that company. In fact, I'd stay the fuck away from any shady shit going on at the station and focus on my hauls."

"No kidding," Matt muttered. It was a damn good piece of advice; unfortunately, like pretty much every other instance of good advice throughout history, it had come too late to be useful. He forced a smile and changed the subject.

"Listen, I sorta have a job offer for you. Have this guy who's hankering to get off this station by the jumpgate, all quiet-like. I'm a bit tied up right now, so no can do. Could you take him on?"

Randy huffed and stroked his neatly trimmed beard.

"Tell you what, Spears. You're a nice guy, so I'm gonna help you out. I'm scheduled for a jump to the Salua sector in a few days. If your passenger can wait till then, I'll pick him up once I get to 73 for the jump. A thousand creds, and you're all set up."

A thousand Fed credits were way more than Matt could realistically afford, and it was a steep sum for transporting a single stowaway passenger. No doubt Randy had sensed his desperation and was not above profiting from it. But it wasn't as if Matt had a lot of choice. His options were limited, and at least with Randy involved, he could be reasonably sure he'd be getting what he was paying for, without the man flapping his mouth to the wrong people.

"It's a deal," he said. That would leave them with absolutely no extra cash for luxuries like food and technical upkeep, but other concerns were more pressing. "Send me the details of your jump, and he'll be waiting for you."

"Sure thing," Randy said. "Good luck with…whatever. Make sure you stay alive to pay me."

"Will do," Matt said as he disconnected. He sincerely hoped he wasn't lying on that part.

Chapter Sixteen

"I DON'T LIKE this at all," Matt said.

"Need I remind you this was your idea?" Tony said and took a sip of her cocktail. They were sitting at the bar in the Broken Stairway Canteen, waiting for Tony's new friend to arrive. Having splurged on her drink, Matt was nursing the cheapest beer on the menu. It was encroaching on undrinkable territory, but at least it gave him an excuse to keep his place at the bar, even though there weren't many patrons there. The seat between them was strategically left empty.

"My idea was you cajoling the *Medusa*'s entry code from the fuel tech guy, not actually go on a date with him."

"Well, I had to convince him to meet me, didn't I?" Tony threw her long braid off her shoulder in an annoyed gesture. "If you didn't want me to do it, you should have been the one doing the leg work and contacting his fuel company in the first place. Besides, it isn't really a date. All I told him was that I wanted to chat about some stuff over drinks."

"That's a date. Trust me, I've been on enough of those to know. And when it's a very good date, you usually end up in—"

"Ew, spare me the details," Tony said, making a disgusted face.

"It's a date, is all I'm saying."

He checked his comm for any messages from Ryce. Now that they'd established a connection between Griggs and the mysterious yacht—even if it was pure hearsay from a source some would call questionable—acquiring the entry code had become imperative. But a lot of other prep work needed to be done, and since Ryce was to use his aerojet again in the upcoming race, he had to make sure it was in perfect working order. Matt wanted him to take all the time he needed for repairs and charge Tex for every little thing which needed replacing after the rough romp.

His inbox was empty, and he went back to crowd watching. The man was running late, and if it had indeed been a real date, Matt'd be in favor of ditching him out of sheer spite. He took a perfunctory swig of his beer, trying to rein in his annoyance.

"Antonia?" a man's voice said, and a guy in a silver-toned shirt that was almost as blindingly glaring as the luminescent countertop plopped onto the empty stool. It was all Matt could do to keep his eyes on his drink, maintaining the guise of a disinterested stranger. An overly musky scent of cologne wafted off the fellow, making Matt gag. He felt sorry for Tony having to bear the brunt of the all-around sensory assault.

"I'm Dan. Sorry to have made you wait. My boss kept pulling some pointless shit for me to do at the last minute."

"Yes, bosses can be assholes like that," Tony agreed with a straight face.

Matt stuck out his tongue at her behind the guy's back. Come to think of it, for some reason, he'd been doing it a lot lately. He decided to blame it on pent-up nervous energy.

They chatted for a bit about nothing in particular. Matt noted that Tony carefully avoided divulging too much personal information, steering the conversation back to Dan, who didn't seem to mind. Talking about himself seemed to be his favorite topic anyway. In the course of a few minutes, Matt had learned all about his favorite pastimes, grievances against his current employer, and future aspirations, in what seemed to be random order.

The beer was not going to be enough to get him through this. Tony's cocktail was definitely not enough to get *her* through this.

As Dan continued with a lengthy account of his college years and what had led him to choose his current career path, Tony must have come to the same conclusion.

"This is all truly fascinating. But I'd love to hear more about your job here on the station. Like that yacht you've been telling me so much about. Is it really that expensive? I've never been aboard a luxury yacht before. What's it like inside?"

Despite his previous chattiness, Matt could sense Dan wasn't eager to broach this particular subject. If he knew, or at least had an inkling of whom the yacht belonged to, his hesitation was understandable.

"It's nice and all," he said evasively. "You know, they don't usually let us roam around in there. I just deliver the fuel and do a maintenance checkup."

"But you still would have seen it," Tony insisted, putting on her best seductive smile and leaning in toward Dan. "It must be so glamorous. I'd do anything to take a little peek at it."

Matt couldn't see Dan's face, but he could imagine the inner struggle. In the end, however, self-preservation won over the urge to impress a date.

"Sorry," he said. "Can't have outsiders on the job. But it's just a ship, anyway. You've seen one, you've seen them all."

Tony straightened, the disappointment evident on her face. Matt cursed inwardly, but at that moment, he caught a glimpse of Dan's commlink sticking out of his pants pocket. He made a motion at Tony to keep talking to distract the man while he zeroed in on the comm.

To Tony's credit, she didn't bat an eyelash at the prospect of being an accessory to petty theft.

"That's too bad," she said smoothly. "But I'm sure it's not the only exciting thing about your job. Tell me more about that off-station delivery to Dinona you've mentioned making. Is the moon really all made of ice?"

Dan launched into the story, which Matt tuned out. He spun around on the stool, holding his beer in one hand and surveying the crowd. Nobody seemed to be looking his way. The bartender was busy fixing drinks for a couple sitting at the far end of the bar. Matt shifted, reaching behind his back with his free hand, and very carefully, very slowly pulled the slim commlink out of Dan's pocket.

Tony, who must have noticed his maneuver, faked a flirtatious laugh at something Dan said, effectively drawing his attention from Matt's pilfering. Being too caught up in his one-sided conversation, Dan didn't catch on to any of it.

Matt hunched over the commlink and tapped the screen. The guy didn't strike Matt as someone who'd put an extra security layer on his work-related files, so he was hoping he wouldn't have to deal with any passwords.

Luckily, the comm wasn't even on lock. Dan and Tony's voices continued behind Matt, which meant he had at least a few more minutes while Dan remained oblivious to the fact he'd had been pickpocketed. Matt ignored the guy's personal inbox and pictures—wasn't gonna touch those with a ten-foot pole—and zoomed in on the folders labeled with the fuel supplier's brand name.

Sure enough, those weren't restricted and contained the specs for the ships currently being serviced by Dan's company. Under any other circumstances, Matt would have scoffed at the breach of confidentiality, but right now Dan's laxness worked in their favor. Matt quickly searched for Dock B11 and found the *Medusa* yacht among the spacecraft docked there. The technical specs pertaining to the fuel type and intake were of little interest to him, but the entry code that granted Dan access to the ship certainly was. He memorized the five-digit code and swiped the screen back, erasing all evidence of intrusion.

Turning back on his stool, he shot Tony a meaningful look over Dan's shoulder. She inclined her head slightly, letting him know she got the message.

Matt wiped the comm screen on his sleeve and dropped the device under Dan's chair. As the guy glanced down at the sound of it clattering to the floor, Tony rose smoothly from her seat.

"Well, it's been fun," she said as Dan's attention divided between fumbling for his comm and peering up at her. "But I don't think it's going to work out between us. Best of luck with everything, though." She flashed the startled man a grin and strode away purposefully without a backward glance at either him or Matt.

Dan stood and shoved the commlink back in his pocket automatically. His expression was so utterly bewildered that Matt kind of felt sorry for him. The guy wasn't altogether insufferable, merely tedious. What they've done was certainly not fair to poor Dan, but there was a reason for what they said about love and war.

"Don't let it get to you, mate," Matt said, slipping off his seat and grabbing his half-finished beer. He didn't wait for Dan's mumbled response as he headed to the exit after Tony.

"I GOT A message from Tex earlier," Ryce said in a low voice.

It was well past midnight, right in the middle of the night shift at the docks. Matt and Ryce made sure to pick a time when none of the ships at Dock B11 were scheduled for departure or a jump, so the area was quiet. Even so, they had to act quickly, getting in and out as fast as they could without anybody spotting them tampering with the dock maintenance terminal which was located close to the lower-level entrance.

"What did she want?" Matt asked, although the answer was pretty clear already.

"The next race is the day after tomorrow," Ryce said. "Oh, and they're docking my second-place prize money as exemplary damages."

"What? Damn, that's soon. Did she say anything about Val?"

"She implied he was still alive, but refused to let me talk to him, or even say if he was getting medical treatment."

Matt gritted his teeth. "Not good enough." Tex certainly knew what she was doing by contacting Ryce instead of him, because he wouldn't have been able to keep his cool during that conversation.

Ryce shot him a quick look and changed the subject.

"It's a pretty tight schedule. I'd estimated a week between the races, but now they're spaced only days apart. I wonder why they're in such a hurry."

"Like you've said, they might be worried about the flood," Matt said, but Ryce shook his head, apparently dubious.

They approached the terminal, trying to stay close to the walls and away from the range of the cameras aimed at the docked spacecraft. Matt counted on the nondescript fatigues they were both wearing to help them blend in with the station maintenance crew. So far, however, they hadn't encountered anyone inside the dock proper.

Ryce knelt in front of the terminal and took out his tool kit. Opening the lower panel below the touch pad revealed a tangle of colorful wires. Matt kept watch, scanning the floor and upper walkways, and the wide, illuminated expanses between the dormant ships. He was tempted to go and take a peek at the *Medusa*, which was docked some ways off. From here, he could only glimpse its finely tapered bow behind the other, larger ships. But being caught loitering around the yacht was a risk he couldn't take.

He glanced at Ryce, who was busy attaching a small black box to a bunch of wires.

"How's it going?"

"This should give me remote control of the Dock B11 camera feed and continuous access to the video data," Ryce said, methodically sifting through the wires. "I just need a few more minutes to install it properly."

"Okay," Matt said. "Wait, there's someone's coming."

He hunkered down next to Ryce, hiding his face from the newcomers and willing them to keep on walking. Nothing to see here, just a couple of tech guys performing routine maintenance. Ryce's hand tightened on his screwdriver, but he didn't stop whatever he was doing with that box.

The footsteps receded into the distance, and Matt risked glancing up over his shoulder. From the looks of it, it was just a crewman from one of the ships coming back home after a long night. Matt let out a relieved breath and got to his feet, dusting off his pants.

"Almost done," Ryce said. He snapped the box shut, tightened the last screws, and pushed the thing as far back as he could, to make it less conspicuous. "There we go."

"Good. Let's get the fuck out of here."

They closed the terminal panel carefully and hurried outside the dock. The outer corridor was busier, even so late into the night, but nobody spared them a second glance as they made their way to the service elevators.

"Do you always have pieces of surveillance equipment lying around?" Matt murmured. "That's handy."

"No," Ryce said absently, shoving the toolkit in his backpack. "I assembled it this morning."

Matt rubbed the bridge of his nose.

"I swear, sometimes I forget how damn smart you are." He glanced sideways at Ryce. "You know it's sexy as hell, right?"

Ryce smiled faintly and shouldered his bag with a look that was close to smug.

"Funny. I distinctly remember you finding it extremely annoying."

"Well, I was wrong. About a lot of things," Matt added softly. "It would seem I'm all-around prone to bad judgment."

"I don't think that's entirely true," Ryce said.

"A fool is a fool."

Ryce shook his head. "I've always considered foolishness to be the conscious refusal to employ critical thinking. You have no such problem."

Matt huffed in amusement but couldn't help preening just a bit at the offhand compliment.

LADY LISA WAS stationed at Dock C24, which serviced small- to medium-sized haulers. Since cargo vessels, unlike private transport, operated at all hours, the C docks were hubs of activity even in the small hours of the morning, but *Lisa* was the only ship there at the moment, so their dock was unusually quiet. However, Matt and Ryce didn't have a chance to reach it.

As they came in the double-door lock-chamber, which separated the entry to the dock itself from the main corridor, the door slid shut behind them, while the dock door remained closed. Usually both doors were open to accommodate the people and goods going in and out, shutting only in cases of emergency, for example, when the air pressure inside the dock was compromised. But now, it seemed, they were facing a different kind of emergency. Three tall and bulky gentlemen stood at the far end of the chamber, apparently waiting for them. One of them, sporting a starburst tattoo on his neck, nodded toward Ryce.

"You Easom?"

"Who's asking?" Matt stepped forward.

Three against two weren't terrible odds, but the men might be armed, and, judging from the painstakingly set trap, they probably weren't inclined to talk things out, whoever they were.

"Been waiting on your ass for a while. Got a message for you from Stahl," the guy said, clearly not impressed with Matt's posturing. He advanced on them with a smirk. The other two came at them from the sides, effectively surrounding them.

Instinctively, Matt and Ryce moved to stand back-to-back just as the men charged at them. Matt ducked and kicked his opponent in the knee while Ryce swung the bag with the heavy tool kit, aiming at the other guy's face. It connected with a satisfying thud, and the man grunted in pain. Matt's attacker staggered, but the tattooed leader sidestepped him and threw a punch that Matt blocked at the last moment. The impact made his forearm go numb, and he hissed. The guy was definitely stronger, and all Matt could do was stay out of the range of his blows, dodging and ducking while trying to score a kick where it would hurt. He wasn't above fighting dirty—not when he was reasonably sure his life depended on it—but he had to admit he was out of practice, and he wasn't always quick enough. Some of the heavy hits found their mark, and pain blossomed where they landed.

Matt's first attacker left the leader to finish the job and rounded on Ryce with his other pal. But unlike Matt, Ryce's close-combat training was apparently still fresh in his mind. He was deceptively lean, his fine elfin features giving him an almost fragile appearance, but Matt knew very well he was much stronger than he looked. His attackers, who must have pegged him as easy prey, fell back under the onslaught as Ryce went on the offensive, his every move calculated with deadly precision to inflict damage. It was like an exotic dance, and Matt would have paused to admire the sheer beauty of it had he not been otherwise occupied. Soon, one of Ryce's opponents sagged to the floor, clutching at a broken arm, while the other hunched over as Ryce's fist drove right into his solar plexus. The man wheezed and fell to his knees, coughing violently.

Seeing that, the leader grabbed Matt by the shoulder, easily crushing his resistance, and threw him across the floor, momentarily stunning him. The blade of an electric knife flashed in his attacker's hand as he lunged at Ryce's back.

There was no time to think, just to act. Without bothering to get back up, Matt rolled across the floor and grabbed the man's ankle, yanking it as hard as he could in a desperate attempt to slow him down. The guy staggered with a curse, the knife slicing a wide arc through the air as he struggled to keep his balance. Ryce spun around and ducked beneath the guy's raised hand, evading the glowing blade, just as his opponent managed to shake his leg free and kick Matt in the face.

For a moment, all Matt could see were bright stars dancing before his eyes. Sadly, those weren't the kind of stars he was so fond of gazing at. Then the pain finally caught up with him. It felt as though his face was going to explode—if it hadn't already. Through the daze, he could still hear grunts and the sounds of flesh colliding with flesh, and he scrambled on the floor that was slippery with something wet and sticky oozing from his nose. He opened his eyes just in time to see Ryce grapple with the larger man, locking his arm in a weird angle as the knife trembled between their bodies, threatening to sear fabric and skin. With a sickening cracking sound, the thug's arm gave, and the knife toppled to the floor.

Ryce applied pressure to the man's broken arm, forcing him to cry out and fall on his knees.

"What was the message?" Ryce asked in a voice that was dripping ice.

"Drop out of the race or you're dead," the tattooed man panted.

"We'll see about that."

Ryce released the guy's arm abruptly, sending him sprawling awkwardly, and kicked the knife into the far corner of the chamber. He then helped Matt to his feet, throwing his arm across his shoulders.

In any other circumstances, Matt would have been embarrassed to be toted around in this fashion, but right now, he was too disoriented and too much of a bloody mess to care. He hobbled alongside Ryce as they hurried to the control panel, opened the door to the dock, and made their way to the safety of *Lady Lisa*, leaving Stahl's buddies to fend for themselves as best they could.

Chapter Seventeen

"OH MY GOD, what happened to you?" Tony exclaimed as Ryce led Matt through the main hatch aboard the *Lady Lisa*. Ryce's quick call to her commlink had woken her up, and she was staring at them, still bleary-eyed from sleep, her hair hanging loose over her shoulders. It was the first time Matt had seen her without her neat braid and in her pajamas. Nonetheless, the call had alarmed her enough that she also had her gun at the ready.

Tony lowered the weapon as they shuffled aboard and helped Ryce usher Matt down the corridor to the infirmary.

"We were ambushed." Ryce lowered Matt gently onto the cot, shoving a plastic-covered pillow under his head. "I wasn't hurt, but Matt was injured while trying to prevent another guy from knifing me."

"Why would Griggs's people try to knife you?"

"These weren't Griggs's people."

"Boy, do you have a knack for getting yourself into trouble." Tony sighed. She nudged Ryce aside and used a roll of gauze to swab the blood off Matt's face.

"Is my nose broken? It feels broken," Matt mumbled around the gauze. It wasn't his first time being kicked in the face, but he'd almost forgotten how fucking painful it was. His entire face was throbbing, and it felt as though his nose now took up at least two-thirds of it. The steady trickle of warm blood into his mouth wasn't helping. The metallic taste of it stirred up unpleasant memories, and for a brief moment, he had to suppress irrational panic. He winced as Tony carefully probed the bridge of his nose and his cheekbones.

"Surprisingly, no," she said. "You were lucky; no bones seem to be fractured. But I wouldn't count on you landing any modeling jobs soon. Let's get you cleaned up and see if I can find something to reduce the swelling."

She insisted Ryce tell her what happened while she tended to Matt, staunching the nosebleed and placing a cool pack over the bridge of his nose.

"Stahl's the bastard who flies the Waxwing jet?" she asked when Ryce was finished. Her mouth was set in a hard line. "Sounds like he went to a lot of trouble to rough you up."

"If he did, this just means he's worried about the possibility of losing," Ryce said. "That speaks of his insecurity. If he was so sure of his superiority, he wouldn't have felt the need to warn me off. He knows I can beat him."

"He wants you to drop out of the next race, so he probably intends to participate in it," Matt chimed in. The pain made it difficult to focus on anything else, but he welcomed the distraction. "We already know he won't stop at anything to win. I'm not so sure it's a good idea for you to go through with it."

Ryce was silent for a moment, simply looking at him. Matt was already bracing for a snappy response, but finally, Ryce just sighed wearily.

"I don't think I can come up with a better one. The race is already set for the next morning. Think what they might do if I don't show up. Besides, your entire plan for rescuing Val from the *Medusa* hinges on my participation. They would assume you'd be watching the race too, not crawling around their ship. Sometimes, there just isn't any easy way out."

Matt bit his lip, which was a bad move, considering how bruised it already was. Ryce was actually being reasonable about this—not cocky, or overconfident, or dismissive. There was nothing Matt could say to counter that, and he knew it.

He docilely waited for Tony to stuff his nose with cotton pads and feed him some painkillers. All he wanted was to pass out in his bed and worry about everything else later. He just hoped the painkillers were potent enough to shut him off for a few hours of dreamless and sensation-free sleep.

"Are we all set for tomorrow?" he asked just to shift his thoughts onto something other than the current state of his visage as he eased himself off the cot gracelessly. Tony only nodded, watchful like a parent whose child was taking their first baby steps.

"There are some minor adjustments to be made on the jet, but other than that, everything is ready," Ryce said. "We should all get some sleep."

"Just be careful when you're working on the jet tomorrow," Matt admonished as Ryce helped him to his room. The painkillers were thankfully kicking in, and the agony receded to a dull pounding behind his eyes. "Who knows what this Stahl is capable of, and who he's gonna send after you next. You shouldn't go there alone at all."

"I'll be fine," Ryce said, guiding Matt into his cabin and onto his conveniently unmade bunk. For the first time in his life, Matt was happy he was such a slob. "That transport bay is always teeming with people. He'd be foolish to try something with so many witnesses around. I'm more worried about you right now, to be honest. How do you know you're not concussed?"

He hovered over Matt's bunk, looking at him with concern, even as Matt tried and failed to curl up in a position that would bring him some sort of comfort. His fatigues were dirty and bloody, but washing and changing would have to wait till he felt he could stand on his own two feet again without falling over.

"I'm all right. Nothing's even broken. Besides, Tony gave me the all clear. I just need to rest a bit, and I'll be as good as new in the morning."

"It's almost morning already," Ryce noted. "Are you sure you're going to be up to breaking and entering?"

"If you can do your part, I can do mine," Matt said, closing his eyes. "See you tomorrow, okay?"

"See you," Ryce said after a heartbeat. Matt heard the door slide quietly behind him even as he drifted off into numbness.

MATT WOKE UP well past noon and stared blearily at his commlink for a few moments, trying to recall where he was and what had happened to him. It was much worse than one of his usual hangovers. At least then he'd have had the advantage of drinking himself into a stupor before passing out. Somehow, painkillers didn't have quite the same effect.

He dragged himself into the shower to change out of yesterday's smelly clothes and wash up. A glance in the mirror showed his face was still a bit swollen (and tender to the touch), and he sported two impressive black eyes. But it actually looked worse than it felt, which was a good sign in his book.

Freshening up and popping two more painkillers went a long way to improving his mood. He checked in with Tony, who again made sure no bones were broken and gave him a fresh cooling pack. He sat down with her, working out the details of the plan.

Their best bet was sneaking aboard the *Medusa* in the middle of the night. As Matt and Ryce had witnessed last night, there weren't a lot of people hanging out at that particular dock during those late hours, and Ryce's device would deactivate the cameras while they broke in. They went over the blueprints of a Javelin yacht, though these were generic schematics Ryce had pulled off the web. It stood to reason Griggs would have made custom modifications on those, but at least it gave them a rough idea of where they were headed.

Matt would have preferred going in alone instead of putting Tony in danger, but he couldn't dissuade her from accompanying him. And as far as backup went, he could hardly wish for someone he trusted more, or who was handier with a loaded weapon.

There wasn't much to do until then. Matt tried to occupy his mind and hands with routine maintenance, which he'd neglected over the course of the last few days. But he had a hard time concentrating on even the simplest task, so he gave up on that eventually. No new messages came into his inbox. It appeared the IMA were still biding their time on deciding whether to hire them, and even Nora seemed to ease the pressure. Ryce was conducting a final inspection of his jet, but he was due back soon, and Matt resisted the urge to check up on him every few minutes. Whatever he'd said about being safe while working on the jet, Matt doubted this Stahl fellow was reasonable enough to adhere to any assumptions.

He moped around on the bridge until he couldn't take the waiting any longer. Patience, like so many other virtues, was not an attribute he could boast.

Matt certainly drew attention on his way to the transit hold where the jet was stowed. Passersby flinched and did double takes, some even shying away as he strode down the corridors.

"Haven't you people ever seen someone who got sucker punched before?" Matt muttered, annoyed.

The Sparrow aerojet was even more battered than the last time Matt had seen it. Sand particles had grazed the hull, leaving tiny scratches in the paint. But performance was more important than appearance, and the little jet had proved its capabilities in Ryce's hands.

As he approached, Ryce hopped down from the cockpit and dusted his hands. After all the side glances he'd been receiving on the way there, Matt was grateful to see a smile light up his handsome face.

"Are you here to escort me home?" Ryce teased, locking up the jet and making a final walk-around.

"It's probably gonna be the other way around," Matt said. "The way you gave these guys a bashing, it was awe-inspiring. I still haven't thanked you for saving my neck last night."

"I should be thanking you too, then." Ryce came up and took Matt's hand into his. Matt was a little startled by the gesture; Ryce wasn't one for public displays of affection. But it made the touch that much more meaningful, and Matt held on to his hand a bit tighter.

"As much as I'd like to take credit for contributing, all I did was get the crap beat out of me."

"No shit," a gruff voice said behind them.

Matt turned quickly, berating himself for letting his guard down enough for someone to creep up on them like that. Being besotted had never saved anyone from being shot in the back.

He found himself face-to-face with a tall, rangy man wearing a dark military-style jacket and cargo pants, and his slim hope of it being Cobb, come to dispense his advice again, evaporated. The stranger was a pilot too, judging from his adapters, but he was younger than Cobb and wearing a scowl that made it perfectly clear he wasn't there to offer encouraging words of wisdom. Matt's hackles instinctively rose at the dangerous gleam in his eyes.

"I see you chose to ignore my message," the guy said.

Matt resisted the urge to step between him and Ryce. He was damned if he'd give Stahl the impression they were afraid of him, even if every nerve in his body screamed to get the hell away.

"You shouldn't let others do your dirty work," Ryce said coolly, his usual haughty mask replacing the earlier genuine smile. "It doesn't have quite the same effect."

"Well, I'm here now," Stahl said with disdain. "You think you can snag that prize? Think again. You race tomorrow, and you won't be leaving the fucking canyon."

"If the canyon isn't big enough for the two of us, I suggest you sit this one out," Ryce retorted.

Matt shot him a warning look. It was a bad idea to antagonize a bully without knowing if he had the means to retaliate—like another squad of goons hiding somewhere in the depths of the hold, just waiting for a sign to pounce.

"First of all, let's all chill," he said in the most pacifying tone he could muster. "Since you asked so nicely, we'll consider it, how about that?"

"You. I know who you are," Stahl said, turning to Matt. "Heard all about you from a friend of yours. He'll be mighty pleased to hear you got that pretty face bashed in."

"Oh yeah? Which friend might that be?"

"Dylan Rodgers."

Hearing that name was like a punch in the gut. For a second, Matt couldn't hear anything else above the white noise in his ears.

Ryce moved closer, touching his arm discreetly. As light as the touch was, it stemmed the flow of bad memories, grounding Matt in the here and now, and it was all he could do not to reach for Ryce and grab him like a lifeline.

"I used to pilot one of his ships," Stahl continued. "Think he'd like to hear about where you've been hiding?"

"Rodgers is in Federal prison." It was a miracle Matt's voice wasn't quivering with tension. "My whereabouts are the least of his concerns and will stay that way for a very long time."

"I wouldn't be so sure about that." Stahl's knowing smirk sent an unpleasant shiver down Matt's spine.

"We're done here." Ryce stepped up between them. "I suggest you leave now, before I find an excuse to call Station Security."

Stahl gave him a once-over and spit on the floor in contempt, barely missing Ryce's feet.

"You mark my words, bitch. Show up tomorrow and you're roadkill."

They watched in silence as Stahl stalked away.

"Are you all right?" Ryce asked quietly. "Don't let the bastard get to you. Rodgers is behind bars; he was only trying to mess with your head."

Matt let out a laugh that was entirely too unconvincing.

"I should be the one telling you to ignore him." He shook his head. Ryce was right. Stahl was just a bully trying to screw with him, and he wasn't about to give him the satisfaction. "But I'm not sure I can. Perhaps it's better if we listened."

Ryce pressed his lips into a hard line.

"He's a tough guy who tries to get all alpha-male on me for stepping on his toes. He'll have to do a lot more than sending hired thugs or get into a pissing match to scare me."

"It's not the thugs I'm worried about," Matt said. The image of the tiny Finch jet exploding against the canyon wall while the racers simply sped past was still too vivid in his mind. Ryce was as excellent a pilot as they came, but even he couldn't anticipate every move his close opponent might make—especially such a vicious and unscrupulous opponent as Stahl.

"We should get back," Ryce said in a more reserved tone.

They returned to *Lady Lisa* without incident, and without exchanging another word about tomorrow's race.

Chapter Eighteen

INSTEAD OF GIVING Ryce some time alone to cool off, Matt trailed determinately behind him to his cabin. The pills were beginning to wear off, and the pain was once again spreading across Matt's face and into his brain. Fuck, this was absolutely the worst possible time to be nursing a persistent headache and bruises. *Way to keep a low profile and not attract attention.*

"I just don't want you to get hurt," Matt said once the door to Ryce's cabin closed behind them, before Ryce could round up on him. "And before you get all defensive again, I know you can take care of yourself, but shit happens. We're already too deep in it."

"Trust me, I haven't forgotten." Ryce turned and opened one of the drawers in the cupboard. He took out a box—a spacecraft first aid kit of the kind they kept in their ship's shuttle. This one appeared newer; Ryce must have purchased it along with all the spare parts needed for the repairs on his jet. "I don't treat the situation lightly. And as much as this goes against my better instincts, I have to make sure I have an advantage in a game that's rigged from the start."

Ryce snapped open the first aid kit. When he straightened, there was a syringe in his hand.

Matt took a step forward. "That's a stim shot."

"Yes." Ryce leveled a look at him. There was a hint of defiance in his voice, as if he was challenging Matt to say something about it.

"Those can be dangerous," Matt said, keeping his voice neutral, treading carefully.

"I need all the help I can get."

"This stuff is addictive. You know that."

"You're hardly the person to lecture someone on addiction."

Matt's hands curled into fists so tightly the fingernails dug into the flesh of his palms. It took every ounce of whatever self-control he possessed not to snap back at Ryce through the red haze of anger that momentarily clouded his vision. But deep, deep down Matt knew Ryce had a point. He'd never done drugs, but he couldn't deny he had a long-standing relationship with alcohol.

"Maybe it means I know what I'm talking about," he said as evenly as he could.

Ryce tsked in annoyance. "I will hardly become addicted from one shot."

It won't be your first, though, Matt wanted to say. He remembered Ryce using stims on Colanta, when he was injured and hard-pressed for time while getting them through an asteroid field in a shuttle. Besides, medications were fine for when you needed them, but stimulants were potent drugs, only to be used in cases of emergency such as serious injury in dire situations. They were restricted for general distribution, approved only for use in medical kits on space- and aircraft, and terrestrial combat and heavy-duty transport.

But he kept the thought to himself.

"You do realize you don't actually have to win this time, don't you?" he asked carefully, in an attempt to steer the conversation back to what he was trying to convey before Ryce announced he had to resort to doping. "Whether we succeed or not, the results of the race would be irrelevant to us. They won't pay you, just like they didn't last time. You don't have to do this—" He gestured toward the syringe. "Just let Stahl have his precious win and leave it at that. Unless it's your professional pride taking over."

Ryce had been a combat pilot, after all. Those folks' egos were nurtured and cultivated from the moment they set foot inside the Fleet Academy. As a former space traffic controller in the Fleet, Matt was all too familiar with their "better-than-thou" attitude.

"It's not about pride," Ryce said sharply. "You don't know what might happen on that ship. Even the best-laid plans are often rendered worthless by circumstances. What if you're so outnumbered you decide not to go through with it? What if Val isn't even on board? We're basing this entire endeavor on the assumption he has to be there, but he might not. It is equally possible Griggs is keeping him somewhere on the station while he's away on his yacht. And what will happen to Val if I return once again without a win? Do you want to get another part of him in a box? What will it be next time? A hand? A foot?"

"Look, you don't have to try and scare me. I was sufficiently freaked out the first time."

"Then let's make sure it's the last."

Matt took a deep breath. It seemed like no matter what he said, it turned wrong. He was all out of tactics—which meant all he had left to fall back on was good old begging.

"Please, baby." The endearment rolled off his tongue automatically, without thinking. Matt had never been big on using sweet nicknames, but somehow, now it felt natural and apropos instead of fawning or condescending, like it had when he'd tried it with other people. Maybe it was because this time the sentiment behind it was real. "Just promise me you'll be careful. That's all I'm asking. I can't bear losing you."

It was the simple, God-honest truth. It would have been different if Ryce had left on his own accord to pursue a better life—Matt would have found a way to deal with it because he wanted Ryce to succeed. But if he died...Matt knew he wouldn't be able to live through that and emerge whole on the other side of grief.

For a long moment, Ryce gazed at him with that inscrutable expression of his Matt had learned to recognize as a veil drawn on conflicting emotions. Finally, he put the syringe back in its place and closed the kit.

"I promise I won't use it unless I feel I absolutely have to. And I will be careful. As long as you promise to do the same. Because when I think of everything that might go wrong with you and Tony being all alone up there..."

Matt stepped closer and took Ryce's hands in his. "We have every intention of coming back. All three of us."

He knew perfectly well love wasn't enough to keep someone safe from harm. There was no mystical force that somehow tilted the odds in your favor because you meant well. But it was so much easier taking on the universe when you knew someone would be there, waiting for you to come back into their arms.

It seemed like Ryce had a similar idea. His jaw worked, and he let go of Matt's hand to gently run his fingers along his swollen cheek. The touch was soothing, feather-light, and Matt closed his eyes for a second, reveling in it, needing it all the more for the ache in his bruised bones.

"You still have a few hours before you have to get ready," Ryce whispered. His eyes were dark, like a wintry sky with the promise of a storm. "Stay here until then. Make love to me."

"Are you sure?" Matt's voice was just as soft, his heart speeding at Ryce's words. There was nothing he wanted more than to hold Ryce and be held by him, to share the heat of their bodies and the beating of their hearts in the hours that might yet prove to be their last. But as precious as it would be to him, such a level of trust and physical closeness meant even more to Ryce. And Matt didn't want their first (and possibly only) lovemaking to be rushed out of desperation, especially if Ryce still wasn't entirely ready.

"I'm sure," Ryce said. He leaned in and touched his lips to Matt's, effectively dispelling his misgivings. "I love you. I want you."

"I love you too," Matt whispered, barely audible to his own ears. The words burned on his tongue like a brand, exciting and terrifying at the same time. "But I'm hardly a picture of desirability right now. I want our first time to be special for you, and I look like shit."

"I don't care how you look."

The kiss, when it came, was sweet, languid, and tinged with pain. When they finally parted, Matt was gasping for air—and not in a good way.

Damn it. Not being able to breathe through his nose put a damper on certain things he was planning on doing.

But the thought slipped from his mind as Ryce caressed his neck and unzipped the front of his fatigues in one fluid motion, exposing the crumpled white T-shirt underneath. Matt did the same, peeling off the layers of clothing from the other man. They paused to touch and admire each other's bodies as they were revealed under the harsh fluorescent lighting, until they both stood there, gloriously naked.

Well, Ryce was certainly glorious. Matt had seen him in various stages of undress in the past, since they often slept together, kissing and cuddling, even if things never progressed further than that. But now it was as if he was seeing him for the first time—the long, elegant lines of his limbs, the reserved strength of his musculature, the expanse of flawless pale skin. He was perfection personified, as beautiful as the stars, cold and unattainable.

But the latter proved false as Ryce threw his hands around Matt's neck and lavished small, heated kisses along the line of his jaw. Matt tilted his head back, allowing Ryce even more access. He was painfully hard, the promise of what was to come making all the blood in his body rush to his cheeks and cock. The fact that Ryce was also aroused, his smooth length rubbing against Matt's, sent excited shivers down his spine. The realization that he could elicit this reaction, that Ryce really wanted *him*, was a heady feeling, a rush no drug in the universe could rival, and he allowed himself to bask in it, get drunk on it.

They backed up to the bunk bed and sank onto it without breaking contact. Matt ran his hands over Ryce's chest and the taut pink nipples, drawing a soft moan and a shiver out of him, memorizing every sensation and sound. It still amazed him he could do this, that out of all the people in the known galaxy, Ryce had chosen him to share this intimacy with, that he cared enough for Matt to have this level of trust. And Matt wanted it all, everything Ryce was willing to give, and there was nothing, not a single scrap of his heart and soul he wouldn't give in return.

While he could.

The thought came unbidden to his mind, and he banished it immediately. He would not ruin the moment by dwelling on the uncertainty of their future, not when the present was so generous to him.

"I want you so bad," Matt whispered, his voice husky with need. "But I haven't come prepared."

Ryce's heartbeat and breathing were fast and unsteady. Considering he'd never done this before, it must have been an even bigger moment for him, and Matt hated putting any breaks on it. But there was no way he could make do with spit and a prayer.

"It's okay; there's no rush. We'll get there next time. Come here." Ryce climbed on top of him, making sure Matt's head rested on the pillow. Matt spread his legs in welcome, and now they fitted just right against each other, despite the narrowness of the bunk, their hands roaming over exposed skin, finding tender spots and sensitive places that made them sigh with pleasure.

His skin was on fire, every nerve tingling, every sense overloaded. His breath came out in ragged gasps—half moans, half sobs.

"Breathe through your mouth," Ryce whispered close to his ear. Heat radiated from his flushed skin, and a smile tugged at his lips, dark and swollen with kisses. For a second, Matt was afraid he was going to lose it right there, simply soaking in the sight. "Otherwise you're liable to pass out, and that would leave us both somewhat frustrated."

Matt snorted. "You bastard. Don't stop."

He bucked insistently underneath him to emphasize his words, and Ryce obliged. He wasn't shy about taking control, and Matt was only too happy to submit. They rubbed against each other, their bodies perfectly aligned, the sweet friction between their cocks sending jolts of pleasure down Matt's spine. It wasn't what he'd imagined, yet so much more than that; the reality of touch infinitely more satisfying than any fantasy he'd ever indulged in. Every move, every stroke was a wave of sensation and feeling washing over him, threatening to drown him, each one cresting higher and higher, until the powerful tide swept him along, carrying him safely ashore.

Ryce joined him moments later with a soft moan that reverberated through Matt, and collapsed on top of him, right into the pool of sticky mess now smeared between their stomachs. Neither of them cared.

"I love you," Ryce said, hiding his face in the crook of Matt's neck.

"I love you too, so much," Matt whispered hoarsely. His hand, when he lifted it to stroke Ryce's sweat-matted hair, was weighted with lead. All he wanted was to stay like this forever, to dissolve into bliss that was so wholly unfamiliar, and yet so right.

Chapter Nineteen

THE *MEDUSA* WAS everything Matt had expected of a luxury yacht. In deep space, the looks of a ship didn't matter, as was evidenced by the wide array of alien ship forms, ranging in shape from boxy to fancifully organic. The *Medusa*, however, was designed to please the human eye, its immaculate hull painted glossy silver and blue. It was slightly smaller than *Lady Lisa*, with most of its bulk reserved for spacious accommodations and recreational areas instead of cargo storage.

Matt and Tony huddled in a shadowy recess behind one of the other ships in the dock. They'd been watching the yacht for the past twenty minutes or so, and had picked up on no sign of activity either from within or around it. No one had entered the dock, either, but this time, Matt wasn't taking any chances, so they were biding their time until he was sure it was safe to make a move.

"The crew is probably asleep, if they're even on board," Tony whispered beside him. "We should get going before the shift changes. The station patrol might get it in their heads to make a sweep of the dock at the wrong moment."

Matt nodded in agreement. Everything seemed quiet, and the time was as ripe as it was ever going to be. He took a deep breath, steadying himself before the irrevocable plunge.

"Ready? Here we go."

He took out his commlink, pulling up the temporary camera controls Ryce had installed on it. Tapping into the feed interrupted the recording, creating the impression of a momentary distortion.

"Come on," he whispered to Tony, and they pounded toward the dormant yacht. Ryce had timed the camera outage for three minutes— short enough to prevent the maintenance crew from coming to check up on them in the middle of the night yet giving Matt and Tony sufficient time to get on board.

The *Medusa*'s entry panel was lit, as if in welcome, but the ship was on lockdown. Tony punched in the key code they'd pilfered from Dan the tech guy. Matt only hoped it hadn't been changed in the interim, because if so, they were about to be royally screwed. The cameras' "malfunction" had probably already drawn the attention of the night security guards, and if they were caught trying to gain unauthorized access to a private vessel—

The entry panel status changed to "Open," and the main hatch doors slid apart, revealing a dim airlock chamber. They hurried inside, and Matt shut the hatch.

Tony drew her gun, but both the airlock and the main corridor leading to the common areas were empty. Matt nodded toward the corridor, and they started that way as silently as they could. It was so quiet Matt was sure their footsteps echoed in the empty space along with their heartbeats, but nobody came to check on the noise.

They needed to stay away from the areas that posed a high risk of being occupied even at the dead of night—the dining room, the huge rec room, and the wet bar. There was no telling who'd be up for a late drink and a movie, even though they were counting on Griggs not being on board. But there was one stop Matt had to make before they were in the clear—relatively speaking.

The deck plan didn't exactly follow the blueprints they'd pulled—some of the spaces were divided differently on what must have been a custom order. But the bones of the ship stayed the same, so they had no trouble following the path to a utility service compartment next to the galley. The open shelves held extra towels, bed linen, cleaning supplies, and, more importantly, spare staff uniforms. Matt and Tony each grabbed a set, which consisted of navy-blue pants and a jacket shirt before hurrying to the stairs that led to the lower deck.

The blueprints didn't disappoint. They quickly found their destination—another utility closet directly adjacent to the engine room. As far as hiding places went, it wasn't a comfortable one. The compartment was small and cramped, filled with spare parts and fluid containers.

"It stinks in here." Tony wrinkled her nose at the pungent smell of the stored coolant.

For once, Matt was grateful for his nose being temporarily out of commission. They changed into the staff uniforms, giving each other as much privacy as the tight space allowed, and stashed their own clothes behind some crates at the far wall. The uniform wouldn't fool the crew if they saw their faces, but they were counting on it making them less conspicuous at a casual glance.

Matt checked his watch.

"Only five more hours to go. Any ideas as to how to kill time?"

Tony scoffed. "Of all the people to be stuck in a closet with. We only just got here, and you're whining already. Val is gonna owe me one hell of a favor for this."

"I'm not whining," Matt protested. He glanced around, but there was nothing sturdy enough to perch on, so he sat on the stained floor, cross-legged. "I just like to spend my free time productively."

"Now you sound exactly like Ryce."

Matt fidgeted. He was trying to take his mind off the upcoming race—so far unsuccessfully. He wasn't sure if he trusted Ryce to take it easy, despite his promises, and he definitely didn't trust Stahl—and other racers—to do the same.

"Some things rub off on me," he muttered.

"Yes, I bet they do," Tony said in a lighter but meaningful tone and lowered herself on the floor beside him. "Is that why you had a silly grin plastered all over your face before we left?"

"It was not silly." Matt had been defending himself way too much in the past few minutes for his liking. "It was a very dignified grin."

"And about time, too." Tony gave him a light, friendly punch on the shoulder.

Matt grunted, an uncharacteristic blush creeping up his cheeks. He was also grateful to her for not pestering him for details. But even if Tony was not aware of the particulars of Matt and Ryce's relationship, she certainly understood how important and special it was to both of them—and she knew better than to pry.

THE NEXT FEW hours passed in relative silence since they didn't want to risk being overheard. Both of them fiddled with their commlinks and dozed off in turns, but as morning drew near, Matt became more and more agitated. He pictured Ryce getting on that transport, preparing to take the aerojet down to the planet. All alone, gearing up for a fight no less intense than one of the skirmishes he'd waded through as a Fleet Falcon pilot. And if Matt and Tony failed, he'd be trapped, with no place to run.

Matt could lie to himself with the best of them, but even he couldn't deny the most likely outcome was all of them ending up dead before the day was out.

A drink—any drink at this point—would go a long way to soothing his nerves, but he doubted he could actually swallow a drop of alcohol, even if he'd brought a bottle with him. Not after having been called out by Ryce on his developing habit, and not after having gotten on Ryce's back about the stims. They all had different ways of handling high stress, but some ways were undoubtedly more destructive than others.

The yacht came alive at about 05:30. They were too far away from the bustle to hear any voices, but some of the louder noises filtered through—doors opening and closing, the sounds of footsteps on the above deck. The race was scheduled for 07:00, and it would take about an hour to get from the Freeport to the lower planetary orbit at a leisurely speed. The yacht would have to get there a bit earlier, taking a position that would allow the cameras to zoom in on the canyon. The race itself would only last a few minutes. It wasn't much of a window of opportunity, but they'd have to make their move then, banking in on the crew's attention being directed elsewhere.

Finally, the engine revved to life, its roar palpable in the close quarters. Matt didn't spend much time in the engine room anymore, more than happy to rely on Val's expertise for everything needed there, and now he appreciated the man's dedication to working under such rough conditions. Still, even if he wasn't a trained engineer, Matt had at least some idea of how things worked in there, and he was about to put that knowledge to the test.

The ship trembled, setting into motion. Matt imagined it gliding out of the dock, taking a turn around the station, and speeding off into space. Tony shifted by his side, looking as uneasy as he felt.

After about an hour, Matt tapped his commlink for the hundredth time. He was waiting for it, but when the encrypted channel for the broadcast of the race came live, showing static and a countdown instead of a blank screen, it took him by surprise.

"T minus ten minutes. That means the ship is already positioned in orbit."

"Let's get moving." Tony sprang lightly to her feet, weapon already in hand, squaring for action after the tedious hours of waiting. "Now's your shining moment, Captain."

"No pressure."

Matt peered out of the door, but the service corridor was dim and empty. Thankfully, the adjacent engine room was left wide open, so they didn't have to waste time fiddling with the control panel. When inside, Matt made a beeline toward the engine capsule. The huge mechanism was humming loudly, the sound almost deafening this close, but he had no extra time to bother with protective gear. He took an electric screwdriver out of his pocket and removed the main maintenance panel, exposing the delicate wiring underneath.

"Can you disable it permanently?" Tony asked. She remained close to the door, watching the entrance. Matt strained to hear her above the noise.

"Not in two minutes," he shouted back. "But this should be enough to slow them down for a while."

He replaced the screwdriver with a cutter and ripped into the wires.

Fixing a broken engine was a challenge that called for expertise and finesse, but wrecking it required nothing more than a basic understanding of its inner workings and the willingness to inflict damage—neither of which Matt lacked. He dug deeper into the engine's exposed guts, cutting and tearing out the connections he knew were the most crucial. As he'd told Tony, he couldn't really break the engine itself—not to the extent that *Lady Lisa*'s was broken, for example—but mending the now-tattered electrical system would take quite a lot of work in itself.

The engine shuddered, faltering, and made keening noises that reminded Matt of death rattles. Sparks flew from the open panel, and Matt took a step back, shielding his eyes. The engine gave a final shake and died down.

The sudden silence was as deafening as the earlier noise. Matt drew his handgun, set on low impact to incapacitate rather than kill, and joined Tony by the door, both of them with their backs plastered to the wall on either side of the opening.

His gamble paid off. After a few long, tense minutes, they heard footsteps and voices approaching from the service corridor, and two crew members came in. One guy's grease-stained fatigues marked him the mechanic, while the other's uniform was crisp and clean, and there was a holster strapped to his hip.

"Let's see what the problem is—"

The mechanic stopped midsentence as Tony and Matt moved in unison, shutting the engine room door behind them with their guns trained on each man.

"Hands up," Matt ordered.

The mechanic complied immediately, but his buddy—probably a security guard—hesitated, his hand fluttering uncertainly above his own weapon.

"Don't even think about it," Tony said.

The guard must have gauged her scowl correctly because he raised his hands while Matt divested him of his blaster gun and both their commlinks.

"Hey, man, that's mine!" the mechanic protested.

"Sorry, gents. Can't have you tattling to your boss just yet."

Matt held them both at gunpoint while Tony tied their hands behind their backs with the zip ties she'd brought with her—starting with the sour-faced guard.

"Now I need your access code," Matt told the mechanic after both of them sat on the floor, huddling in the corner by the hamstrung engine.

"I'll get fired," the man whined.

"Well, I ain't got much time, so it's either your job or your kneecaps," Matt said, hoping he was convincing enough. He'd never actually shot anyone in the kneecaps, and he wasn't about to start now, but the other man didn't have to know that. "Your choice."

Thankfully, his battered face must have lent him the necessary credibility to go along with his weapon.

"157 dash 143," the mechanic said sullenly. The guy beside him muttered something unflattering under his breath, which Matt ignored. None of it mattered anymore—with the universal code which gave the engineer instant access to even the most security-sensitive areas, they could now gain entrance to any part of the ship.

"Where do they keep the prisoner?" he asked the guard. He was sure the man knew exactly what he was talking about—he didn't even appear startled by the question. In fact, Matt was more surprised their guess about Val's whereabouts proved correct, and they hadn't pulled this elaborate scheme for nothing. "And by the way, same deal goes for your kneecaps too."

"Upper deck, guest accommodations. Cabin 3," the guard said reluctantly and glared at the mechanic, as if it was all his fault.

"Classy. I'm sure Val is a valued guest. Let's go," Matt told Tony, and they stepped out into the corridor, using the access code to lock the engine room door. Matt only paused to toss the crewmen's commlinks into the storage compartment where they'd been hiding.

MATT AND TONY hurried toward the staircases leading to the upper deck. Matt checked his watch as they ran; it was now 07:02. The race must have begun already. He itched to check its progress on his comm, but there was simply no time. The next few minutes were crucial and would determine the success or failure of their "Crime and Punishment" mission, regardless of what was happening in the Pit.

They didn't encounter any of the crew or staff in the living quarters. If Matt had to venture a guess, he'd say there were currently no guests staying aboard the yacht, and the owner was probably watching the race on the bridge, enjoying the view on the big panoramic screen. That's what they were counting on, at least, as they turned toward the row of cabins.

These were suites, really, nothing like the cramped little rooms they'd grown used to on the *Lisa*, so there were fewer of them. As they were about to turn the corner, Matt spotted a guard stationed outside the far cabin on the left. This one wasn't wearing any sort of uniform, and by his rugged looks, he wasn't part of the yacht's professional crew. He also appeared bored, which was completely understandable. No one wanted to be stuck on a posh cruise ship just hanging out in an empty hallway doing absolutely nothing.

"Distract him," Matt whispered in Tony's ear, and she nodded. She handed him her weapon and walked purposefully toward the cabin door. Matt hid behind the corner, peering out ever so cautiously, Tony's gun in hand and his own tucked under his waistband.

The guard drew himself up at Tony's approach and adjusted his grip on his plasma rifle, but her blue uniform and her deceptively nonthreatening appearance gave him pause.

"What is it?" he inquired roughly.

"I was sent to check on the prisoner," Tony said. Matt couldn't see her face, but he bet she was wearing a sweet smile to match her voice.

The guard, however, wasn't falling for it.

"I've got my orders. Nobody's allowed in."

"But he might be hungry," Tony insisted. "I'm sure nobody remembered to feed him this morning."

"Who are you again?" he asked suspiciously. "I ain't seen you around before."

"I'm new. Only started two days ago."

"Let me check in with the bridge," the guard said, reaching for his commlink.

That was their cue. Tony stepped aside in a smooth motion, and Matt threw himself into the corridor, taking aim and firing before the guy had the chance to raise his weapon. The charge hit him square in the chest, and he toppled silently, the comm clattering out of his hand. Tony caught his rifle before it could discharge and poked at the unconscious guard with the tip of her foot to make sure he was well and truly out of it.

"Nice shot," she told Matt when he joined her by the door. "I thought for sure I'd have to tackle him."

"Why is everybody always so surprised I can use a gun?" Matt asked, addressing the universe at large. "I *was* trained at the Fleet Academy, you know."

"Must be your mellow disposition, Captain. Can we open the door now, please?"

Matt scoffed and punched the mechanic's code in the entrance control panel. The door slid open without so much as a hiss.

Tony moved in first, rifle at the ready, and Matt followed her, glancing behind to make sure nobody was sneaking up on them from the corridor.

The cabin must have been intended as guest accommodations in the past, much like the others, but now it was stripped of any luxury furnishings. The spacious room was bare of carpeting, and the oval screen window was dark. Only the built-in cupboards and the en suite bathroom remained untouched. An old mattress was tucked into one corner, occupied by a large man who was just pushing himself into an upright position, his hands tied behind his back.

"Val!" Tony strapped the rifle behind her back and rushed to his side.

Matt allowed himself a sigh of relief. Up until this very moment, he hadn't been sure they were going to find Val in any kind of shape—or indeed alive. The odds had rarely been stacked in their favor, but it seemed they'd finally caught a break. Val was here, and while it looked like he'd taken a beating or two, his condition wasn't as dire as Matt had feared. His eyes had lost none of their sharpness, and he appeared anything but defeated.

"How are you feeling?" Tony asked, gently untying Val's hands. The left one was bandaged, clearly missing the index finger. Matt winced and busied himself with dragging the guard's limp body inside, where he wouldn't be spotted so easily.

"I'm all right." Val's voice was rough with disuse, or perhaps screaming. "How did you get here? And what happened to your face?"

"Long story," Matt said. "We should get a move on before they send a search party to the engine room and then here. Can you walk?"

"I can walk." Val proved his words by rising to his feet and hobbling toward the door. "Let's get the fuck out of here."

They spilled out into the corridor, locking the door behind them. Tony took the lead while Matt helped Val along. He glimpsed the time on his watch—07:11. Was the race over already? He couldn't pause to take out his comm, not even for a second, not when they were on the move. Once the race was over, Griggs's attention would shift to the next urgent matter—namely why his ship's engine was still shut down. Resisting the urge to check that channel or send out a quick message was one of the hardest things he'd done in his entire life. *Please, let Ryce be safe. Let him be alive.*

The two lifeboats were nestled on the sail, so, fortunately, they wouldn't have to go anywhere near the bridge and the lower deck again. They hurried toward the escape ladder leading upward from the end of the corridor. It was hidden behind a decorative panel that slid aside easily when Tony touched it.

"Go, go!" Matt let Val climb the ladder first, giving him a push to compensate for the impaired grip in his mangled hand.

"Hold it," a vaguely familiar male voice said behind them. It wasn't a shout, but there was something grating and unpleasant about the timbre, and it carried in the confined empty space.

They turned to the newcomer, Val still poised with his leg on the lower rung and Tony with her finger on the trigger of the rifle. They all froze, staring at Eddie Ander and two guards, aiming their weapons at them.

Chapter Twenty

"I HAVE THEM," Ander said into the commlink he was holding in one hand, never taking his eyes off Matt and the others. He had a handgun in the other, trained in their general direction, but with the guards' plasma rifles it seemed a bit redundant. "Surprise, bitches. Now, drop your weapons."

Matt complied, bending to lay Tony's gun, which he was still holding, on the floor, and taking out his second one as well. There was nowhere to hide, and a shootout in a narrow hallway wasn't going to end well for any of them. A split second later, Tony followed suit, putting down the rifle. Behind them, Val hopped off the ladder and came to stand between them. Even without looking, Matt could feel waves of tension rolling off his body. Matt's own heart was trying to claw out of his chest like a frightened animal in a cage.

"Good," Ander said when they were done. His snow-white hair stood up in tufts that would have been comical on anyone else. "Hands up, and get your asses over here. Slowly."

The three of them did as they were told, slowly crossing the corridor with their hands in the air. It was so unfair, Matt thought bitterly. They were so close to making a clean escape, just a step away from the lifeboats, exactly on time. Who knew Ander would be on the *Medusa* and that his hunches would be right on the money?

Every step away from the ladder brought them closer to their deaths—not just them, but Ryce as well. If they allowed themselves to be taken now, it would be well and truly over for them. The only possible reason they were still alive at this point was because Griggs probably wanted to question them on how they slipped aboard his precious yacht before pushing them out of the airlock. Matt was aware that if he so much as glanced at either Tony or Val, let alone whispered something, he'd be shot on the spot.

But they were his crew. They'd been together for years, as friends, as family. And close-knit family didn't always need to communicate verbally to understand each other. He'd just have to trust them to play along, even if that meant staking all of their lives on it.

"Close enough," Ander said when they were only a few steps away. "Boys, take them in."

The guard on the right shouldered his rifle and moved to cuff them, taking plastic ties out of his pocket.

One less rifle pointed their way was in no way evening out the odds—not even at this close range that made this specific weapon more cumbersome to use. But it was the best they could hope for, and Matt was going to take what he could get. It was now or never.

When the guard reached to grab his hands, Matt went with the motion, dropping to the floor while yanking the guard's outstretched arm so the man lost his balance and fell on top of him with a strangled curse. Matt didn't pause to check what the others were doing, even though, judging by the sudden eruption of shouting and the sound of bodies colliding with brutal force, all hell had broken loose. A gunshot resonated through the corridor, the charge emitting a familiar heat wave, but Matt didn't dare look at who or what might have been the intended target. He might have been only slightly better than absolutely useless in their wretched tussle with Stahl's thugs, but now, sheer desperation spurred him into action. He didn't let go of the guard's arm, instead, rolling over, pinning him to the floor with his weight, and punching him in the face with all the force of his frustration. Pain spread from Matt's knuckles up to his elbow, but he ignored it, punching again and again until the man went limp in his hold, his head lolling from side to side. With a grunt, Matt heaved him aside and pulled a handgun out of the guard's hip holster, opting for a lighter weapon rather than the rifle. Only then did he look up from where he was crouching on the floor.

It seemed the only reason he hadn't been shot in the head in the middle of his desperate struggle was because their other opponents were too busy trying to contain his crew members, who, indeed, had followed his lead, driven by the same incentive. Tony was still struggling with the second guard, both of them clutching his rifle—which was now swinging in a wide arc, pointing at the ceiling. Tony was petite, but she'd had bodyguard training a few years ago when she was searching for a job in spacecraft security and, when she wanted to, could boast the tenacity of an attack dog.

Val, unsurprisingly, had gone for Ander. Ander's gun was the one that had gone off, but the high-intensity blast had strayed, charring the pristine silver wall. Apparently, close combat sometimes had advantages over the use of longer-range firearms—that, and sheer luck. After a long bad streak, it favored Val again, because the larger man was crowding his enemy, pushing him back toward the mouth of the corridor, their hands locked on the butt of the gun.

There were far too many weapons ready to discharge in unpredictable trajectories for Matt's liking.

"Tony, duck!" he yelled, and she did, abruptly releasing her grip on the guard's rifle and dropping to the floor without so much as a backward glance. The man stumbled, and Matt took the opportunity of his momentary confusion to shoot him. This time, his aim was somewhat shaky, and the charge only grazed his side rather than hitting him front and center, but it was enough to bring him to his knees as he cried out in pain. With a sharp kick to his face from her squat, Tony sent him sprawling, hopefully unconscious for the next few minutes. Matt winced in instinctive sympathy—that kick must have hurt.

Unconcerned, Tony sprang lightly to her feet and grabbed the rifle.

"Val!" Matt shouted, but he already saw it was useless. The engineer was locked in a standoff with his nemesis, quite oblivious to everything else, and he wasn't about to let go. Ander's gun clattered to the floor as the two men grappled, so close that neither Matt nor Tony could possibly shoot Ander without risking hitting Val as well. Not that their help would be in any way welcome. It was Val's fight, and it was a fight to the death.

"Tony, get upstairs, fire up the lifeboat," Matt ordered. "Get it ready to go as soon as we step through the hatch. I'll get Val."

This time, she hesitated, looking uncertainly between them. Val somehow managed to pin Ander to the far wall, but he was struggling to maintain his hold. He was strong, but his injured hand and the beatings he'd sustained were slowing him down.

"Go!" Matt repeated, and Tony ran to the escape ladder. Matt raised his handgun, holding it firmly in two hands. Personal vendetta or no, he was determined to take a shot at Ander as soon as an opportunity presented itself. At that moment, Ander turned, twisting in Val's grip, and landed a precise punch to Val's solar plexus that made him grunt and take half a step back. Pressing his sudden advantage, Ander whipped out an electric knife, as sharp and deadly as the glint in his eyes.

"I shoulda killed you when I had the chance," he spat out, never taking his eyes off Val. "Griggs's too soft. But you're not getting away now."

As if to underscore his words, the bright illumination in the corridor dimmed, and red emergency lights flashed along the bottom of the walls.

"Intruder alert," a computer voice announced from somewhere overhead. "Intruder alert."

Griggs's crew were definitely onto them now, if that somehow wasn't clear enough already, and it would only be a matter of minutes, if not seconds, until reinforcements arrived. Matt hoped Tony had the right idea and would make her escape if they didn't get out in time. Ryce's life hinged on the lifeboat picking him up on Elysium-5. He couldn't go back to Griggs's transport vessel, and the aerojet wasn't built for outer space travel.

Ander lunged at Val then, too quick for Matt to take proper aim. He cursed and ran toward the fighting men, as Val countered and deflected the strike with his injured hand. The blade sliced through his forearm, but it didn't give him pause. With his other hand, Val reached under the knife and seized Ander's throat, squeezing so hard his knuckles turned white, relentlessly crushing his foe's windpipe.

Ander made a choking sound, and his face turned red, his eyes bulging. Matt reached them in time to knock the knife, which Ander still tried to swipe at Val, from his hand. With a savage growl, Val lifted the man a few inches off the floor and hit his head against the wall with a hard bang. His fingers dug into Ander's throat with crushing force. Thankfully, Matt couldn't hear the sound of breaking cartilage over the repeating alarm, but Ander's raspy gasps were bad enough. Finally, his eyelids fluttered and shut, and he sagged like a marionette with its strings cut.

"Val, we need to go," Matt urged. He didn't care if Ander was dead or merely unconscious; either way, a crushed trachea meant he would be unable to give chase.

The engineer didn't respond, still applying pressure to his opponent's neck. Blood seeped through his sleeve from the fresh knife wound, dripping on the floor as his mangled hand hung uselessly to his side, but he didn't seem to notice. He scowled ferociously, intent on Ander's now-purple face to the exclusion of everything else.

"Val!" Matt grabbed him by the shirt and pulled. He could hear loud noises and someone running up the staircase. It was high time for them to haul ass. "Come on!"

His desperate plea seemed to penetrate the angry haze because Val blinked and released his choke hold. Ander's body folded and crumpled like a broken doll. Matt didn't bother checking for a pulse; however, on a momentary flash of inspiration, he hunkered down to reach into the man's pant pocket and fished out his commlink.

"Let's go!"

Val let him pull him along, and they ran toward the escape ladder. Matt pushed Val forward, following on his heels, and slammed the hatch just as more guards spilled into the corridor below them. He hurriedly turned the bolt, closing it even though he couldn't actually lock it from outside, and ran toward the starboard lifeboat airlock, which was open and waiting. As soon as he and Val were inside, he shut the outer hatch, leaning against it and breathing heavily.

"Tony, get us out!" he shouted, and nearly fell over as the tiny vessel shuddered and took off at full throttle, speeding away from the immobile yacht.

THE LIFEBOAT WAS slightly bigger than *Lady Lisa*'s shuttle, but a bit more cramped as well since it was meant as a rescue vessel for a greater number of people. Matt replaced Tony at the control panel, tapping the adapters on his temples to link to the ship's computer and setting the course to enter Elysium-5 atmosphere. His hands were still shaky with adrenaline, and he took a couple of steadying breaths to calm himself and focus on the task at hand. The lifeboat responded readily, changing trajectory and veering gracefully toward the designated point of entry above the vast equatorial desert.

"What happened to Ander?" Tony asked, taking a seat in the copilot chair.

"He's dead," Val said dully. He had lowered himself into the closest passenger seat, hunching over. "I felt his hyoid bone snap."

Tony threw Matt a quick look, but he only shrugged slightly. He wasn't at all sure Ander was really dead. Choking the life out of somebody was a lot harder than as portrayed in movies. And the man probably received top-notch medical assistance as soon as the yacht's crewmen found him in that corridor. But he wasn't about to say it out loud in front of Val. If he believed his long-time enemy had met his demise, so much the better. Perhaps now he'd be able to find some peace within himself and change his perspective on what life still had to offer. Either way, if the rest of their plan worked as it should, they'd have seen the last of Mr. Ander.

"You're bleeding!" Tony exclaimed, just noticing Val's knife wound, and busied herself with finding a first aid kit and tending to the nasty cut. Val voiced no objections, docilely letting her do her thing with disinfecting and bandaging his forearm. Matt suspected he was in a bit of a shock, both physically and emotionally.

With the course set, Matt allowed himself to relax a fraction. He checked the rearview cameras. The *Medusa* grew smaller and smaller until it was only a tiny speck in the black void. Whatever was happening on that yacht, it seemed they'd refrained from using the remaining functioning lifeboat to chase them—which was a break Matt had counted on.

He still couldn't quite believe his outrageous plan had worked and they'd made it off unscathed. A single flesh wound and a few bruises were definitely a fair trade-off for getting out alive. But they weren't in the clear yet. The relative safety of the Freeport station was a long way off, and even if they managed to pick up Ryce and reach it without incident, they'd have to hurry to make sure they were one step ahead of Griggs. They were still running against time, and being unexpectedly waylaid by Ander had set them back quite a bit.

Matt took out his comm. The one he'd snatched from Ander was stashed in his other pocket, but he was content to leave it there for the time being, having turned it off. The race channel had long gone silent, of course; there was no way of knowing what the outcome had been. His earlier anxiety, which had been pushed aside by survival instinct, was back in full force. Tapping on Ryce's contact, he typed a quick message:

On our way to the rendezvous point. All ok?

He waited, but no answer came. He wasn't even sure his message had been received. Perhaps there was some technical problem with communications. Or maybe Ryce was simply too distracted or preoccupied to look at his comm. There could be a hundred reasons for him not answering; there was no need to stress about it and jump to long-reaching conclusions.

No matter how he tried to calm himself, it wasn't working. Matt increased the speed, directing more energy to the thrusters. *Come on, come on, come on,* he urged, as if he could really compel the ship with the power of his mind.

The lifeboat shook as it entered the planet's atmosphere, and Matt had to divert his attention to keeping it nice and steady. The ship tore through the dense layer of clouds, coming out on the other side under the glare of the Elysium sun. The sky was an intense indigo blue, which made the sand and the rocks below appear bleached white.

They were right on the spot. The long, wide gash of the canyon sinuated below, marring the otherwise pristine expanse of sand dunes and occasional rock formations. Matt turned on the scanners, searching for abnormal heat patterns on the ground. Ryce was supposed to be waiting for them a little way off, where he wouldn't be easily spotted, but Matt was worried about discovering the traces of a fresh explosion within the canyon. There'd be no way of knowing who the unfortunate jet had belonged to, of course, but in any case, he didn't pick up anything on the scanner. It served to settle his nerves a bit; however, his heart rate still refused to return to normal.

He slowed down as the lifeboat descended further, skimming the terrain at a safe altitude that still allowed good visibility. The mouth of the canyon dwindled into the distance, and the desert stretched before them in all its barren glory.

Tony took the second seat again, swiveling to face the window display.

"How is he?" Matt asked, not taking his eyes off the scanner's data feed at the bottom of the screen.

"A bit shaken. But he'll be all right."

In Matt's experience—and if his recurrent nightmares and memory loss were anything to go by—it took a while to be "all right" again after living through captivity and torture, even for someone as stoic and resilient as Val. But time, they said, healed all wounds, and Val, at least, had his friends to help him through it.

"I'll get the IMA to surgically reattach his finger," Tony continued.

"It might have to wait. Our top priority is getting Val off the Freeport as soon as possible. We don't know what happened to Eddie Ander, and I'm not taking any chances. Hell, if it wasn't for *Lisa*, I'd be happy to skedaddle myself."

The risk of staying on the station with an angry crime boss most likely clamoring for retaliation was perhaps too high. But Matt couldn't leave his ship to be either taken apart by Griggs or impounded by the authorities. *Lisa* was as much a part of the family as any of them, and you didn't abandon family. Not the one that wanted you, anyway.

"What's there?" Tony pointed to the screen just as Matt picked up something on the scanner. His heart leaped, as if he could actually recognize Ryce's presence from a string of data. He zoomed in on a large outcrop of jagged rocks and boulders sticking out from the white sand.

Sure enough, there was the outline of an aerojet, which upon closer inspection turned out to be Ryce's Sparrow, behind one of the larger boulders. Whatever had happened during the race, it meant Ryce had managed to survive it, that his body wasn't lying somewhere at the bottom of the canyon among the debris of his jet.

Reining in his excitement, Matt carefully lowered the lifeboat, landing on a relatively flat patch of craggy ground and shutting the thrusters off.

"Stay here," he told Tony just in case. "I'm going outside to meet him."

She only nodded, but Matt was already heading to the lifeboat entryway. The planet's environment wasn't hostile enough to require a full space suit, so he just picked up an oxygen mask from one of the emergency kits, and barely waited for the pressure chamber to lock before opening up the main hatch and stepping out onto the sand.

Chapter Twenty-One

MATT RAN TOWARD the jet, leaving footprints in the gravelly sand. The oxygen mask chafed on his swollen nose, but he hardly noticed the discomfort. The jet's engine was turned off, and there were no other life signs he could discern, and for one awful moment, Matt was terrified something had gone wrong after all. But then the jet's hatch opened, and Ryce sprang to the ground. He was wearing his flight suit and a far more elaborate oxygen mask which covered half his face and was vaguely reminiscent of alien armor.

Matt closed the distance between them in two long strides and threw his arms around him, locking him in a powerful embrace with a vigor that made Ryce stagger. Forming a coherent sentence that would make sense of all the jumbled emotions swirling inside him—joy, relief, pride—proved quite a challenge for the current state of his faculties, so he settled for a simple:

"I love you. God, I love you so much."

Ryce's arms tightened around him in response. "Had I known this would be your reaction to life-threatening situations, I would have found some sufficiently risky hobby to engage in a long time ago."

There was amusement in his voice, but he seemed in no hurry to release his hold on Matt.

"Don't you fucking dare," Matt breathed. "I think we can safely say we've had quite enough close calls to last us a lifetime."

"True. I love you too," Ryce added in a much more serious tone.

Matt briefly weighed the dangers of breathing potentially toxic air against the benefits of ripping their masks off and kissing right there and then till they were both dizzy, but he couldn't contradict his own words regarding those close calls. As much as he wanted to feel the press of Ryce's smooth lips against his, it would have to wait until they were both safely on the lifeboat.

"I'm just glad you're okay," he said. "I was worried there for a while when you didn't answer my call, I must admit."

"Sorry about that," Ryce said. "There must be something in the local atmosphere interfering with transmissions."

"Fuck this planet sideways. Let's just go home."

He couldn't say where home actually was, but perhaps it was true what they said about it not being a place at all. Maybe it was just a feeling you got when you were surrounded by the people who loved you most.

They broke apart and started toward the ship, hand in hand. The sun continued its climb in the rich blue sky, and it was getting hotter and dryer by the minute. But they'd only made it a few steps when the ground in front of their feet erupted in a barrage of gravel. Both of them stumbled backward, clutching at each other and instinctively ducking.

Several more laser blasts, directed from above, hit the sand around them. The violent bangs shattered the relative silence of the desert, preceding the roar of another aircraft's engine as it came swooping out of the sky. For a second, Matt was sure Griggs had somehow caught up with them, using the second lifeboat or some other proxy vessel. But when he raised his head, he saw the silhouette of a Waxwing jet, massive at this short distance, outlined against the glare of the sun.

Ryce pulled him behind one of the larger boulders of the outcrop. They crouched in its shadow as the Waxwing soared upward and sideways, preparing for another pass.

"What the fuck!" Matt's heart felt ready to explode, along with his head. The flow of pure oxygen inside the mask, mixed with yet another surge of adrenaline, was making him slightly dizzy, and he fought to maintain focus. "That's Stahl's jet!"

"I know," Ryce said grimly, following the plane with his eyes.

"This is supposed to be a no-fly natural reserve, not the fucking Sawyer Strait! And since when are racers allowed to install laser guns on their jets?!"

"I hardly think he asked for permission. He must have waited till the race was over to seek out my aircraft and get rid of the competition once it became clear I wasn't going back to the transport vessel."

Matt glanced at him. "Why is he so pissed? You won, didn't you?" he said accusingly.

Ryce actually managed to look sheepish despite the mask. "I did. But it wasn't as difficult as I'd feared it would be this time. And if you're worried about me using stims—"

"I worried because they're dangerous," Matt interjected in exasperation.

"Whatever. I didn't use them. Watch out!"

They ducked, plastering themselves against the stone as the Waxwing dived again, showering the outcrop with a hail of laser shots. Matt threw his arm up to shield his face against the shrapnel of rock chips.

"What is he even doing here?" He had to shout to be heard over the terrible noise.

After all they'd gone through, he refused to believe they were in this situation. It was almost surreal. This part was supposed to easy, but now they were trapped, unarmed, while precious minutes were trickling by. They were supposed to return to the station before Griggs had the chance to intercept them. Now, that possibility was looking less and less solid—provided they'd survive the impromptu aerial attack.

"He missed the transport," Matt said. "Now he's stuck on the planet with his damn jet, even if he manages to take us out."

"The fact that he's a homicidal egomaniac doesn't mean he can't have friends or at least paid associates who would fly a shuttle to his rescue, much like you did," Ryce reasoned. A sharp piece of stone hit his forehead, and he hissed. A streak of blood welled just beneath his hairline.

"We've gotta do something," Matt said. The Waxwing pulled up again, ready to go on another strafing round. "Right now he's focusing on us, but if he hits the lifeboat..."

He didn't have to finish the sentence. Even if everyone survived the attack, damage to the lifeboat meant they'd be effectively marooned, with no means of getting off the planet—and then it would be a gamble on who found them first, Griggs or the Freeport authorities. Neither option was particularly appealing.

"I'll draw him away." Ryce got up, dusting himself off. "You get to the lifeboat before he makes another pass."

"Draw him away in your jet? Seriously?" Matt demanded. "He'll shoot you right out of the sky! Stop trying to be a damn hero!"

"I'll dodge him," Ryce said with a confidence Matt did not share in the slightest. "Just go!"

Without waiting for Matt's response, he ran toward the discarded Sparrow. But he didn't get very far. When he was merely yards away from the jet, the Waxwing came in again, this time forgoing the hiding spot amidst the rocks to focus on the stationary jet. Ryce threw himself on the sand as a volley of laser beams hit the aircraft, several of them penetrating the hull. A sharp smell of jet fuel wafted in the dry air, the fetor of absolute bad luck.

"Get back!" Matt yelled at the top of his lungs and bounded toward Ryce's huddled form in complete disregard of his own command. "It's gonna blow!"

Ryce managed to heave himself up and run back to Matt a split second before an explosion shook the desert. The blast tossed both of them to the ground, leaving them stunned by the impact, as a wave of fire billowed across the taller rocks.

Matt rolled on his back, gulping the sweet oxygen in his mask, staring at the indigo vastness above. Heavy smoke rose from the charred remains of the jet, blocking the sun.

Ryce stirred beside him, and Matt took his hand, the two of them helping each other stand on unsteady feet. Ryce was saying something, but Matt couldn't hear anything over the ringing in his ears. Warm fresh blood seeped from his nose to his mouth underneath the mask.

Ryce pointed to something behind his back, and Matt turned to see Tony jump out of the lifeboat hatch, laser rifle in hand. She shouted something, and then, when they failed to respond, waved at them frantically to join her. She pointed the rifle in the Waxwing's general direction and fired a few shots.

A rifle was no match for a fighter-jet caliber laser gun, but it gave them some semblance of cover as they sprinted toward the lifeboat. Matt felt rather than heard the engine already purring as he reached the hatch and unceremoniously shoved both Ryce and Tony inside.

"He's coming!" he yelled, glimpsing the jet gaining altitude before slamming the hatch shut. He hoped Ryce had heard him because his own voice was coming to him as if from under water.

Ryce headed straight to the tiny bridge as soon as the pressure chamber door opened, taking off his mask and linking his adapters on the run. He didn't waste any time getting the lifeboat in the air. The thrusters strained at liftoff, going at full capacity, but the angle of ascent made them a vulnerable target. The laser beams cut the air around them in rapid succession, several of them grazing the hull but none hitting the ship directly as Ryce swerved among them, sacrificing speed in his struggle to dodge the shots. The control panel beeped in alarm.

Matt flung himself into the copilot's chair, tearing the mask from his face.

"Strap up!" he ordered, and did so himself, without bothering to look back. Tony and Val knew what to do; right now, his biggest worry was to avoid sustaining a direct laser hit. The lifeboat wasn't robust enough to withstand it, and it was no match for an aerojet when it came to speed and agility—as long as they remained in the lower layers of the atmosphere. Their best bet was to reach escape velocity as quickly as possible since the jet couldn't follow them into the mesosphere. But attaining it seemed as impossible as reaching the sun when they had an angry fighter jet hot on their tail.

Getting into the lifeboat and off the ground was a tactical mistake, but it was hardly one they could have somehow avoided. Their chances of survival, however, didn't look great at the moment.

The lifeboat dropped abruptly as the Waxwing fired another volley of laser beams at them, and Matt clutched at the chair armrests. They were definitely at a serious disadvantage and losing altitude rather than pushing upward. There was nowhere to go, nowhere to hide, and the other jet was locked on target.

"Those stims could have come in handy right now," Ryce said pointedly.

"No time. You said you could dodge him anyway."

"I wasn't talking about a lifeboat."

"When life gives you lifeboats, you make the fucking lifeboats work!"

Ryce barked a laugh, and the ship sped up again, taking a sharp turn to the right. The desert stretched far beneath them, an endless sea of sandy dunes peppered with stone formations, barely visible in the distance. The Waxwing followed, dogging them every step of the way. This was another race, but this time, there was no set course, no time frame, no prize. This was about survival, and Ryce was doing everything he could to stay one step ahead of the laser beams coming his way—with varying degrees of success. Each glancing blast shook the small vessel, and it was only a matter of time till one of them hit the fuel tank or took out the electronics.

"Let's make it work, then," Ryce said, once again as cool and collected as Matt was used to seeing him when he was helming a ship. "I'm going to try a disengagement maneuver. Here's hoping this thing can take it."

He switched to full manual and took hold of the control stick. The lifeboat sped up, simultaneously tilting to the side. Matt grabbed the chair, even though he was strapped into it. The lifeboat rolled over, and everything that wasn't affixed to the walls tumbled down. Tony cursed from the passengers' seats in the salon.

The lifeboat dived, now flipped at a 180-degree angle. Matt's stomach jumped all the way to his throat as he hung upside down from his chair. The Split-S was a tried-and-true move in aerial combat, going back centuries to the very first human-invented aircraft. But a lifeboat was not a fighter jet, as Ryce had already made abundantly clear.

Matt kept his eyes on the screen, just in time to see the Waxwing overshoot them from above, speeding on its original trajectory while they nosedived. Then Ryce pulled the control stick. The thrusters keened, fighting against gravity. For a split second, everything seemed to be suspended midair, and Matt could have sworn the lifeboat was going to stall and plummet, losing momentum. Angry red alarm messages flashed across the screen. Ryce ignored them, keeping his hold steady. The ship's bow lifted, and it came out of the half-loop, once again aligning horizontally. But Ryce, uninterested in keeping a straight course, kept the pressure on the stick. The engines roared, emitting a totally different sound to their earlier wail, and the lifeboat soared, cutting through the gradually thinning air and the wispy layer of clouds, taking advantage of the Waxwing's momentary lag to make its escape upward.

Chapter Twenty-Two

MATT SLUMPED IN the chair and closed his eyes. The dark embrace of outer space had never felt sweeter. The lifeboat shot out of Elysium-5 atmosphere, leaving the planet behind. Stahl, at least, was off their list of things to worry about for the time being.

Ryce exhaled softly beside him. Matt opened his eyes and turned to him. A slow smiled spread on Ryce's face, warming his gray eyes.

"I guess you were right about those lifeboats," he said.

Suddenly Matt couldn't care less about Stahl, Griggs, Ander, and the entire damn galaxy. He undid the straps, and pounced on Ryce, practically climbing into his lap and claiming his lips. Ryce responded eagerly, throwing his arms around Matt, holding him painfully tight, deepening the kiss. Their teeth clashed, and Matt tasted blood again from his abused nose, but neither of them could get enough, drinking each other like air.

"Ahem," Tony said, entering the bridge. "Sorry to spoil the party, boys, but it'd be nice to get a status report."

They broke the kiss reluctantly, and Matt sat back in the copilot chair, mainly to hide his body's involuntary reaction to Ryce's proximity.

"Why do you always have to be the responsible adult?" he complained.

"Do you really have to ask?"

Ryce tapped the control panel, still grinning. "We should be back at the Freeport in little over an hour." He glanced at Tony." How is Val?"

"As well as he can be at the moment."

"Good. We need to get him on board Randy Reid's ship and off the station right after we dock," Matt said. "I'll give Randy a call to make sure he's ready to bolt as soon as his passenger arrives."

The unexpected altercations with Ander and Stahl had cost them precious time. The plan was to get back to the 73 before Griggs had the chance to return and raise hell. He could still do it long-distance, of course, but in Matt's experience, things ran much smoother when the boss was around to oversee them.

Sending Val off was their top priority since it stood to reason he'd be the main target of both Griggs and Ander's wrath (provided Ander was still alive to be angry). But realistically, they were all in the same kind of danger. If it weren't for his poor stranded *Lisa*, Matt would have them all evacuated in a heartbeat. But a captain didn't abandon his ship if he could help it, and he had this thin, barely tangible thread of hope that, somehow, he could make everything all right again—if his plans panned out.

"You should both go with him," he told Tony and Ryce. "I have to sort things out on the Freeport, but I'd be much calmer knowing you were all safe somewhere else."

"Didn't we already have this conversation?" Tony scoffed. "I'm not going anywhere."

Ryce said nothing, merely giving Matt a very pointed glare.

Matt's throat closed. If this was what it felt like to have a family that had your back no matter what, it was the best feeling in the world.

"Thanks, guys," he said when he was sure his voice wasn't going to betray him. "And in case I won't have the chance to say it later, I love you all and I appreciate the support. Truly, I do."

He looked them both in the eye to make sure they understood he was being sincere. They nodded.

"Okay, then. Now—" Matt fished Ander's commlink out of his pants pocket. He hoped it had survived him rolling around on the craggy ground, and there was no time like the present to check. "Let's see what the dead man has to say."

REID'S SHIP, THE *Siren*, was berthed at Dock F13, and after talking to him en route, Matt requested the Station Control's permission to land there. To his relief, the lifeboat was yet to be reported as stolen. He was cleared to come in—not before the operator reminded him there were docking fees pending in his name for his Phaeton vessel, registration number 050420 slash 11.

"Kinda hard to forget," Matt muttered. Unpaid fees were low in priority right now, but he knew he'd have to somehow address that issue—if he lived long enough for it to matter.

"Is everybody ready?" Ryce asked as he navigated the curve of the outer ring of the Freeport station. The adjacent jumpgate, built and left there by the mysterious Mnirians millennia ago, was active, its four detached corners glowing bright against the dark backdrop, dimming the distant stars. Ships were already queued up, waiting for the precise space-folding technology to take them to their respective destinations throughout the galaxy.

"Ready." Val was the one to answer in that low, rumbling voice of his. His tall, broad figure seemed to occupy all the available space as he stepped onto the tiny bridge, but the presence of all four members of their little crew, finally together, filled Matt's heart with undiluted joy. He didn't mind sharing cramped quarters, eating canned soup, and desperately hunting for the next underpaid job, as long as they were all safe—even if some of them eventually chose to follow a different path.

He glanced at Ryce, but this time, the thought didn't carry anger, only deep sadness.

"And thank you all. For everything. I mean it," Val said. "I'm sorry I got you in trouble, and—"

"Don't sweat it," Matt said. "We all get in trouble from time to time, and we're here to have each others' backs."

Val's mouth quirked. "Aye, Captain."

A few minutes later, the lifeboat glided into the open mouth of the dock and then through the huge pressure doors into the main area. It landed softly on its shock absorbers without so much as a jolt, which made Matt a little jealous of the quality. *Lady Lisa*'s shuttle was much more cumbersome in comparison—not to mention a lot less luxurious when it came to interior design.

"All right, let's get the hell out," Matt ordered after Ryce shut down the engine. He could see the elegant silhouette of the *Siren* behind a few other ships, beckoning with a promise of safe passage (for one of them, at least). Its main hatch was open, as if in welcome, and the ship's thrusters were already glowing, warming up before the anticipated takeoff.

They all spilled out onto the dock, looking like they'd indeed been in some sort of shipwreck—Tony and Matt still in the dark blue uniform of the *Medusa* crew, both he and Ryce covered in a thick layer of brown-gray dust, and Val with his bloodstained clothes and bandaged hand. Dock F13 was a busy one, and they must have drawn some startled glances, but Matt didn't get the chance to find out if that was true.

A small group of people was waiting for them as they stepped onto the ramp—and it didn't include Randy coming to greet them. There was Tex, her arms folded across her chest, an unreadable expression on her face, flanked by three large men in nondescript gray clothing, their hip pockets bulging with the shape of concealed blaster guns.

Another man stood beside and slightly ahead of her. He was middle-aged, of average height, his dark hair graying elegantly at the temples. His suit was much too expensive to be worn at the docks. Matt could only presume this was the elusive Griggs himself, finally gracing them with his presence. Eddie Ander was notably absent from the party.

"You've gotta be kidding me," Matt muttered wearily. He wasn't even really surprised; being ambushed when they thought they were in the clear was only par for the course for how the day was going.

"Captain Spears," Griggs said. His cultured voice, like his attire, was incongruous with both the surroundings and his brutish entourage. "I see you're in quite a hurry, but I do believe we need to talk."

"Do they wanna talk too?" Matt nodded toward Tex and the armed men. The tension in his friends was palpable, and he didn't have to turn around to see Tony and Ryce's hands hovering above their own weapons.

"After some of your recent antics, I must take the necessary precautions," Griggs said almost apologetically and then gestured toward the lifeboat. "Shall we? This should give us all enough privacy."

Matt was reluctant to go anywhere with so many guns present, but settling the score on the shuttle definitely beat disappearing into the bowels of the station.

"After you." Tex nodded toward the lifeboat, and they had no choice but to file back inside. Tex brought up the rear and shut the hatch closed when everybody was on board.

At Griggs's gesture, they sat in the passenger seats. Val was glaring at Tex, Tony was sizing up the three guards, and Ryce was focused on Griggs, his lips tightly pressed. No one had actually drawn a weapon yet, but the air crackled with impending violence.

"I'd say it's a pleasure meeting you all, but that would hardly be true under the circumstances." Griggs came to stand in front of them. "In fact, Captain Spears, you and your bunch have been quite the pain in the neck."

"I'm sure you'd agree not all of it was our fault," Matt said. "It's not like any of us actually wanted to find ourselves in this situation. In fact,

I'm known to be a very reasonable and amiable person—as long as nobody kidnaps my friends and threatens me with their body parts."

"Be that as it may," Griggs said, unimpressed. "I'm a businessman, and you have done more than enough damage to my business. As well as my private property."

"I don't think killing us is going to solve that," Matt said cheekily.

"Indeed, it's not. But I must say it would bring me no small amount of satisfaction," Griggs said with a pleasant smile. "As well as serve as a warning to others not to interfere with my enterprises. And all I have to do is report finding your bodies on my stolen vessel, apparently having killed each other in an argument gone wrong over the division of the loot."

Ryce tensed in the seat next to him, and Tony shifted uncomfortably in hers. Matt didn't know if Griggs was being completely serious (after all, it would have been easier to just shoot them outright instead of sitting them all down first to be scolded like misbehaving schoolchildren), but he didn't want to test whether the man would carry out his threat.

"Now, I had a feeling you'd see things this way," he said, doing his best to match the put-on civil tone of the conversation while hoping Griggs didn't notice how sweaty his palms were, or how fast his pulse was. "I hate to be a pain in the neck again, as you put it, but I don't think this'll work at all. As a matter of fact, I think you'll let us all go."

Griggs raised a perfectly manicured eyebrow. "I'll play along. Why would I do that, exactly?"

"Because it just so happens I have your buddy Ander's commlink." Matt produced the incriminating piece of evidence from his pocket. "The one where he kept detailed records of everything pertaining to the organization of the illegal races on Elysium-5—including the recordings of every single race and the stakes made on it. That kind of information will be hard even for our status-quo-loving station authorities to overlook if it fell into their lap, wouldn't you agree? And before you try to pry it out of my cold dead hands," he added hastily at seeing the dangerous gleam entering Griggs's eyes, "you should know an encrypted transmission of all the relevant data has already been sent to Admiral Cummings of the Federal Fleet, to be opened in the case of my untimely demise."

A deathly quiet settled in the cabin as everybody seemed to hold their breath. Griggs stared at him, and Matt held his own gaze steady, drawing on every ounce of courage he had in his body to weather the other man's scrutiny. He'd sent a copy of all the files stored on Ander's commlink to *Lady Lisa*'s computer before they touched down on the station, but he was lying through his teeth about getting the same transmission out to his father. Admiral Cummings would in no way welcome anything that came from his wayward son unless it was a humble apology. Matt just needed a name which sounded impressive enough not to be easily dismissed—and a plausible one, in case Griggs had done his homework on Matt's background. For some reason, he was reluctant to bring Nora into this, even if it was only a bluff.

"It seems I've underestimated you, Captain," Griggs said finally, breaking the silence. He was smiling again, but it was the kind of smile that sent shivers down Matt's spine. "Well played."

"So can we go now?" He was perhaps pushing it, but Matt didn't want to spend a second more in these people's company than he had to.

"Not so fast. As I said, I'm first and foremost a businessman. Assuming I'd be willing to forget about you damaging and stealing my property, not to mention assaulting my men, there is still the small matter of our original deal. Funding for the repairs on your ship in exchange for your assistance with transporting special goods along with IMA shipments, I believe it was?"

Shit. Matt really didn't need that. He opened his mouth, frantically searching for the most diplomatic way to put it into words, when Tony unexpectedly came to his rescue.

"That deal is a bust."

Everybody turned to look at her, and she rushed to explain: "I got a message this morning from Dr. Yang informing us they've decided to go with a different hauler for their moon shipments. Sorry, Captain," she added, turning to Matt. "We were kinda busy, so I forgot to mention it earlier."

"No worries," he muttered. Right now, he was grateful for what was undoubtedly Prof. Brinan running interference against them. The Onorean could be as spiteful as he wanted, as long as it got them off the hook with Griggs.

"Well, it seems we are both out of luck today," Griggs said. "You are free to go, lady and gentlemen. I don't think I have to remind you to stay well away from both my associates and my ventures on this station from now on, do I?"

"Got it," Matt said, suppressing his sigh of relief.

"Wait," Ryce said. "I did win the race this morning. And as I recall, the winner was promised a cash prize of twenty-thousand credits."

Matt almost groaned with frustration. He could understand Ryce's eagerness to score the money they so badly needed, but couldn't he see Griggs was already pissed off enough? It was beyond risky to aggravate him any further, especially by trying to twist his arm in front of his subordinates.

"Indeed," Griggs said, without batting an eyelash at Ryce's audacity. "And I will be holding on to that money as recompense for all the inconvenience your bunch had caused me—not to mention the cost of repairs to my yacht. I think it would only be fair, wouldn't you agree?"

"Yes," Matt hurried to say. "Very fair. Thank you, sir."

Griggs nodded and made a sweeping gesture toward the main hatch. "Out you go, then."

The four of them got up and proceeded toward the exit. Matt brought up the rear, not daring to look back, his shoulder blades itching with the expectation of a gun blast hitting him in the back.

But nothing happened. They stepped out of the lifeboat again, right onto the dock. The noise of the surrounding vessels undergoing maintenance and people milling about was overwhelming after the dangerously low tones of the conversation they were lucky to have escaped.

"Is he really letting us go?" Tony asked in a hushed voice, glancing in disbelief toward the lifeboat.

"For now, he is," Matt said, just as quietly. "But let's not forget he's a vengeful bastard with a grudge. I can guarantee he won't let this slide. The longer we stay on this station, the bigger the chances he'll seek some sort of retribution. Don't let that refined crap fool you. He'll make it look like an unfortunate accident instead of ambushing us around a corner, but we'll end up dead all the same."

"Then we either all leave now, or we all stay," Val said. They turned to him, and he shrugged. "There hardly seems to be any point in smuggling me out alone now. He gave us a pass, even if it's a temporary one. And frankly, I'd rather not leave you guys."

"Val's right. Not to mention he's in need of medical attention that I doubt Mr. Reid would be able to provide," Ryce said. Tony nodded vigorously.

"All right." Matt threw his hands up. Any life-changing decisions would have to wait till they all got their food, rest, and, yes, medical attention. "We stay together. I'll let Randy know we had to cancel Val's trip. Let's go home, get our shit together, and see where we stand."

Chapter Twenty-Three

"I NEED A shower," Matt said, starting down the hallway of the *Lady Lisa* after depositing Val and Tony at the infirmary. Deep weariness settled into every bone and muscle in his body, and all he could think about was washing himself in blissfully hot water before passing out in his bed. Even the hunger already gnawing at his stomach had to take a back seat to some well-deserved shut-eye. "A fucking long one."

"Wait," Ryce said.

He was walking beside Matt, but now, he halted in the middle of the corridor, forcing Matt to turn to him. He couldn't quite read Ryce's expression—both apprehensive and determined at the same time. Cold dread coiled at the bottom of Matt's stomach.

"There is something I need to do first, and I'd like you to be there with me," Ryce said.

All thought of sleep fled. Judging by Ryce's tone, whatever he was talking about was not going to be particularly pleasant for either of them, despite the slightly suggestive wording. Knowing Ryce, he probably had no idea it was suggestive at all.

"Sure. Whatever you need."

He meant it, but it must have come out a lot more reserved than intended, because Ryce rushed to explain: "I've scheduled a call with Major Cummings, to give her my answer. I felt it's something that should be delivered face-to-face, not in a comm message."

"All right," Matt said, his heart sinking. He was hoping for at least a few more days of respite before the inevitable parting—a few more moments of shared happiness, especially after everything they'd been through—but it seemed Ryce had other plans. "Are you sure you want me to be there, though?"

"Yes." Ryce started toward the bridge, and Matt had no choice but to drag himself after him with all the eagerness of a death-row convict. A familiar craving stirred at the back of his brain, drying his mouth, but he could hardly make a pit stop for a shot of whiskey.

"I want you to know I didn't take the proposal lightly," Ryce said as he sat in the pilot's chair. The clock at the bottom of the screen showed two minutes to 13:00 hours. Ryce was nothing if not punctual. "And I'm absolutely confident in my decision. There are no regrets."

"Okay," Matt said, sounding dead to his own ears. Really, there was no need to drive the point further.

One minute remained. Matt took a deep breath. There was still time, however brief, to make his case. To beg Ryce to stay, to plead to give their love, their strange new bond, another chance. But the words died on his tongue, unspoken. If you love someone, let them go, an old saying went, and the bitter truth of it lanced through his soul.

A loud beep indicated an incoming transmission, and they both turned to face the screen. Nora and Colonel Mensah appeared before them. This time, the officers were sitting in a different room, with rapidly shifting star-map holograms on the walls. Muted voices and computerized announcements filtered through, too low to make out clearly, as if coming from somewhere beyond the room itself.

Nora's eyes widened slightly, and she actually did a sort of double take as she took in Matt and Ryce's disheveled appearance. Colonel Mensah appeared unperturbed.

"Nice to finally hear from you, Mr. Easom," the Colonel said pointedly.

"Colonel. Major." Ryce nodded, assuming his usual polite yet slightly aloof demeanor. It was quite astonishing to witness the difference between the cool facade he presented in public and the vulnerability he only dared display in his most intimate moments.

"I apologize for tarrying with my response. There have been... extenuating circumstances—not that it's any excuse."

Matt couldn't help but sneer. Being blackmailed into criminal activity was a good enough excuse for tardiness, in his opinion, but he wasn't about to regale Nora and her Colonel buddy with it. They were already getting what they wanted; any further placation would be adding insult to Matt's private injury.

"I wish to thank you both for this opportunity," Ryce continued. "To work on something of this magnitude and scientific significance—previously unknown Mnirian technology—would be a dream job for any qualified xenohistorian, let alone an amateur like myself."

Here we go, Matt thought dully, bracing for the blow. He looked away, pretending to study something on the side control panel, which was currently switched off.

"That being said, I must respectfully decline the offer."

For a moment, Matt was sure he misheard. He turned toward Ryce sharply, but he was focused on the screen.

Colonel Mensah seemed no less startled by Ryce's declaration. Nora, on the other hand, appeared much less surprised, for some reason. She glanced at Matt but said nothing.

"That is very unfortunate," Colonel Mensah said, unwittingly echoing Griggs's earlier words. The set of her mouth conveyed the same level of displeasure. "I'm assuming this is your final answer?"

"Yes. I'm sure you'll find someone as qualified, if not more. In fact, I'd be happy to recommend several Mnirian technology and linguistics experts who would be suitable for this project."

"I won't ask for your reasons, Mr. Easom," Nora said. "I only hope that whatever it is, it's worth it."

She pointedly raised an eyebrow at Matt, and he flushed. God, he hoped she was right too.

"It is." Ryce didn't look at him, but simply hearing his words made Matt's heart skip a beat in a much different manner than it had only minutes ago.

"That's the end of that, then," Nora concluded. "We shall have to find another consultant for the excavation project. Good luck and Godspeed, Mr. Easom. Matthew."

"You too," Matt managed to get out before the call disconnected.

"What?" Ryce asked when the awkward pause, during which Matt did nothing but stare at him, stretched on.

"Why did you do that? I know you wanted to take the job. I *know*. That's why I didn't say anything. If anybody deserves a second chance at having their career reinstated, it's you."

"I can't deny I was tempted." Ryce swiveled in his chair to face Matt, gazing into his eyes. "And you'd seemed so nonchalant about the possibility of me leaving... Well, let's just say we were both wrong in that regard, but it made me seriously consider accepting the offer. I've been interested in studying the Mnirian civilization for as long as I can remember. It's partly the reason why I was so eager to help Commodore

Archer with his plan—war effort aside. A discovery like the one we made seven months ago—an untouched Mnirian base with likely military application—is astounding. Who knows what else lies beneath the surface of that moon apart from the weapons? Just imagine the possibilities. It could easily be as groundbreaking as the jumpgates. As a scholar, I would love to work on something like that."

His eyes gleamed as he spoke. Matt had no doubt as to Ryce's passion regarding this subject. He'd never been a scholarly type himself, but he could well understand the scientific curiosity that drove researchers and explorers on their quests.

"But it's a military project, first and foremost," Ryce continued with a small sigh. "And I made a conscious decision to not follow that path again. Even if I no longer serve in the Fleet, while being a part of this endeavor I'd be forced to play by their rules again. As much as I hate disappointing Major Cummings, I don't think I'm ready for that, not yet, even if it's the smart, sensible thing to do."

Matt listened in silence. Judging by the uncharacteristic verbosity, this was something Ryce had longed to get off his chest for some time.

"Besides, I've made decisions based on logic and common sense my entire life. When I joined *Lady Lisa*, I made a choice to follow my heart instead—and I don't regret it." Ryce reached out and took Matt's hand, lacing their fingers together. His gray eyes still shone, but now they were brimming with a whole different kind of emotion. "I'm following my heart again, wherever it may lead me. One day at a time, for as long as we're together."

Matt squeezed his hand. It felt like receiving a death sentence pardon—a second one within the space of a few hours.

"I love you," he said, his voice raw. "You know that, right?"

"I do. And I love you too."

"Come here." Matt got up, pulling Ryce after him, and heading determinately toward his cabin.

"I thought you wanted some rest," Ryce remarked, trying not to laugh at Matt's renewed vigor.

"Fuck rest. I want to shower, and then prove there are at least some things worth sticking around here for."

SOMETIME LATER, THEY were lying in Matt's narrow bunk, their bodies cooling in pleasant languor, their limbs intertwined. Matt was happy to drift off on the waves of satiated slumber, but despite both the contentment and the deep weariness, sleep wouldn't come.

This had been a day of close calls and miracles, but even resting now in the safety of his lover's arms, he wasn't entirely at peace. Their lives hadn't ended, but they weren't going to pause, either, and the problems which had haunted him a week ago, before it all went into a tailspin, didn't just disappear. Griggs was not about to leave them be, despite Matt's little victory (or perhaps because of it), and he was reasonably sure Stahl wasn't going to either. Revenge was a damn powerful incentive for a certain type of people, and Matt had met plenty of those in his lifetime to recognize them for what they were.

Then there was still the little matter of the broken-down engine. With Tony's IMA job lead going bust and coming out of Griggs's races by the skin of their teeth but with no money to show for it, their hope of obtaining the needed funds was effectively dashed. Their spat with Griggs made it virtually impossible to get any sort of job on the station, which left them in a hopeless quagmire. With no other viable solution in sight, Matt suspected he'd eventually have to heed Tony's advice, swallow his pride, and beg Nora for help. Now that they were on speaking terms again, he was reasonably sure she wouldn't reject him outright—but asking his big sister for cash was something he'd hoped to never have to do if he could help it.

That alone was enough to lose sleep over, but there was something else that was bothering Matt, something he'd somewhat successfully put out of his mind while there were more pressing concerns to worry about, but which now he couldn't help but be reminded of.

The problem was, he didn't know how to begin broaching the subject—and if he should bring it up at all. Brinan's words regarding Ryce's father were forever seared into his brain, but did he really want to dump something so potentially painful on Ryce? It was enough that he had to carry the doubt. It wasn't a burden he yearned to share with the man he loved.

But Ryce had the right to know, didn't he? Matt didn't have the privilege of withholding something so important from him. Ultimately, this should be Ryce's decision.

"Can I ask you something…personal?" he said finally, lightly stroking Ryce's arm.

Ryce turned his head to face him with a lazy smile that melted Matt's heart. Damn everything else; he was the luckiest person in the galaxy for being on the receiving end of that smile.

"Isn't it a little late in the game for us to be shy about asking personal questions?"

Matt chuckled. "Yes, but it's not *that* kind of personal."

"Now I'm intrigued."

"If you had the chance…would you like to know who your father was?" Matt asked carefully. "Your biological father, I mean."

There was a long pause.

"I already know who my biological father was," Ryce said tersely, and Matt's heart dropped. How could have Ryce possibly found out? And why didn't he say anything about it before?

Ryce continued, oblivious: "He was a monster. A criminal. A pirate. A rapist. I don't care what his name was; I know what he did, and it's enough to never refer to him as my father. I had parents—real parents. They didn't always understand me or agree with my choices, but they loved me with all their hearts, unconditionally. John Easom was my father, and Sofie Easom was my mother. That's all I ever need to know."

Matt pulled him closer, Ryce's muscles tensing and flexing under his touch, and planted a soft kiss on his sweat-dampened hair.

"I didn't mean to upset you, baby. I'm sorry."

"That's all right. I meant what I said. You can ask me anything."

Matt drew the thin sheet over both of them, and they once again settled into a comfortable, warm silence. He couldn't help but be relieved at not having another difficult conversation with Ryce, even if it still felt like he was withholding information, despite the man's unequivocal answer. But some things were better left well enough alone, weren't they? And besides, other than the Onorean's mention of the pirate ship's name, he had no absolute proof it was actually Dylan Rodgers who was Ryce's— That there was any connection between them. It would be too much of a coincidence, wouldn't it? Many pirates and outlaws roamed the galaxy, and most of them were, as Ryce said, monsters. Any one of them could have been the one who'd assaulted Ryce's mother twenty-three years ago. And even if it was Rodger's ship, the culprit could have been any one of his crew rather than Rodgers himself.

don't want to lose the chance of getting to know my birth mother because I was too proud to give her a break."

Matt hugged him before planting a kiss on his temple. "She'd be lucky to know you."

Ryce leaned into his embrace. "My complicated relations aside, we need that money."

That "we" sent a warm shiver through Matt. But it still didn't feel right to him.

"It's your money," he insisted. "I can't possibly take it."

"If it's mine, then I can do whatever I please with it," Ryce countered. "Like buying a new power converter for my ship. If you want, we can call it a loan for upkeep purposes."

"It would take me forever to pay you back," Matt said, smiling.

"Then it's fortunate I'm not going anywhere," Ryce whispered and drew him into a kiss.

Epilogue

THE FREEPORT 73 IMA branch waiting room hadn't gotten any more welcoming since the last time Matt was here. It was busy, with a lot of tired and concerned humans and aliens occupying the uncomfortable plastic chairs or pacing nervously. A large screen displayed a muted edition of the news, which was met with general disinterest.

Matt tried to follow the recap of the political situation and the war updates across the galaxy but quickly gave up. Most of it was predictably grim, and he didn't need any bad news spoiling his mood.

Things were actually looking up for all of them, for a change. Val had already put in an order for a brand new power converter, which was scheduled to arrive tomorrow. With the engine (hopefully) operational again, and their station docking fees paid in full, they could go wherever they pleased, and Matt, for one, couldn't wait to get out of this miserable system and as far away as he possibly could.

He was still undecided on their new destination. Every sector and star system held its own opportunities and risks. Perhaps, this time, it would be prudent to choose a more central location. Matt usually avoided working in places with massive Federal presence, but he was quite fed up with backwater authorities' approach to organized crime. Maybe going by the straight and narrow for a change wouldn't be such a bad idea. Ryce would certainly welcome it, even if it meant being somewhat restricted in their job choices.

He fiddled idly with his commlink. Minutes seemed to crawl by with agonizing slowness. God, he hated waiting. Tony was right; he had all the patience of a toddler.

"How much longer is this going to take?"

"It's a complicated procedure, you know." Tony was sitting in the chair next to him, sipping some atrociously healthy beverage she'd concocted using fresh produce. Matt shuddered at the vibrant green color, clearly visible through the transparent plastic.

"They only have to sew his finger back on, not attach a different head," he muttered.

Tony didn't deign to respond to that, and Matt went back to his commlink. They could try the Gemel system. It had plenty of inhabited planets and moons, as well as several military outposts and remote environmental research facilities. That, along with a fairly strategic location on the edge of the disputed space between the humans and the Alraki in the Scutum–Centaurus Arm of the galaxy, promised stiffer competition in the runners' job market. But Matt had no problem with working for less than lucrative fees if it meant staying afloat for a little while longer.

The clinic door opened, and Val finally emerged into the waiting room limbo. Matt and Tony surged to their feet.

"Everything all right, big guy?" Matt asked, eying him critically. Val's left hand was bandaged in swaths of silicone elastics, and he was pale as a sheet, but otherwise, he appeared to be his usual healthy and reserved self.

"Yep. The surgery went well. The doctor said I should be able to fully use the finger again in a week or so." He waved his wrapped hand in the air vaguely and winced. "Gave me pain meds and everything." He sighed. "I really owe Easom for paying for all this."

They all owed Ryce in one way or another, there was no doubt about it; but this time, Matt was surprisingly chill with being indebted to someone. He supposed it all depended on the person in question and their attitude toward helping friends in times of need. Unlike Matt's family, there were no strings attached to the money.

"Drinks are on me, gents," Tony offered graciously. Val side-eyed her cup, and she mock-slapped him on the shoulder. "I mean real drinks, in a bar. We need to celebrate you getting out of surgery, among other things."

Val shrugged. "I'm good with that. Captain?"

"Sure. Let's just all stay out of trouble this time, okay? I'll call Ryce and tell him to meet us there."

A voice-message alert popped up on screen at the exact moment Matt tapped his comm. He frowned at the unfamiliar number, but he couldn't afford to ignore any calls. The chances of a potential client seeking him out at just the right time were slim, but not nonexistent.

"You go on," he told Tony and Val. "I'll see what this is about and catch up with you."

As they exited the waiting room, Matt hit the message icon.

"Long time no see, Spears," a deep rough voice said, and Matt had to sit back in his chair for the sudden weakness in his knees. It was a voice he'd hoped never to hear again, a voice out of his nightmares.

But how could this be? Federal prisoners weren't allowed to make personal calls or send messages, not even high-profile prisoners like Captain Dylan Rodgers, who, as far as Matt knew, was currently detained at a secure correctional facility in some godforsaken hellhole. *Wasn't he?*

"Heard you've been stirring up some shit again," Rodgers continued. "Makes you an easy man to find. See you soon."

The message ended abruptly. There was no other information attached, just a number which led nowhere when Matt tried to search it.

He put the comm back in his pocket and wiped his hands on his pants as if the palms were sweaty or dirty. His mind reeling, it took conscious effort to slow his breathing and calm down as he stared at the plain white wall with unseeing eyes.

Perhaps he could ask Ryce to trace the call—but no. He didn't want Ryce involved in his feud with Rodgers, whatever other link there might exist between his partner and the notorious pirate. What Ryce didn't know couldn't hurt him, and that applied to whatever mindfuckery Rodgers was indulging in.

Because that was all it was—Rodgers simply toying with him, trying to scare Matt for putting him behind bars. Matt had no idea how Rodgers had managed to find him and reach out from his prison, but he didn't care—nor did he want to dig any deeper into it. It didn't matter anyway. Soon, they'd be far, far away from here, and even if Rodgers had any informants on this station (such as Stahl, most likely), he wouldn't be able to track them down again so easily.

Matt took one last deep breath and got up. To hell with Rodgers and his threats. He had so many things to be thankful for—he had the man he loved by his side, his friends were safe, his ship was ready to fly again, and they were all happily and gloriously alive. The universe was there at the touch of his fingertips with its infinite possibilities, full of mysteries and untapped opportunities yet to discover—that they all could discover together.

"One day at a time," Matt whispered, recalling Ryce's promise, and hurried to join his crew's celebration.

About the Author

A voracious reader from the age of five, Isabelle Adler has always dreamed of one day putting her own stories into writing. She loves traveling, art, and science, and finds inspiration in all of these. Her favorite genres include sci-fi, fantasy, and historical adventure. She also firmly believes in the unlimited powers of imagination and caffeine.

Email: info@isabelleadler.com

Twitter: @Isabelle_Adler

Website: www.isabelleadler.com

Other books by this author

Adrift (Staying Afloat, Book One)
The Castaway Prince (The Castaway Prince, Book One)
A Touch of Magic (Fae-Touched, Book One)
Frost

Coming Soon from Isabelle Adler

The Exile Prince

The Castaway Prince, Book Two

The warm morning breeze carried the smell of sea salt, exotic spices, and the promise of a distant sand storm.

Stephan breathed deeply, closing his eyes against the gentle currents, and leaned on the windowsill, offering his face up to the sun. It was not yet noon, but the heat was already building up. Soon the busy streets of the port city of Varta would empty, the denizens taking a brief respite during the midday hours to hide in the relative cool of their homes, away from the glare of the ruthless sun. At dusk, all activity would renew with rekindled vigor, the streets around the harbor filling with the cries of peddlers hawking their wares, the music of wandering performers, and the general hubbub of a large city going about its business. But for now, Stephan simply enjoyed the bright sunshine, which had been so rare in his native Seveihar, before he'd be forced to retreat to the shade of his rooms.

No, *their* rooms. He'd been living with Warren, his former footman and current lover, for the past six months, sharing the two cozy rooms in one of the quieter districts of Varta. The modest appointment of the space was a far cry from the richness of his father's royal palace in Sever, but luxury was low on Stephan's priority list. These short months were the happiest he'd been in his entire life. Granted, at twenty years old, he was still at the beginning of his journey, but with his father gone and the rest of the family actively persecuting him, he'd had his fair share of misery.

Stephan sighed and closed the wooden shutters. Even so, the room was still softly illuminated, filled with translucent, soporific light. The hem of his white silk robe trailed after him as he made his way to the large writing desk, cluttered with sheaves of paper and different-colored inkwells. Warren, being the son of a merchant, was the one with the experience and a practical grasp for business, and he had been the one to suggest they invest the money left from selling Stephan's extensive collection of jewelry in local commerce. For centuries, Varta, the second largest city of Segor, had been a crucial junction for the passage of goods between the deep south and the northern countries and provinces—including Seveihar and rival Esnia. With trade burgeoning in recent years, investing in independent shipping ventures seemed like a sound plan, although they were only now beginning to see any returns. None of it was enough to make a fortune, but for now, at least, they were able to live comfortably.

Stephan settled in a chair and pulled out a stack of letters he wanted to sift through one more time. While Warren was responsible for the finances, Stephan handled the records and the correspondence. As a member of the royal family, he was well-versed in several languages, including Segati—a dialect spoken in Segor and along the long stretch of the southern coast. But reading and writing with a teacher weren't the same as practicing the language among native speakers, and Stephan wanted to brush up on his communication skills as much as possible to be able to navigate the often-equivocal patterns of business negotiations with Segorian merchants and ship owners.

He was writing down some notes on a piece of paper when the door opened, and Warren stepped in, letting out a long-suffering sigh as he closed the door and took off his sweat-soaked scarf.

Stephan smiled and rose to meet him, throwing his arms around Warren and planting a quick kiss on his lips. Warren's skin, flushed and hot, still carried traces of salt and fish smell.

"I missed you," Stephan said playfully.

Warren grinned in response, taking Stephan's hand and kissing his fingers. "I've only been gone a few hours. And I still stink from the docks."

"I don't mind." Stephan nodded at the leather-bound ledger sticking out of Warren's coat pocket. "Any news?"

"The ship should arrive any day now. With the price of silk going up, we should make a nice profit off this consignment."

"You might be the one to blame for the increase in prices," Stephan teased. "You didn't have to buy me quite so many dresses."

"Of course I did. They make you happy. And I love seeing you in them."

Warren let go of Stephan and threw the ledger on the desk. He was still smiling, but Stephan could sense tension in the rigid set of his shoulders and the way his smile quickly turned from genuine to strained.

"What's wrong?" Stephan asked. "Are you worried about the ship being delayed?"

Warren shook his head and sat on the long bench beside a low dining table. He picked an orange from a fruit bowl and began peeling it.

"I've heard some bad news from Seveihar," he said, avoiding meeting Stephan's eyes.

Stephan sat back at the desk, tucking his long hair behind his ear in a nervous gesture. He knew he wasn't going to like it.

"The war has started, hasn't it?" he asked quietly.

Warren nodded. "Rumors spread fast in this city. It seems the first thing your brother did after ascending to the throne was declare war on Esnia."

Stephan swore softly. His older brother Robert had been warmongering to garner political support, but until now, Stephan had clung to the naive hope he wouldn't go as far as actually starting a full-blown territorial war with their neighbor. Or at least that his advisers would stop him from making such a foolish move, if he wasn't prudent enough to restrain himself. Even after fleeing his homeland and abandoning his title, Stephan couldn't help but feel somehow responsible for the wellbeing of its people. Waging a war when most of them were already struggling with the increase in waterway taxes his uncle Rowan had decreed last fall would only add insult to injury.

"That wasn't what got me worried, though. There's more." Warren dropped the peelings on the table and frowned at the naked fruit, as if surprised it turned out to be an orange after all. "There's talk about Seveiharians in Varta. Apparently, an envoy arrived at the Governor's palace two days ago. They were trying to keep it secret, but again, Varta is anything but surreptitious."

Stephan shrugged. "So? They must be here to amend trade agreements. War changes demand, and the usual shipping routes would need to be altered if the Zenna River proves too dangerous now for regular transport."

"No doubt." Warren handed him a few orange slices, and Stephan popped them in his mouth. He flicked his tongue across his lips to lick away the juice, noting the way Warren's gaze took on a familiar intensity as he followed the tiny movement.

Warren's unmistakable interest sent a jolt of heat down his belly, triggering his own arousal. He licked his lips again, this time in an involuntary response to the thought of what he and Warren could be doing to while away the sultry midday hours. But apparently Warren wasn't done yet.

Also Available from NineStar Press

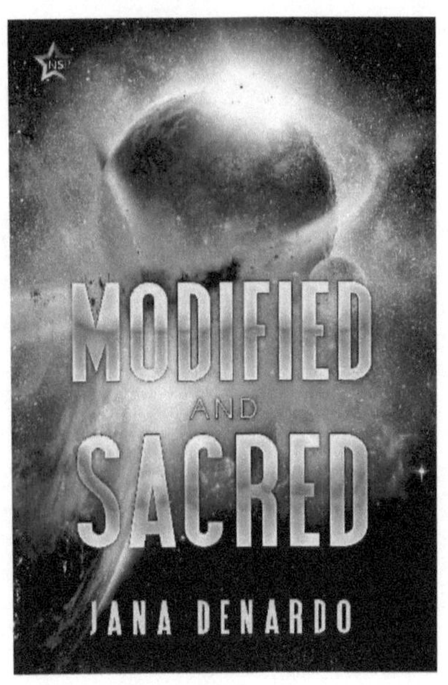

Connect with NineStar Press

Website: NineStarPress.com

Facebook: NineStarPress

Facebook Reader Group: NineStarNiche

Twitter: @ninestarpress

Tumblr: NineStarPress